Best Short Stories from **Stand Magazine**

Best Short Stories from
Stand Magazine

Edited by
Lorna Tracy, Jon Silkin and John Wardle

A Methuen Paperback

A Methuen Paperback

BEST SHORT STORIES FROM *STAND MAGAZINE*

British Library Cataloguing in Publication Data

Best short stories from *Stand magazine*.
  I. Silkin, Jon, *1930–*   II. Tracy, Lorna
III. Wardle, John   IV. *Stand magazine*
  823'.01'08 FS

  ISBN 0–413–18410–2

First published in Great Britain 1988
by Methuen London Ltd
11 New Fetter Lane, London EC4P 4EE
Printed and bound in Great Britain
by Cox & Wyman Ltd, Reading

The editors' thanks are due to the copyright holders of the following stories for permission to reprint them in this volume:

Elizabeth Baines and A. D. Peters Ltd: 'Star-Things', copyright © Elizabeth Baines.

The David Mercer Estate and Margaret Ramsay: 'Huggy Bear', copyright © The David Mercer Estate.

Lorna Tracy and *Stand Magazine*: 'A Shetland Set', copyright © Lorna Tracy.

Peter Carey and Deborah Rogers Ltd: 'I Know You Can Talk', copyright © Peter Carey, 1975.

Angela Carter and Deborah Rogers Ltd: 'The Borden Family Murders', from *Black Venus*, copyright © 1985 by Angela Carter published by Chatto and Windus.

Dennis Silk and *Stand Magazine*: 'Costigan', copyright © Dennis Silk.

Michael Wilding and the University of Queensland Press: 'The West Midland Underground', from *The West Midland Underground*, copyright © University of Queensland Press, 1975.

The B. S. Johnson Estate and MBA Literary Agents Ltd: 'Everybody Knows Somebody Who's Dead', copyright © The B. S. Johnson Estate.

The G. P. Elliott Estate and Georges Borchardt, Inc, New York: 'The NRACP'

Igor Pomerantsev and the translator Frank Williams: 'Aubades and Serenades', copyright © Igor Pomerantsev and Frank Williams.

Emanuel Litvinoff and David Higham Associates Ltd: 'Enemy Territory', from *Journey Through a Small Planet*, copyright © Michael Joseph.

Neil Jordan and Douglas Rae Management Ltd: 'Last Rite', copyright © Neil Jordan.

Georgina Hammick and Methuen London Ltd: 'People for Lunch', from *People For Lunch*, copyright © Georgina Hammick, 1987.

Iain Crichton Smith and *Stand Magazine*: 'The Dying', copyright © Iain Crichton Smith.

The Sid Chaplin Estate and David Higham Associates Ltd: 'Tom Patrick', from *The Blackberry Time*, copyright © Bloodaxe Books Ltd, 1987.

Tony Harrison and *Stand Magazine*: 'The Toothache', copyright © Tony Harrison.

Contents

Foreword by Lorna Tracy

To adapt some words of Donald Barthelme: through the imagination one can resist even the greatest temptation, which is 'ordinary life'. In this selection of stories from *Stand Magazine* the editors hope to offer readers both that temptation and the means for resisting it.

Stand Magazine has been appearing quarterly every year since 1952, with the exception of a period in the late 1950s while Jon Silkin, its founding editor, was getting a university education in Leeds. Since 1965 the magazine has been published from Newcastle upon Tyne after accepting an invitation from Northern Arts to receive an annual grant towards its running costs in return for publishing from a base within the Northern Arts bailiwick. This arrangement continues and the editors gratefully acknowledge it.

Little magazines are not part of Official Culture, whose attitude to such enterprises as *Stand* is one of (largely) benign neglect. Nevertheless the little magazine is the seed-bed and nursery out of which the glory of the garden eventually comes. The authors published in *Stand* are seldom famous writers – at least, they are seldom famous when *Stand* publishes them. When early fiction by Peter Carey, Neil Jordan and Georgina Hammick appeared in *Stand* they were promising new writers, relatively unknown, just as in *Stand*'s earlier days Tony Harrison and David Mercer were.

A truly 'little' magazine physically as well as generically, *Stand* has never achieved an issue with more than eighty pages, but it has covered the world. It has no aspirations to grow fat and glossy, or to spray its readers with the stink of fashionable writing. A necessary reliance upon public subsidy helps maintain its modesty, its good standard of production, and above all, keeps the editorial eye focussed upon First Things: poetry, fiction and criticism of high quality by both new and established authors, local and international.

This volume is the first gathering in book form from the fiction

Stand has published. The stories are representative of nothing but minute, collective editorial decisions over thirty-odd years – and it is not even representative of *them* when one is aware that *Stand* has always given generous space to *translations* of modern short fiction from the world over. For lack of space this important aspect of the magazine is entirely absent from the present volume. The one translated story here is by an author who, although he writes in Russian, lives and works in England.

A second enduring feature of *Stand*, its hospitality to the long short story, can only be hinted at in these pages, as obviously it would take only five or six such stories to fill the book completely. It has been a particular sorrow to the editors not to have space to represent the remarkable and horrifying trilogy by Francis Fytton concerning the Algerian war, but that would have been a book in itself. Indeed, after our first publication, it was.

One way in which this selection unhappily reflects the composition of the magazine in general is in the disproportionate number of male to female writers. *Stand* has never attracted nearly as many potential contributions from women as from men. This has been consistently true over the years, and continues to be, even though women are sending out more of their work to publishers in the 8os than ever before. For whatever reasons – and *Stand* has recently opened its correspondence columns to a discussion of these reasons – women continue to be seriously under-represented.

If there *were* any such animal as 'a *Stand* story' (and the editors do not believe that, in pure form, there is) it might be a fiction that rejuvenates the presentation of content while at the same time it 'strikes through to the reader's senses', in Johnson's phrase – not forgetting the sense of humour; it would, as well, be aware of the fact that even the lonely individuals who populate so much of short fiction ultimately inhabit some kind of human society. Such fiction would call for readers willing to perform an act of sustained attention, and would reward more than one reading. None of this has anything to do with sex or class or (beyond literacy) with education; it has everything to do with the commitment of one's attention and imagination – reader in collaboration with writer – to completing and criticizing the fiction. That, at any rate, might be the ideal.

Star-Things by Elizabeth Baines

'There's things like stars in the stream.' Angela Johnson nudges the gate. That's not the way home.

'Come on,' says Angela Johnson, lolling her eyes about. Angela Johnson has socks that disappear down her sandals. She jumps on the gate and makes it swing inwards.

You should go straight home.

'Come and see the star-things.'

My Daddy's got a star-thing, a thing called a meteorite, out of the sky.

At Angela Johnson's, when you call in the morning, there's a man sitting in the shadows who Angela Johnson ought in all decency not to call Daddy. Sunshine lops across the breathless dust of the sideboard and over the table, making bacon rinds oozy. The shadows around seem to wriggle. Angela Johnson's mother, still in her dressing-gown, hardly says anything, and nothing at all about going straight home.

Angela Johnson's mother gets children while she's blinking.

Angela Johnson gets her clothes handed down. As she leans on the gate her dress that used to be her sister's goes up at the back and down at the front right to her ankles.

'No one will know.'

The wood is black and yellow bars dipping over the hill-crest.

No one knows where the Johnson children come from. No one knows where they go. Everyone knows what the business was their father went away on; some can guess why he broke down the back door with a hatchet.

In the wood there's something cracking.

Angela Johnson leaves the gate swinging. Down the hill there are boys, Johnson boys and others, breaking branches and slinging them. They jump, knees bent, swinging, till the whole tree winces; twigs and leaves spark and sizzle as they hurl them down the slope.

'Don't worry, no one will come.'

My Daddy might come.

My Daddy might come looking.

For children like the Johnsons the Welfare State comes looking. Children like the Johnsons have heads that are alive.

The boys come round, fists like pebbles in their pockets, legs in corrugated socks, their cropped hair bristling in the sun.

'Your Dad's a Jew, then, isn't he?'

My Daddy's got a star that fell out of the sky.

'What star? Hah!' Doubled up, snorting, kicking the tree-trunks, throwing sticks looping upwards.

'Got a star, my eye!'

Yes he has, he's got a meteorite he found while he was walking.

'Get out, what's it look like?'

Split across, and in the middle there's a wheel-shape all in silver.

Elbows leaning on the tree now. 'What's it made of?'

The meteorite lies in the glass-fronted cabinet. No one knows where it came from, no one knows what it's made of. Perhaps you better hadn't touch it.

Don't go too close to children whose bodies might be crawling. Don't let them get too near. Just in case, let's do your hair with a fine-toothed dust-comb; scrub your nails and keep them short or you might catch worms.

'Your Mam wears a hat, I seen her, and goes to church on Sundays.'

The Johnson children's mother wears a coat with half its buttons, no wonder when she's passing she turns her head as though she's wincing: you wonder really how she dare to walk abroad at all.

My Daddy's got a star that fell while he was winking.

'What's the colour of the star, then?'

Once it was red-melting, but now it's black and silver.

'Ha!' Dancing off, sending currents of stone-flight out through the bracken: 'Her Dad got birdshit in his eye!' Flicking back: 'What's it feel like?'

You're not supposed to know, remember, better hadn't touch it. Once it was on fire, but it must have been cooling when he put it in his pocket.

'So where did he find it?'

No one knows. No one knows how far he'd been to when he walked abroad. And by the time he brought it home it had gone stone cold.

And weren't there lots of questions? And didn't someone call out in the night-time? And then they made the rule about the glass-fronted case.

Now the boys are off, lolloping, spinning sticks at blackbirds to make them go cack-crackling, looking for a spot that's flat enough for marbles.

Angela Johnson's tugging: 'Let's go to the stream.'

The sun's getting lower, the air fizzing with midges, flicking on and off in pin-points. Baubles of stained sunshine smash across the ground.

One of the Johnsons has a scar across his forehead.

Johnson children get dropped from their prams.

'What's the meteor's shape?'

Like a chopped-off finger, a knobbly knuckle.

The Johnson boy's scar jumps like forked lightning: 'Ha! Someone threw her Dad a knuckle-bone!'

My Mummy's got a scar that she covers up with powder. Powdered skin smells sweet and dry, has a perfume that lingers after someone's gone to church. Be careful near the dressing-table, all those bowls and cut-glass bottles: scent that's been spilled stains the polished surface, and powder makes a pale breathless cloud. . . .

Angela Johnson slithers off down the tussocks. Golden king-cups in the water, oily with the sunshine.

Stars that ooze and bubble from mud that you could slip on.

You can slip on the mud and badly scar your cheek-bone, lose your hat and scar your cheek-bone; run through mud with a pushchair, banging, slipping on the mud-slope, suddenly tumbling backwards, wheels up-ended, spinning. You'll be lying cheek-down, sobbing: there's no running away, you can't undo the mistake you made.

Now the boys come swaggering, lice in their heads and wriggling worms inside their bellies, throwing pebbles, knocking king-cups, punching holes into the water.
  Don't throw stones.
  Don't throw anything.
  Don't throw powder-bowls and bottles. . . .

  'Hey, here's your Dad, here's the Jew-boy!'
  Run, and the sun's clip-clipping the branches; nearer: light slicing the grasses; grasp his knuckles: it's so late, the way home now has different shadows.
  My Daddy's got a star that hit the earth and died.

Elizabeth Baines was born in 1947. Her short stories have been published in numerous magazines and anthologies. Her novels are *The Birth Machine* (Women's Press, 1983) and *Body Cuts*, to be published by Pandora in spring 1988. In July 1987 her first radio play, *Rhyme or Reason* was broadcast on Radio 4.

Huggy Bear by David Mercer

Hooper stomped up the oilcloth treads to his surgery and kicked open the door, to stand belching with harmless truculence just inside the waiting-room. It was empty. No people, no Hoop-bound mouths. He rolled off a last belly shaker (High Street caf: steak pie two veg. 2/3d.) and looked at the clock. No watches for Hoop, he has his own internal rhythms. Dawn and dusk, seed-time and harvest. No watch, but a grumbling acquaintance with reality, and therefore note the time. It was ten minutes to two. Janine Lasso time. Hoop stumbled into his room, pumped up the dental chair and flung himself into it to stare at Janine, who was applying mascara by the window. Outside and below, the stagnant backyards of Kilburn festered in the usual *sfumato*, ignored by Hoop's teenage receptionist.

''lo Janine,' offered Hoop.

'Ya-Yo,' Janine said. Her tongue was between her teeth. Its pointed tip adhered to the inside mucosa of her lower lip. 'Yot ya hum hack so early hor?' She took her mirror off the dental tray, breathed on it, polished it on her sleeve and began to scumble powder over her dead white cheeks.

Hoop picked his nose, rolled a little black pellet and thoughtfully chewed it. Strong and silent, for Janine certainly knew what he had hum hack early hor.

The sharp click of a compact lid. Snap. Then in the crisp tones of aggression which were Lasso's surgery voice: *'Must* you do that? You know it's common and just because you think it's working class. Things have changed a bit since your day you know –' And, as if safely delivered of a much constipated resentment, she fell silent.

It was true, Hoop mourned inwardly. Things had changed since his day. He spoke to himself inside his own head – where else such privacy? – Mi Slassoo. Miss Lassoo. Misslass OOO. You dizzy little painted ikon. And not even a painting, a daub. And take that starched uniform: a projection of the will to dominate, that's what. Sadist Lasso. And Hoop, slobbering grateful object of pleasure.

'I don't know whether I can face Barbara's parents,' Hoop said. There.

'Well-it's-a-bit-late-now-isn't-it?' Burrowing in her bucket bag, Miss Lasso sniffed. She knew Hoop. She knew his old tricks. Coming in every day at two o'clock with that look in his eye. But his prestige value had long ago carried away her token objections – and, his line was digital sex, which posed no ethical problems. Janine fiddled with a probe and relaxed. The vacant, languorous semaphoring of her eyes let him know that the Barbara Business had failed to register against the almost total anaesthesia which she substituted for consciousness.

'Barbara militates for marriage,' hoo-hoo-ed Hoop.

'Jer mean she wants to get married?' Janine inspected her silver fingernails. ''s only natural, in it?'

They both examined Hoop's half recumbent body, as if in search of testimony.

Heterodox dentist, in sandals, greasy socks, bagged-out made-to-measures, ragged jumper, eggy tie – mounting to the huge chubby face cast in something like mobile Caerphilly. Annihilator of conventions topped with short stiff bristles and a baby frown. Was this a nubile Hoop, their eyes quizzed? Was this a tame and commuting species? Was all lost?

Janine took in the portly datum in her neutral way, whilst Hoop recapitulated in elegiac mood.

Barbara would take this helpless ensemble and knock it in to shape. She was tall, clean, would devour his self-indulgence like a vacuum cleaner. He saw himself like some prisoner in the delousing room, stripped to the basic Hoop and re-processed on Barbara lines. She would make him buy all the things he could afford . . . taboo his atavistic pleasures . . . turn him into a dispenser of sherry. No more Lasso, no more saving coupons for the Weetabix Atlas . . . no more, for example, anti-Semitic jokes for pro-Semitic Hoop. Barbara's calm liberal world would engulf him in reason, in points of view, in tastes, in abomination of Lasso the Yahoo . . . just as she coolly ignored the breaking of wind, putting it down to inverted snobbery.

Propelled by fear and drawn by the exorcising image of Janine,

6

Hoop leapt up, took his receptionist in his arms and sucked her ear. Rocked backwards and forwards, sucking and analysing, Miss Lasso remained snugly passive, leaned away a fraction till Hoop's puckered lips went *pop* and he nuzzled the glistening lobe. She patted her hair at the back with her free hand. Over his shoulder her eyes roamed the surgery endowing all things with a minimal existence. Now he had the other ear and shook it playfully between nibbling teeth.

Hoop always rejoiced at the feel of a real live mammal in his arms. Ho-ho, tumescent Lasso. Inside her overall, as hard and swollen as gumboils pointing upwards at an angle of roughly twenty degrees from the horizontal . . . which compensates for their poverty of size. Could eat them. Would like to have them framed. Could snuffle about between them till kingdom come and never draw another tooth. And whilst Hoop blissfully toured her thorax Janine shifted her weight to the other foot, turned a yawn into a swallow, mentally set a deadline of ten minutes of this. She was picked up and plumped down on his lap as he fell backwards growling into his dental chair. It's funny, some boys don't know when to stop . . . but with him it's different. Funny to think, I didn't even have them four years ago and now he's . . . one of these days shouldn't be surprised he'll bite them off, the big baby.

Barbara had set aside the afternoon for cleaning his flat. She stepped from her Baby Austin and locked it. She took a holdall containing her Electrolux from the boot and checked: brush for dusting, thing for carpet, thing for upholstery, flex. Hydra-headed machine to gobble up Hoop's traces, it lay coiled in the bag, only a vacuum cleaner to Barbara but the voracious enemy of Hoopness. She let herself in and stood with a tender fastidious smile in the hallway of the Hooporium.

The doors leading to various rooms had been bounced open that morning and left, reeling from the shock. As Barbara moved from room to room her expression became more tender, and more fastidious. Colin such a darling, but this? His friends had confided that it differed in no way from previous tenancies, either. It looked disembowelled, as though in the morning dash from bed to front door Hoop had encountered and bitterly fought with every object he possessed. And from last evening, things were scattered about in the brutal postures with which only toys can define their capricious and impatient owner. Barbara walked round the telly, which dangled its broken antenna as reproachfully as any crushed insect; in the search for a plug she traced its plastic flex back to a splintered bakelite fixture in the wall, and pondered the arrangement of matchsticks which held two quarter inches of denuded wire in position. Between the telly and the gramophone: a bent poker, a polythene bag containing hair and labelled 'moustache 2nd March 1959', crumpled pages of Hoopscript (one headed 'Novel'), an eviscerated Russian alarm clock, a condom (gossamer), and a dusty half-eaten teacake. Raising the lid of the gramophone she found that Hoop had dispensed with the inconvenience of hinges; it swung free in her hands, and beneath, a saucer of jammy butter revolved gravely on a cracked recording of 'Songs from the People's Democratic Republics'.

Oh Colin!

Who would think he averaged eighty pounds a week? She plugged in the vacuum and tried to decide where to begin. The tactful thing would be to leave the place spotless without disturbing anything, then he would never notice. Begin as we mean to go on. And yet, Barbara disliked that sort of thing . . . the feminine conspiracy. She lunged at the cigarette ends in the hearth, then held up the flexible tube to hear them go flap-flap-flap down into the whirring inside of the machine. She detached the fitting from the tube and pressed her palm over the rim. Sssssponk . . . it made her tingle. She sat down and thought about Colin and the meeting with her parents that evening. She knew he wouldn't pick his nose or break wind, or any of those things he fondly believed to represent freedom from inhibition . . . she was pretty sure of the things he *wouldn't* do. But what *would* he do? Say? No telling. A defensive Hoop might threaten decorum in such a way that even Mummy and Daddy's social expertise would prove inadequate. It was this dreary pride he had in his working-class origins. Snobbery, really. And worst of all sentimental – sentimental about working-class people, despite the fact that he was really quite cruel when he described them.

Why did she love him? Why, to be more objective, was Hoop lovable? She didn't know. Couldn't think. But the chaos of his existence held the same nervy fascination for her as a picture askew on a wall. Had to be put straight. To do this without disturbing or alienating the essential Hoop would combine the deep satisfaction of interfering with a sophisticated sense of knowing what to leave alone. In this, Barbara was conscious of the dangers but felt that since her intention was to trim rather than to re-model, Hoop would remain tolerantly passive. Lacking a coherent image of himself he tended to take the view that his very shapelessness made him formidable. Like the fragments in a kaleidoscope, he could be manipulated – but the last turn of the screw was his own, returning the pieces to the original jumble where they really belonged and where his sense of his own value was nourished in a secret, satisfying confusion. Dimly, Barbara perceived this. Much less dimly she reaffirmed to herself the wisdom of becoming Mrs Hooper.

She vacuumed the living-room and the bedroom, and with a slight diminuendo of zeal opened the door of the bathroom. A Hulot-esque pattern of shoe prints meandered from basin to bath, from the lavatory pan to the door. In and around the lavatory pan was a bad smell and quantities of screwed-up newspaper. Grey Terylene pants hung from a piece of string arranged in such a way that anyone sitting on the lavatory would be demurely veiled about the face in limp cascades of Hoop skinwear. On the edge of the bath, next to the lavatory pan, was a book squashed face downwards between the taps . . . a copy of *Reflexions sur la violence* . . . and sopping wet. A stack of papers and magazines below: *Daily Mirror*, *Guardian*, *Encounter*, *New Left Review*, *The Probe*, *Tit Bits*. Surely, from the merest practical point of view, less comfortable than Bronco? Barbara scooped them up, took a roll of Bronco from her holdall and balanced it on *Reflexions sur la violence*. She scrubbed and scoured. She pulled the chain six times and poured in half a bottle of Domestos. Washing the floor, she cut herself twice on rusty old razor-blades which Hoop had thrown down secure in the knowledge that on *his* bathroom floor they were harmless.

Only the kitchen taxed her confidence in her own stamina. It was like a cross between a private slaughterhouse and a festering rubbish dump. On the bloodstained cutting-board, a plate of crimson offal buzzing with flies. On the floor: bacon rind, smears of fat, fish skins, a condom (gossamer), an eviscerated English alarm clock, lumps of stiff mashed potato, bones of various animals. The walls around the

9

gas cooker were spattered with fat in layers, as lovingly preserved as the waxy hock bottle from that party. Pinned on the wall over the table, a coloured portrait of Her Majesty with inked-in beard and spectacles. Bismarck loomed impassively opposite. Hitler stared out of his eye corner at Her Majesty, conferring on his bit of the kitchen an air of gaga malevolence and permanently gnashed teeth. In one corner were stacked three headless mops, a pop gun and a stick with a piece of cardboard saying BAN THE BOMB tacked on to it.

Barbara almost gave up. She sterilized a cup in a pan of boiling water and made herself a strong cup of Maxwell House. Mentally she cased the intricate labyrinth of Hoop's dear and complex soul. What to make of a man who was communist, fascist, labour, conservative, liberal, humanist, pacifist, militant, intelligent, ignorant, vulgar, sensitive and cuddly? She sighed, swigged her coffee, rolled up her sleeves again and got to work. It was four o'clock, and at seven she was meeting Hoop for dinner before going on to her parents' house in Hendon.

We'll have dinner together she had said, and then you can come back with me just for coffee. You don't have to stay long . . . only to meet them. As Hoop blundered up and down in front of Giacomo's restaurant he played off his mental reel of impressions of Barbara's parents, masochistically edited from what she had told him about them in the past few months. The Lasso's dead white mask intervened. What was the Lasso Secret? A little music, then. Oh Miss-slasso Hi love you . . . Hi'm al-ways drea-ming o-hof you. But I don't and I'm not. What it was, he told himself, the *frisson Lasso* so to speak . . . she was a doll for delinquents. Hoop had felt internally delinquent for years. Had felt both guilty and exhilarated on that account. He liked dolls too, though no shabby and skulking nympholeptic. And just as the inner Hoopness radiated its nursery glow, there was a counterpart out there in the world . . . incarnate in Lasso, the cool absence of the usual bundle of greedy needs. Janine was a simple vaso-motor system. Nothing plus. A swathe of hair (bouffon), a stiff petticoat or two, arms and legs sticking out and all that (all *that*), barely animated by the harmless obsessions of her status: the funny music, the cosmos rendered finite by the Inner Ring Road, the engaging mannerisms of the teenager circa 1959 (cosmosis).

To a hungry man a girl who could be enjoyed through the fingertips; none of that suffocating bond between the taker and the taken. Hoop scanned his inner screens with amazed enjoyment, with all the gurgling pleasure that had accompanied his discovery of his big toe on some timeless pre-tot occasion. And Barbara rounded the corner, just as inevitably as Hoop found himself (woke up to catch his eyes in the act) gazing at the volumes of nudes in the shop next to Giacomo's.

The Hooper reaction at moments of exposure was to brazen it out rather than succumb to the temptation of pretending that things were anything but what they were. Trapped with his finger up his nose or his attention focussed on some monochrome teat, he would compel the otherwise perhaps indifferent observer to notice, and do his best to drive them to confessions of disapproval. Barbara was used to it but had learned to withhold the satisfaction of her distaste. As she approached he stared harder and harder at the nudes. He squinted, stepped back as though to take them all in at one go, stepped forward and pressed his nose against the window. His back announced, his pose advertised, his stance bellowed: Barbara look at me I'm looking at nudes.

Oh Colin!

'*That* one's rather good,' she said deflatingly over his shoulder.

'What? Oh! You! I was, I was *just looking at some* NUDES,' Hoop shouted.

'Yes, darling, I know. There there . . . it was *very brave* of you,' soothed Barbara. She turned in the direction of the restaurant door.

'No wait a minit c'meer c'meer look at *this* one. Dugs like melons. Been looking at them for ten minutes –'

'Have you sweetie? Well let's go in, shall we? I'm starving –'

And as they entered Giacomo's she covertly watched the Hooper Metamorphosis. His back straightened, his chin went up and out, Punch-like. His eyes glazed over and swept the tables with calculating *hauteur*. A hovering waiter was ignored, a cigarette detached from its case and lightly tapped. Smoke was sparingly trickled down the Hooper nostrils. We are upright, intelligent vertebrates. Unashamed of our simian forebears, we need not carry the evolutionary tree on our backs. Still, we have class class class. It's everywhere, but money talks, Jack. Hoop's face was impassive throughout, his manner curt. They selected a table and were deferentially settled in.

In a restaurant, as in most public places, Hooper felt somewhat at bay. He found it difficult to get it into his head that the outside was *there*. He would sit and watch his hand lying crabwise on the table, watch it advancing cautiously towards a glass. Then, looking round him as though he had nothing to do with the hand at all, he would let it have its way. When it pushed the glass over he would jump, and exchange glances with nearby diners as though sharing a universal astonishment that cause and effect enters the lives even of the humble.

When eating, it struck him as absurd that what had formerly been *out there* was now *in here*. It made him dreamy. You take that spud . . . carve it . . . spear a bit . . . there it is under your nose (*outside*); and suddenly it's *inside* and you're *outside* it. Aware of this peculiar carry on, Hooper felt extremely philosophical. For a moment or two he watched things disappear into Barbara. Then he thought: there is no mystery. Anything which was inside Barbara was still outside Hooper. He took a gulp at his Chianti and felt it chuckling down into his stomach. The odd thing, surely, was that anything should be inside Hooper if *you* were Hooper? How could anything really be –

'Colin darling, there's wine trickling all down your chin. Some on your collar –'

Now, there was a bitch who took it all for granted, if you like. He wiped his chin with the back of his hand. He focussed on Barbara an expression of bland neutrality . . . thought: old Barbara's an *object* too, ha ha. Having torn the meat off his chop he picked up the bone and ground it ferociously, at the same time searching for wax in his left ear.

'Colin *must* you sweet?' But Barbara's eyes strayed to her own discarded bone, where a few succulent bits remained that would have been eaten in the privacy of her flat. Am I a hypocrite?

'Some of these buggers –' Hoop laid the bone to rest, 'some of these buggers who wouldn't be seen eating a bone in public, they eat each other in private –'

Still, he didn't really hold that against them. He had often thought how pleasant it would be to eat Lasso. The mammaries anyway. Bishop Berkeley would have had a point if human beings were totally omnivorous. Hooper took out a little notebook and entered up the thought, examining Barbara from time to time and wondering if she were edible in this exciting way. He veered off sharply from the speculation.

'Colin, you do *want* to come home this evening?'

And meet the Barbara-Makers? That must have been a riot, when they conceived *her*. Hooper had a vision of a naked man in a bowler hat and a woman in W.V.S. uniform cohabiting, with averted faces. Unfortunately, Barbara's parents could never have attained even a comic originality. The crisply tailored girl in front gave the impression of having been born under aseptic conditions in a laboratory (and likewise conceived).

'I dunno. I dunno whether I do. Now.' Hoop knew at last that he had never intended to meet them.

'Darling what do you mean, *now*?' Tiny spasms of impatience took Barbara by surprise, for during Hoop's ingestion of his meal her face had felt becalmed and unwanted.

'I'm frightened of them.' Hooper forced half a pear into his mouth and looked wistful about the upper half of his face.

'Of Mummy and Daddy?'

'Big people. Frightening,' said Hoop, through the sweet and liquid mash.

How to put it? To explain that he had delusions of other peoples' grandeur? It was a question of physical size only, though. Since Hoop had found himself technically an adult, it had not been easy to cope with . . . what was it, an hallucination? An hallucination that although he was as tall as he was ever likely to be, other adults were taller. The big people. Another species. Giants going about their mysterious, compulsive business.

Barbara leaned across the table, and with her paper napkin wiped a trace of pear from Hooper's cheek. 'I hate women who do that sort of thing,' she said. 'But you *are* a messy eater. I suppose it's all part of the act.'

'Act?' Hoop was outraged. 'What do you mean, *act*?'

'Darling, you know what I mean, don't pretend you don't –'

'But bugger it! Act?'

'You're *quite* capable of getting on with people you know –'

He was, he knew it. So if that was what she meant. Hooper

reviewed his accomplishments: could dress, wash and shave self; could get about, though a little shy of busy crossings and preferred countries where the policeman whistled you across; could earn living to tune of four thousand a year; could hold his own in conversation, at least as well as a foreigner; could control excretory functions within reason. Yes, she was right! It was an act . . . all an act. Oh, admirable Babs! Hooper felt that his middle-class hoyden had caught on to his innermost sense of division.

'So all you need to do is, well, just be nice to Mummy and Daddy . . . they won't eat you –' Barbara began to integrate herself with her possessions: purse, cigarettes, umbrella (red, long handle), shoes.

Hooper had been fondling those shoes for ten minutes without realizing that they lacked feet . . . just nipping them affectionately under table cover, by way of reassurance. He stood up, beckoning the waiter. 'What makes you so bloody sure they won't eat me? We, we live in a predatory world. And then.' He screwed up pound notes and dropped them on a saucer. Two.

'And then what, darling?' Barbara was making for the door.

'What do you mean "and then"?'

'Well you just said "and then".'

'And then what?' Hooper felt reality becoming insubstantial.

'That's *precisely* what I was asking you, Colin –'

Outside, Hoop hovered. He had spied a Peeporama. In the muggy summer twilight of Greek Street there was a nostalgia . . . incongruous and not to be savoured at Barbara's side. Her expression suggested that his problem was Hendon or bust. Shall we bust? Get over the street, say, and take in the stills? Then telephone Lasso.

'I'm not coming. Not coming, No. You can tell Mummy and Daddy to get stuffed.' Having shouted this at Barbara, Hoop leapt back a foot or two, wheezing with fright. Psychosomatic asthma, he'd been told.

'Colin!' Barbara stared at her big muddled man in horror. 'Colin!'

From outside, nothing seemed amiss. Hoop was sombrely and respectably clothed . . . tie no more than half an inch from stud . . . shoes polished. Yet from this decorous image of conformity there issued the vulgar demotics of the street corner! Barbara gave him one last long look which combined disbelief with I should have expected it, and walked away.

Hoop giggled inside his head. From the rear, she was a shade scrawny, no? Living up to that? What had been the attraction? Before you knew where you were, house . . . kids . . . gracious living etc. . . . one Thames Green wall in the living-room. Hoop belched loudly and hysterically, went over to peep at Peeporama. He had three pints in the 'French' and rang Lasso, who sacrificed the evening's television without a murmur. For Lasso, no single activity had a superior claim to any other; she appeared at the meeting place in Piccadilly Circus and took Hoop's arm as laconically and dumbly as if it had all been prearranged. On the tube, that gratifying silence all the way – since a vestigial training in manners coupled with mental hiatus allowed Janine to speak only when spoken to.

At his flat, Hoop supplied the chocolates, the couch and the 'What's My Line'. In the semi-darkness, Janine supplied the anatomical parts most coveted and venerated in the Hooposophy. They wriggled and writhed and 'gumsucked' as Hoop laughingly termed it, before the flickering screen. At one point, Hoop got up to make cocoa – emerging from the kitchen with steaming mugs, and wearing a woolly dressing-gown.

'What's that you got on?'

'That's my sexographer's uniform –' Oh, Hoop in form.

'You don't half talk daft . . . mind, you gone as far as you're going wi' me –' She sipped her cocoa, and absentmindedly permitted the removal of certain critical garments. ''ere, has somebody been doing this place up?' But Hoop was beyond recall. Janine took his hairy dressing-gown by the lapels. 'Jer know what you are?'

A question so directly involving his identity was capable of arresting Hoop. 'What? What did you say?'

'You're a huggy bear,' said Janine, 'you're a real *huggy bear*.'

David Mercer was born in Wakefield, Yorkshire in 1928. He was educated at King's College, Newcastle upon Tyne. He served as a laboratory technician in the Royal Navy and then became a teacher. He took up writing full time in 1962. Although he was a playwright and published some twenty-four plays, his early work was in short fiction, some of which he subsequently turned into drama. He was the recipient of the Writers' Guild Award for a television play in 1962, 1967 and 1968, the *Evening Standard* award in 1965 and the British Film Academy Award in 1966. David Mercer died in 1980.

A Shetland Set by Lorna Tracy

Harbour still as glass. Warm sunshine, dazzle flowing down from the windows of Lerwick far into the bay at 6 am. By eight, when our car has been winched onto the pier, cirrus is forming. By nine the wind has pounced. At noon the sky's solid, the sun just a sore spot in that generalized pain. It is raining hard by three. After that come two days of gales, then a sunset like an accident. We will be healed in one night.

Winds scour these islands like water daily; the sea's door-stones.

Drained-off tides expose, day and day after day at twilight, the mess the sea walks on when it comes ashore: flattened rocks thickly stacked with lung-like orange weed formed of tubes and minute bladders, sucker-shaped, swollen, that fatly spring back whole the moment the foot is lifted. The sight disgusts, like hair clogging a drain, sieving off the scurf and saving it; choking nightmare of the sea's underlife, and the intimate water rubbing through it all, coming back.

The third morning in the dark the gale threw rain in fistsful at our window. It struck the pane like tossed pence and rattled off. I woke as if it signalled me and remembered my dream, while the wind poured down on the roof like one endlessly breaking wave that can neither move nor disperse itself. I had been dreaming of you that you sent me your expense account. In red ink at the bottom you had written: *I love you*. It seemed clear that an expenditure of feeling left you in considerable debt.

Wherever it is mean, stony, skint; wherever it's laid its traps for life – bogs, cliff-drops; wherever in the hömin light its crushed hills are beautiful Shetland's earth matches our lives, inert under the stooping moon.

The examining light of evening searches the land. The shadow of every straw is drawn long, tested. Walking among the water-eyes in the pewter-coloured dream's air every grain and bell of heather is sharp and clear but you cannot tell whether that stone will stumble up and sheep off, or whether that sheep will prove a stone to sit on. The wind worries at everything; even the stones shiver. The earth is cracked and sore with peat-cuts. Ronas Hill is a perpetual shadow on the northern sky. I continually hear voices (the wind in my balaclava, I suppose). Also organ music, and brass bands and string quartets and choirs and someone calling my name and crowds in a plaza and trolley cars.

The ponies, who live in rumpled pastures, come to the wall. We stare at one another for a long time.

On Sunday morning, moved by the spirit of sociological investigation, you wanted to go to church. When we found one in Walls that wasn't locked up the first phrase of the hymn sent you scurrying back to the car, disgusted that 'English conformity' had overtaken Shetland. Later, on the warmest day in nearly thirty years you went into a shop in your swimming trunks to buy our bread and cheese. The woman who served you was shamed by your public undress, the counter between hiding you from the waist down, but she was too polite – or else too canny – to refuse your custom. Shetlanders are good starers. The stares they served you then, those two men working on the roof across the road. You didn't notice.

The way you wave from the car at everyone, standing in fields, in doorways.

The islands in the mouth of Weisdale Voe are fair as words that go to gentle love. The first spoken are the mistiest; the breath gathered round them.

2

Something that's between gas and ashes; beyond the suffering Midlands rivers stiffened beneath their loads of poison and stuffed with rusting junk that's helpless even to sink; beyond the cooling-towers of Ferrybridge, the eleven concrete corsets; beyond the solid steam and the thin, shredded steams, the gross unabdomened guts of spewing industry fleshed with nothing but rags of steamy air – a working model in Hell's Museum of Science & Technology converting nourishment into waste; chyme into chyle and that into the end product which is excrement: adding plastic to the tides of Shetland and Yell; rust to the shallow lakes where the rare duck rises, her footprints on the clean water dissolving, linked wrinkled rings broken on a reef of beer cans and detergent bottles. So that anger rises in me like bile in a sick stomach, not bio-degradable, though; permanent as this plastic trash, swept under the Arctic Circle.

The refineries at twilight glitter like a consort of oboes at concert rest; incandescent notes gather all round them.

Leaves of unnatural green tangle the sea stones at Grobsness, entwine the plump pink thigh of a storm-dismembered doll.

Won't crack! Won't dent! Won't rust or stain! It washes up on the beaches of Shetland white and whole after three years in the sea. It comes ashore on Vaila perfect, and the voes of Unst yield strange alphabets. Metal corrodes and glass shatters; wood cracks, stone dissolves, but the white plastic bottle remains perfect, indestructible in seven languages. No deposit, no return! No return? What's the sea doing, then? Depositing them in their thousands; returning them to every shore it visits; and in every empty bottle a message from the castaway world: bury this before it buries you – whatever you can think of you can do.

Lorna Tracy is the author of *Amateur Passions*, a collection of short fiction published by Virago Press in 1981. Her stories and other prose have recently appeared in *Passion Fruit* (Pandora Press), *Bête Noire*, *Panurge* and *The Gamut*. For the past seventeen years she has been a co-editor of *Stand Magazine* in Newcastle upon Tyne, where she lives with her husband, the poet Jon Silkin. Lorna Tracy was born in Oregon, raised in Idaho, educated at Hastings College (Nebraska), the University of Denver and the University of Iowa Writers' Workshop. She has been a frequent tutor for the Arvon Foundation and in 1986 was Visiting Writer in Residence at Cleveland State University.

I Know You Can Talk by Peter Carey

I

The yellow lights of the pedestrian crossing flash regularly on/off, on/off below the window of the room where the Proprietor lies beside his wife. The yellow lights are the heart-beat of the town, the only indication that it hasn't died in its sleep. There is other movement but it is not the movement of the town itself which lies, passive, while large interstate trucks hurl themselves up its main street and out the other side, their tarpaulins flapping and their heavy tyres singing dangerous songs in the wet.

The Proprietor's wife snorts loudly in her sleep and turns suddenly. He turns also, to accommodate her, and fits his small body inside the curve formed by her large one, like a dessert spoon inside a table spoon.

This room on the upper floor contains the Proprietor, his wife, twin dressing-tables, two windows, one of which contains, in turn, a rusted air conditioner; the other opens onto a balcony from which an aluminium extension ladder can be lowered in the case of fire. The ladder is contained in a large built-in cupboard together with various items of clothing.

This is the heart of the Proprietor's territory, his inner sanctum. There are other rooms. In the next room the Proprietor's father-in-law sleeps one more night of his eighty-sixth year. His room contains a white-painted wooden chair on which sits a yellow vinyl cushion, a dresser with a tilting mirror, and a built-in cupboard. On the chair, like discarded dressings in a surgical ward, are items of clothing, to wit: one large pair of grey woollen trousers, one pair of long woollen underpants, a truss, one white drip-dry shirt with size 17 neck, one pre-tied snap-on tie, one pair of long grey socks, one grey cardigan, one dirty handkerchief and one pair of black leather slippers. A walking stick with a brass tip inscribed 'To H.H.' hangs from the handle of the closed door.

Beyond is a larger room in which discarded office furniture seems to float, lost in such a large space. The room is neat in the way of offices. It is not an office. It is the Proprietor's living-room. In one corner of this large room is a table. It is on this table that the Proprietor eats his meals.

Beyond is a long passage off which are smaller spaces: bathroom, toilet, laundry.

The long passage widens to become a narrow, galley-like kitchen and beyond the kitchen is the back porch where the Proprietor's dog scratches the hard linoleum floor.

Below is the spare parts and accessories section where the Proprietor's wife works each day from 7.30 am to 6.30 pm, and beyond that is the large car-yard where twenty-seven used cars now gleam silkily under eight tall lights.

Further, is the showroom where eight new cars, under cover, can be viewed from the street through plate glass windows.

All around stretches the town, a flat town with wide streets and large plane trees which now, in mid-winter, drip water from their leafless branches. All this town is the Proprietor's territory, granted to him by the Ford Motor Company.

Beyond, to the east, is wheat country. It stretches flat and monotonous for sixty miles. All this is the Proprietor's territory. Forty miles to the north, also wheat. Twenty miles to the south: wheat, mixed farms, two small towns, a few unsuccessful dairy farms. Forty miles to the west, including the straggling edges of the city.

All this is the Proprietor's territory. Within this zone he claims 53% of all cars sold, new and used. Beyond, there are greater princes, lords, powers he doesn't understand. Outside the territory there are wars, deaths, greater poverty and wealth than he could even try to imagine. Outside the territory are men who go to the moon, men who make atom bombs, men who control giant corporations, men who make jokes on television. They all walk their tightropes in a huge and complex circus, a vast circus full of dark spaces in which, crossing at fantastic angles, congested, frightening to behold, are the tightropes.

The news of the big circus is reported in the newspapers, but the

Proprietor no longer reads any of it except the advertisements for used cars, comparing prices beyond his territory with those within it.

In truth, he is preoccupied with his own circus where he walks his own tightrope. He is aware of the meanness of his circus, the unspectacular nature of his act. The falls in this tent are not so devastating, the injuries, perhaps, less severe, but it is lonely in the dark spaces which envelope the wires. There is no audience. Strong men with broken bodies lie groaning on the ground. They fall continually from their pitiful wires, like rain on the day of judgement. And all the while the Proprietor, small, weak, with a bad heart, no sense of smell, one blind eye, with weak arms and short legs manages, somehow, to keep his balance. He knows, he believes that he belongs with the maimed, the weak, the crippled, the half-dead who crawl and brawl and beg on the vermin-infested floor of the circus. He knows he belongs there. It was always expected of him and he grew to expect it of himself. As the smallest, meekest son of a large aggressive family it was assumed, a foregone conclusion. But instead, by some accident, he discovered the one talent that could keep him off the floor – he could sell motor cars. He could sell the arse off everyone in this territory. But the more cars he sold the higher they set the wire so that sometimes he wished to fall, simply to end the fear of falling, to have it over and done with.

The performers crawl, run, walk and hop along their wires like spiders in a forgotten cave. And the audience is not in the seats, which are empty, but on the rocky floor which is littered with decaying garbage and old car tyres, and the audience can only curse the performers for their success or applaud their downfall. On the floor his brother passes shiftily among the crowd, passing dud cheques. His sister is there, weeping quietly, harbouring disappointments too large to mention. His father lies there too, a tough old man dying of cancer throwing bricks at the rats who wait, like vultures, for his death.

The voices of the floor abuse him, attempt to distract him, call to him to come down.

But he knows that he wouldn't last a minute on the floor. On the wire, he survives on a nervous mixture of fear and skill. On the floor it is simply a matter of brute strength.

And on the floor he would be destroyed.

Once, a long time ago, he had loved his act. He had sold the first T models, the first A models. He lived and breathed motor cars. He had thought Henry Ford was a genius. He had never dreamt, in those days, that selling cars would become, finally, a matter of juggling finance, of being prepared to walk a thin line that separated a competitive deal from financial disaster. Each day brought new decisions on how much to allow for a trade-in and it seemed a long, long time since he had had to sell a man on the benefits of a motor car. He spent his days doing small calculations on scraps of paper. He kept the scraps of paper in his shirt pocket and at night they drifted through his mind like ghosts flying through the vaporous aftertaste of the whisky that had brought him through the day.

2

The morning, as usual, tasted stale in the Proprietor's mouth. His night had been filled with calculations and dress rehearsals for the day ahead. As usual he had slept little and had spent much of the night walking around the empty spaces of the house, coming always to stand at the picture window in the living-room. It was the same window he always stood at. It framed the car-yard which was filled with the pressed metal shapes that formed the foundations of his nightmares; dreams from Detroit shipped across an ocean to lie here in a country town in Australia, objects planned in minute American detail so that they might glide through the dreams of a sixty-two-year-old man who would stand, night after night in a woollen singlet and a large soft pyjama coat, to rehearse the moves and counter-moves that would result, finally, in their all being sold.

The Proprietor sat at the long table at breakfast and checked the spaces between his fork for scraps of food. It was a habit he had developed in the boarding houses of his youth, a habit he had sustained because the fast, nervous movements of his wife extended into all areas, from driving cars to washing dishes. He accepted the pieces of food without thought, accepting them as the natural result of the pressure his wife worked under. He was continually amazed by her energy. She was last to bed and first to wake. She ran on thin nervous legs through rooms filled with hard vinyl chairs and electric

24

radiators, bustling through the narrow kitchen, clattering, cooking, washing-up. By seven thirty she would be behind the counter in the spare parts section, ordering stock, finding the right fuel pump for an old model Ford, the right head gasket for a trade-in Plymouth. It was she who wrote the letters to people who hadn't paid their bills; she wrote in thick red pencil on the unpaid bill and earned a reputation as a tough old bitch. And while his wife presented the town with a hard exterior he knew it was an exterior built by fear of her own sentimental nature which continually erupted in unexpected and sudden charity. She was an erratic and confusing woman, the only daughter of the man who sat opposite the Proprietor at breakfast.

The Proprietor's father-in-law was a tall old man of eighty-six. A fringe of white hair clung to the sides of his bald, freckled head which had become more and more like a walnut. He had light blue eyes which suggested, alternately, a keen intelligence and a senile indifference. His eyes were like the waters of a lake on a clouded day, sometimes sparkling with reflected light when, unpredictably, the sun broke through.

He had become sloppy in the way of old men, dribbling food onto his large cardigan which his son-in-law could have worn as an overcoat. His limp white shirt was buttoned at the throat but seemed a size too big. His snap-on tie hung limply, revealing its tired elastic neckband.

The Proprietor's father-in-law said, 'Sleep well, Race?'

'Yes, very well.' Anything else would have been too complicated.

The old man took out his hearing aid and placed it carefully on the table, propping it up against his tin of De Witts Antacid Powder. The antacid powder irritated the Proprietor beyond belief, a premeditated insult to the food his wife had cooked. The Proprietor cleaned his fork with the sharp starched edge of the tablecloth and tried to find a place to rest his mind. He could see only the smug face of the Reverend Abrams whom he was going to have to see today.

'I had a devil of a time,' said the old man, 'a devil of a time. Couldn't get to sleep at all.'

The Proprietor snorted. His father-in-law's snoring provided a grating muzak for his sleepless nights. 'The old leg was playing up.' The old man had a bad leg.

He rubbed Rawleigh's Balsam on his bad leg. RAWLEIGH'S

25

BALSAM – FOR MAN OR BEAST. His room stank of the balsam, the smell crept out from under his door and drifted around the house, a constant reminder of his infirmity. 'There was a terrible racket,' the old man said, 'oh, a terrible noise. I thought it was someone trying to break in. A *drunk*, trying to break in.'

'You old bastard.' The Proprietor said it very softly. The old man's face registered nothing. He played with his scrambled eggs in a half-hearted sort of way, suggesting that he was too unwell to manage the food although he would, eventually, eat every scrap on the plate. The Proprietor guessed that he had heard, and felt, at once, remorse.

The old man's complaint had been directed against the Proprietor. It was a complex complaint. It involved the Proprietor's drinking and his habit of walking around the house in the middle of the night when everyone was meant to be asleep. The old man disapproved of both these things and somehow attributed one to the other, the walking to the drinking. 'A *drunk*,' he had said, talking in code to the Proprietor.

Now the old man was disconnecting his hearing aid, because he had heard what the Proprietor had said, or because he hadn't, or for some other reason the Proprietor would never know.

He watched the old man eat his scrambled eggs. A small piece of egg had fallen among the whiskers in a fold of the old man's face.

The table they ate on was large, but it seemed, in the empty space of the living-room, to be very small. The room was furnished with left-over furniture from the business and was dotted with numerous ashtrays advertising brands of petrol, tyres and motor accessories. There was no concession to comfort in the room. It was like a waiting-room, a place where people stay before moving on to other more interesting places.

The Proprietor had lived here for thirty-two years. But it was only now, this morning, as he watched the old man finish the scrambled eggs and mix his glass of De Witts Antacid, that the barrenness of the room struck him, and even then he saw, not the room, but his life in the room.

It had not always been like this. There had been earlier years, before the old man arrived, when his two sons, who he had always assumed would go into the business, had still lived at home, when the room had been full of noise and the empty spaces between the office chairs had not been visible, or had been filled with noise and the sound of music. The pianola still stood where it had always been, beside the picture window, and on top of the pianola were the rolls ('The Student Prince', 'Turn Back the Hands of Time', 'Enjoy Yourself – It's Later Than You Think') they had always played. But now the pianola had become a dark heavy piece of furniture and the rolls were untouched. It would have been wrong to play them. It would have been false, a pretended happiness.

In any case, the old man would have objected to the music. To him it would be a 'dreadful racket'.

The old man had been a fine, dignified old man. He had never scrambled on the high wire but had walked calmly, his head erect, never doubting himself or the wire on which he stood. The Proprietor wondered if the old man had ever been aware of the wire. He had taught school until it was time to retire and then he had retired and come to live in this town in his own house with his own wife. He had grown his own vegetables, kept his own fowls, and valued his independence. But he grew older, his wife died, and his daughter, the Proprietor's wife, insisted that he couldn't be left alone. So he had come, tamely enough, to live in the house above the Proprietor's business. And there, in the house of two tired, busy people, he had been reduced to a child and had only a child's weapons to assist his independence and to assert his will.

So he became sick when the Proprietor drank whisky because he disapproved of drinking and had never lived in a house where it had occurred. He could only communicate his disapproval by becoming sick.

He thought that all honest people were in bed by eight o'clock. Everyone who had ever lived in his house had gone to bed by eight o'clock. So when the TV was switched on at night he groaned loudly from his bed, and continued to groan more and more loudly until it was finally switched off.

He had effectively taken from the Proprietor the few small freedoms that had afforded him some illusion of comfort and release from the tensions of the wire. And now, unable to play darts, watch television or even drink openly in his own home, the Proprietor was confronted endlessly with the spectacle of the circus. There was nothing to take his mind away from it.

The Proprietor found himself, at breakfast, sitting in a waiting-room. He realized, slowly, what he was waiting for.

He was waiting for the old man to die.

He didn't imagine for a moment that the old man's death would bring him any happiness, but rather that it would return him those few small freedoms which would make his life bearable, which would return his house to what it had been before – a fragile oasis in a town that was filled, not with friends, but with acquaintances who were all prospective customers.

The old man looked up and nodded to him, as if he had read his thoughts. The eyes seemed bright blue and clear. They pierced the Proprietor who felt, before those eyes, mean and sordid. It seemed to him then that that was what the old man's eyes had always said to him as long as he had known him.

The Proprietor averted his eyes and stood awkwardly, nearly knocking his chair over backwards as he did so. He went out to the kitchen where his wife was washing dishes while she waited for the breakfast to cook. A diabetic dessert for the old man, freshly made, was cooling on top of the refrigerator. The toast was burning. He took it out of the toaster and said, 'Will I scrape it?'

She took the toast from him. 'Did he eat his eggs?'

'Yes.'

'I'll scrape the toast. You talk to him. He's lonely.'

The Proprietor returned to the waiting-room.

The old man's eyes had clouded over once more. The Proprietor sat across the table from the old man and tried, conscientiously, to think of something to say to him.

3

The Proprietor's face, at eight o'clock, was hard and humourless as he began, once more to set the wheels of the business in motion. The business was like a large eight-cylinder engine on a cold morning. He saw it like that in his mind. Cold, viscous oil clung clammily to the moving parts. He could feel the cold in its steel walls, an inertia which almost amounted to hostility. Each morning he cranked that engine until it came, each day more unwillingly, into life.

The mechanics who waited outside the workshop saw a plump little man with a red face and well-shined shoes lean against a large cyclone gate and push it slowly open. They waited silently for the man to walk to where they waited, unaware that he viewed the coming day with as little enthusiasm as they did. The Proprietor locked the padlock onto the open gate for safe-keeping and walked to where the mechanics stood. He unlocked the huge wooden doors of the workshop and helped the men push them open. The smell of the workshop engulfed him: a smell of heavy oil and petrol vapour which seemed to fill every crack and opening in his life.

The men greeted him but he was thinking about the Reverend Abrams and their greeting didn't reach him until he had already crossed the used car-yard and begun to open one more heavy door – the door of the new car showroom. It was here that he had his office, a glass cubicle separated from the rest of the showroom like a sound-proof booth in a quiz show.

He stood behind his desk and took a number of small pieces of paper from his shirt pocket. These he spread, like a hand of patience, on the office table. The pieces of paper were covered with his strange uneven handwriting, an eccentric mixture of large and small letters which spelt out the names of prospects, contacts made, contacts to be made. He was checking these pieces of paper, mentally ordering them, when Hubby Lloyd wandered into the office like a man who had lost his way. Hubby's large stomach was covered by a grey cardigan; the cardigan was covered by an old green sportscoat; the sportscoat was decorated with worn pieces of leather on the elbows and cuffs.

Hubby said, 'What's on today, Chief?' Which is what he had said every morning for fifteen years, as if each morning were his first day at work. And today, as usual, he would have to be told what to do, to be reminded of what happened yesterday.

Hubby was a large fat man with a large almost featureless face and a love of obscure words, or words which were obscure in this town which managed to function with the shortest of words. But Hubby (whose real name was Hubert and who never referred to himself as Hubby) had educated himself by reading a page of the dictionary every day for many years, many years ago. It seemed to the Pro-prietor, who professed to know about nothing but motor cars, that

Hubby knew about everything but motor cars. He was painful and ponderous and produced his scraps of knowledge with agonizing slowness. He was, however, loyal to the Proprietor and the Proprietor, who never forgot his own precarious position on the wire, forgave Hubby his inefficiencies and inabilities for this one rare quality.

Hubby breathed out slowly and lowered his bulky arse onto the edge of the desk. The Proprietor, watching from the corner of his good eye, thought that he looked like a punctured dirigible. Hubby was holding a newspaper in his large meaty hands. Now he carefully spread it over the desk, obscuring the pieces of paper the Proprietor had spread there. 'Shocking business,' he said.

'What?' The Proprietor gazed unseeingly at the newsprint, still reading the small pieces of paper he could no longer see. He was wondering whether to send Hubby to see the Reverend Abrams or to go himself. The Reverend Abrams had been running his Falcon with the speedo disconnected for more than a year. The Proprietor thought that the minister was a prig and the very thought of the disconnected speedo made him furious. He thought that Hubby might be able to handle it tactfully, if only because he was a member of Abrams' congregation.

'The bridge,' said Hubby, 'a shocking business.'

The Proprietor now saw the newspaper on the table. A bridge had collapsed somewhere in the world outside. A large number of people had been killed. The photograph was grey and muddy in the manner of disaster photographs. To the Proprietor it could have been a photograph of the planet Mars. He said, 'I want you to go and have a yarn with Abrams.'

Hubby breathed out loudly and folded the paper with exaggerated care. 'Not an easy assignment. In fact,' he drew in a new ration of air, 'in fact, an intrinsically difficult assignment, in view of the speedo.'

'Don't go over eight hundred,' said the Proprietor, 'there's not much in it even then. But if you keep under eight hundred we won't get in the shit over it.' He nodded to Frankie Phillips who had just come in and was stuffing some Fairline brochures into his briefcase.

'The only problem I can see,' said Hubby, 'is that I was expecting Mrs K. L. Humphries to come in about the station sedan.'

'Frankie can handle Mrs Humphries.'

'I've got to go to Wallan,' said Frankie. 'Snowy Morton is quacking like a duck. I can write the deal today for sure.'

'OK,' said the Proprietor, 'well *I'll* talk to Mrs Humphries.'

'Very well, Chief,' said Hubby, 'but if you don't mind me saying so she's a personal friend of ours. Her sister is married to . . .'

'I know,' said the Proprietor, 'but Abrams is a friend of yours too, isn't he?'

'He's our minister if that's what you mean.'

'That's what I mean.'

Hubby banged the folded newspaper against his leg and looked miserable. 'Well, actually, that's the problem, if you get my meaning. It could be a bit tricky . . .'

4

The old man was in the far corner of the living-room holding his wet handkerchief in front of the electric radiator. It was his way of saving his daughter work – if he could dry his wet handkerchief he could save her the work of washing it.

Crouched over the radiator with his back to the door he didn't notice the Proprietor pass on his way to the bedroom.

The Proprietor shut the bedroom door behind him and took a new bottle of scotch from the dresser beside his bed. He poured himself a drink and lifted the telephone receiver.

'Yes, is that you?' His wife was working the switchboard down-stairs. Her voice sounded anxious. She was worried that he was sick, that his heart was playing up again.

'It's all right. I want to talk to Abrams.'

'Are you sure you're all right?'

'I just wanted to talk to Abrams from up here, it's quieter.'

'If you're feeling sick you better lie down.'

'No, I just want to talk to Abrams.'

'Who?'

'The Reverend Abrams. Will you get him for me?'

'The Reverend Abrams. Hold on, I'll get him for you.'

He heard his wife's shop voice ask someone to wait and then the noise of dialling. She came back to say, 'It's ringing. I'll hang up.'

The Proprietor thanked his wife and finished his whisky in a gulp. He was trying to soothe the irritation that he felt at the very thought of the minister. He poured himself another glass and thought, if I go on like this I'll kill myself.

Finally the minister answered. He sounded sleepy.

The Proprietor thought, the bastard hasn't even got out of bed yet.

'Oh, it's you is it?' said the minister. 'I've been wondering when you'd get around to calling.'

'Ten o'clock,' said the Proprietor, 'how about ten o'clock?'

'I'll expect a good price from you, Race. She's in good nick.'

'Is ten o'clock all right?'

'Yes, ten o'clock will be fine.'

'All right, I'll see you then,' said the Proprietor and dropped the phone back on the hook, surprised at the intensity of loathing he felt for the minister. The reasons for his feelings were complex. It was because he himself tried to be honest when everyone expected him to be dishonest. It was because the minister was dishonest when the Proprietor expected him, of all people, to be honest. Finally it was because Abrams obviously thought he was simple.

He poured himself another drink, and looked at himself in the mirror. The booze, he thought, wasn't doing much for his complexion. He raised his heavy eyebrows so they stood, arched, above his black-framed bifocals, dropped his false teeth, and pulled a strange face at himself. He could hear the old man moving around the house. The floorboards creaked, but it sounded to the Proprietor as if the old man were creaking. The creaking came closer and stopped outside the door. He popped his false teeth back into place and turned to face the door which opened slowly. The old man seemed to fill the doorway.

He felt immediately guilty, a child caught in his solitary sin, a glass of whisky in his hand. He held the glass woodenly, unsure of what to do with it, unwilling to hide it and equally unwilling to expend any emotional energy in a scene which he would regret later.

'Not at work yet?' said the old man. He seemed vague. The Proprietor wondered what he had been looking for in this bedroom.

'I've been making a phone call.'

'What?' The old man began to fiddle with his hearing aid. He put his walking stick in the crook of his arm and took the hearing aid out of his cardigan pocket. He held it towards the Proprietor.

'What's that you say?'

'A phone call. I came to make a phone call.'

'Oh.' He still hadn't heard. He advanced with the hearing aid as if it were a Geiger counter. The Proprietor stayed where he was but felt alarmed, suddenly, by the size of the old man. He almost expected to be attacked with the walking stick, to be driven from his own bedroom in righteous anger. The old man edged closer with the hearing aid and then seemed to notice the whisky for the first time. His lip actually curled. His face registered hurt and disgust. 'You're not drinking that stuff again are you, Race?'

'Yes,' said the Proprietor, 'I am.'

'Does Mary know about this?'

'Oh God save me,' said the Proprietor. He brushed past the old man and walked from the room. In the kitchen he downed the rest of the drink and rinsed the glass in the sink.

5

The Reverend Abrams was short and squat, a little shorter than the Proprietor, but with broad shoulders and muscular forearms. His round moon face had a strange transparent quality, a soft untouched face that seemed strange on top of such a hard body. The Proprietor found him in front of the Church Hall putting black boot-polish on the tyres of his Falcon. In any circumstances this would have made him suspicious – only dealers blacked the tyres of motor cars.

'Just shining it up for you,' said the Reverend Abrams who was wearing a cassock. The Proprietor wondered why he was wearing the cassock. Did he think it was going to get him a better price?

The Proprietor smiled. 'It's a nice day,' he said.

The Reverend Abrams slipped the tin of boot-polish into a hidden pocket in his cassock and frowned. 'It's a little early, isn't it?'

The Proprietor ignored that and concentrated his attention on the car. Certainly it was a good-looking vehicle. The minister had, at least, looked after the duco. But that was the sort of man he was. As he walked around the car the minister followed closely behind him, a pair of working boots sticking out from under his cassock. It was his belief that the boots, somehow, made him more down-to-earth and thus more acceptable to the locals. His belief was without foundation.

The Reverend Abrams smiled too often and too easily and today, as the Proprietor talked to him, he detected a smirk in the polished corners of the minister's smile.

The Proprietor sat behind the wheel and looked for a long time at the speedo: 32,478·6 miles.

Eventually the minister came and sat beside him in the passenger's seat. The Proprietor started the engine and listened to it. It was not a good sound. He put the car into gear and winced when the gears grated. He repeated the action. The gears grated again.

'First time it's ever done that,' said Abrams, 'have you got the clutch in?'

The Proprietor ignored him. He'd take the car out to the silo for a test drive. He didn't need to test the car anymore, he needed the time to calm down and work out what he was going to offer.

As they pulled out of the churchyard Abrams said, 'You're all right, are you?'

'All right?'

'All right to drive.'

The Proprietor stopped and pulled on the handbrake. 'Mr Abrams, I've been driving cars for fifty-eight years, drunk and sober, and I'm not drunk now.'

'Of course not . . .'

The Proprietor released the handbrake. 'Good.'

The silo was at a railway siding about three miles out of town. The two men travelled there, and nearly back, without speaking.

Finally it was Abrams who turned and placed his pastoral hand along the back of the seat and said, 'Well, what do you think of the old bus?'

'Have you been having trouble with the speedo?' He hadn't intended to say that. Even Hubby wouldn't have been stupid enough to say that. He had been so obsessed with not saying it that he had said it.

'No, no trouble.'

The Proprietor was sure, absolutely sure, that Abrams had smirked. Abrams was a fool if he thought the Proprietor didn't know

34

about the speedo cable. He had seen the disconnected cable himself, the last time the Falcon had been in for service. It was a joke in the workshop. Everybody, even Hubby, knew about it. But he gritted his teeth and decided to swallow the lie. 'I can offer you seven fifty.'

'I've been offered much more than that, much, much more.'

The smug bastard was really sure that he didn't know.

'By who?'

'Oh come, that'd be telling tales out of school.'

'The best I could do would be eight hundred.'

Even while he said this he was trying to work out if that would leave him any margin at all. He might have to spend a hundred, maybe two hundred, getting it into reasonable condition. Even then he'd be lucky to get nine fifty for it. If he made a loss that'd take the profitability from the new Cortina Abrams wanted. Still, if he could just keep calm . . .

'Have you noticed that low mileage . . .?'

'Noticed it?' The Proprietor looked at Abrams incredulously. He thought if I were a strong man I'd kill him with my bare hands. I'd put my hands around his neck and I'd fucking well kill him. 'Noticed it! Oh, for Christ's sake, I know you've had the speedo cable off. Every bastard knows you've had the speedo cable off.'

Abrams said nothing, but he was grinning like a schoolboy.

The Proprietor concentrated fiercely on the road, narrowing his good eye so he could see little but the white line. The minister was on his blind side.

'You can't top eight hundred then?'

He knew that he could make a deal now. He knew that tone of voice. He had heard it a thousand times. It was the voice of defeat. He tried to choke back his rage and turned to look at the minister.

The bastard was still grinning.

They were almost back into town. The Proprietor felt he was going to explode. He swung the car off the road and screeched to a halt in front of a small fibro cement house. He said, 'I've got to see someone here. You take the car on.'

'I'll wait and give you a lift,' said the Reverend Abrams.

'No,' the Proprietor shook his head. He was going to say more but he stopped himself.

Abrams grated the Falcon into first gear and lurched away, leaving a trail of blue smoke which remained hovering over the road long after the car had disappeared.

The Proprietor began to walk. He began to do one more calculation. He calculated what he would get if he sold the whole business, lock, stock and barrel. He knew the answer before he began. He had made the calculation often. Once he'd paid off his loans and fixed his overdrafts there might be enough to live on for two years, maybe three.

He had no choice but to continue on the wire, to keep calm, to be patient, to tolerate the dishonesty, worse – the hypocrisy, of the Abrams of this world, to put up with all the shit and to move, one foot after the other, from one sale, to the next sale, to the next.

Five years ago, even twelve months ago, he wouldn't have lost his temper.

The Proprietor wondered if he wasn't losing his grip. As he walked along the dusty gravel shoulder of the road he imagined he was already on the floor of the circus.

And he didn't understand what that damn grin meant.

6

In the afternoon the Proprietor did penance for the morning.

He had returned from his long walk to find Mrs Humphries about to leave the showroom. Hubby Lloyd was shuffling catalogues and making them stand in neat piles.

Mrs Humphries was a tough, lean woman whose husband had run away with the girl who worked in the butcher's. She ran a small cartage contracting business singlehanded. Now she was edging towards the door mumbling something about coming back later.

The Proprietor summed up the situation immediately. He nodded to Mrs Humphries and began to abuse Hubby.

'Mrs Humphries doesn't want the station sedan.' Mrs Humphries lit a cigarette and narrowed her eyes. She looked from the Proprietor to Hubby and back again.

Hubby looked at the Proprietor beseechingly.

'It's got a whine in the diff,' said the Proprietor, 'and Mrs Humphries doesn't want it.'

Mrs Humphries, in jeans and a plain woollen shirt, was pinning back a loose strand of her untidy red hair. 'Hang on,' she said, speaking around the cigarette in her mouth. 'Hang on, I didn't say I didn't want it, I said I'd think about it.'

'I wouldn't sell it to you anyway,' said the Proprietor, 'not with that diff like that.'

'Hubby's going to fix the diff,' said Mrs Humphries, 'aren't you, Hubby?'

'Yes,' said Hubby, 'you told me you'd fix . . .'

'What use would you have for a station-wagon?' said the Proprietor.

'Don't tell me what I'm going to buy,' said Mrs Humphries. 'I'll buy what I want, not what you want.'

'Suit yourself,' said the Proprietor and walked out of the show-room, leaving Hubby to get the sale finalized.

He spent the afternoon across the road in the Royal Mail Hotel where, in the course of an afternoon, he took an order for a new Fairlane from Wilbur Duncan and collected a cheque for the deposit. He listened patiently to old Joe Morgan while he talked, at length and in detail, about the liver fluke which had infected his herd, and finally, at five o'clock brought him across to show him a '69 Dodge. While Joe took the Dodge for a drive he rang Ford and discovered that they had one Aztec White Fairlane, which was the colour Wilbur wanted. He arranged to pick it up tomorrow.

Joe Morgan returned with the Dodge and the Proprietor told him to take it for the night and show it to his wife.

He returned to the showroom to find that Hubby was, at last, writing out a Hire Purchase contract for Mrs Humphries.

'You're a lovely woman,' he told Mrs Humphries.

'You're an old bastard,' she said.

'I'm not a young bastard anymore, that's certain.'

'You'll kill yourself with all that booze.'

'I've got Liver Fluke,' said the Proprietor, 'It's a fluke I've got a liver at all.'

Mrs Humphries threw her head back and shrieked with laughter. The Proprietor grinned. He was firing on all eight cylinders. He was at home on his high wire, safe and sure-footed.

As Mrs Humphries drove away in the station-wagon Frankie

Phillips arrived back from Wallan with a new trade-in and announced that he'd bled the cocky blind. The Proprietor didn't like that. He didn't like the way Frankie Phillips operated. He was too fast, too slick, and in the long term it would be the Proprietor who would have to pay for his sins. Although the Proprietor was sometimes devious in his approach he never cheated anyone. As he watched Frankie talk to him he knew that he would lose him anyway. He would be a big success in the city.

His father-in-law wandered into the showroom and walked painfully over to where the Proprietor was talking to Frankie.

'How are you?' said the Proprietor.

'I'm all bound up.'

'You should take some salts.'

'What's that?'

'Some salts. You should take some salts.'

'I've used them all up.'

The Proprietor looked up into his father-in-law's face and regretted having lost his temper with him that morning.

'I'll get you some salts,' he said, 'you go upstairs and I'll get you some salts.'

His father-in-law wandered off and the Proprietor told Frankie to lock up everything; then he went to the pub where he knew he would find Nevil Hogan the Chemist.

7

When the Proprietor arrived home with the salts it was seven o'clock. His wife was sitting on a high stool in the kitchen reading an old newspaper. She looked up apprehensively as he came in and, when she saw who it was, burst into tears.

The Proprietor stood unsteadily at the open door of the kitchen, unsure of what he had done. The dog jumped up at his back and licked his hand. He was shocked to see the age in his wife's face, the sagging flesh around the mouth, the blemishes accentuated by her crying. It was as if the old man's age was contagious, a slow creeping disease that had spread through them both since he arrived. She said, 'I thought you were dead.'

He remained at the door, feeling, suddenly, all the whisky energy drain out of him and leave behind a dry, tired scum. 'I went to get some salts. Hogan was at the pub. I had to go there to get Hogan.'

'Frankie said you went to the Chemist's.'

'I had to go to the pub to get Hogan to open his shop.'

She began wiping her tears away with the corner of her apron. She stood and began to peel some potatoes. He could feel the tiredness in her body, a dull exhaustion produced by another day of stock-taking and serving behind the counter and worrying about her sick husband and her unhappy father.

The Proprietor said, 'I'm sorry.'

'Let's not talk about it,' she told the potatoes, 'go and talk to father, he's been annoying me all day with his constipation.'

'I got him some salts.' The Proprietor held up the bottle. 'I had to get Nevil Hogan to open his shop.'

'Good.' She dumped the potatoes in a saucepan of water and tried to light the stove with a dead match. The Proprietor went to help her and she burst into tears again.

He held her until he felt her become still and then he said, 'Would you like me to take him to town tomorrow?'

She was wiping her eyes again. 'You're not going to town.'

'I've got to pick up a vehicle for Wilbur Duncan.'

'Wilbur Duncan!'

'Yes.'

'Isn't that lovely.' She tried, bravely, to smile, to defeat her fatigue with enthusiasm.

'I can pick it up tomorrow and deliver it on Friday.'

His wife lit the stove. 'To Wilbur Duncan. That's lovely.'

'Would you like me to take him with me?'

'Do you mind?'

'No,' said the Proprietor, 'I don't mind.'

'Well, why don't you pour me a drink; it's been a right bugger of a day. I'll come in as soon as I get the peas on.'

On the way to the bedroom he gave the old man his salts. 'That ought to fix you up,' he said.

'What?' said the old man.

'It doesn't matter,' said the Proprietor and went to get the drinks ready.

8

It is night. It is always night in the tent. The Proprietor walks bare-foot across a linoleum floor. The toilet cistern is still filling, making an uneven gurgling sound.

Somewhere, on another wire, the Reverend Abrams performs obscene tricks, swinging insanely from his toes, an indecipherable grin on his shining moon face.

In the back porch, at the top of the stairs, the dog stirs, scratching on his own linoleum floor. The Proprietor wonders if the dog knows that it is the old man who is responsible for his exile.

The Proprietor, in the dark living-room, opens the venetian blinds, lifts the slats, and looks, for the fourth time tonight, at the twenty-three cars in the yard below; hard metallic objects shining in the harsh light of day. He thinks, not of the afternoon's successes, but of the morning's failure with the Reverend Abrams.

The dog sneezes.

The Proprietor opens the door which connects the living-room to the porch. His feet are cold on the linoleum. He squats, puffing as he does so, and takes the dog's black head in his hands. In the half-light the dog's brown eyes glint. They seem very big.

The Proprietor, whispering so that not even the distant unseen audience could possibly hear, says to the dog, 'I know you can talk, say something – I'll give you a biscuit if you say something.'

He rises and goes through a second doorway which connects the porch to the narrow kitchen. He stands on one of his wife's tears. Even when he stoops to examine it and discovers that it is, in fact, a small piece of potato peel it remains, in his mind, one of his wife's tears. Unsure of what to do with it, he places it carefully in the pocket of his pyjama coat.

He finds a dry biscuit but looks for a sweet one which he imagines the dog will prefer, but there are no sweet biscuits except the old man's special diabetic ones which he wouldn't consider giving to the dog.

He takes the dry biscuit and returns to the porch where the dog jumps up at him. He takes the dog by the collar and forces him to sit down. Then, squatting in front of him, the black furry head held between his two hands, one of which also holds the biscuit, he says, 'I know you can talk.'

The dog breaks free and snaps off half the biscuit. The Proprietor stands slowly, his knees creaking. 'I'll give you this biscuit if you say something.' Then, without waiting for an answer, he drops the broken biscuit on the floor and goes back to bed.

9

The Proprietor sits in bed and watches the light of the pedestrian crossing, sliced into pieces by the venetian blind, fall in sickly bands across the ageing face of his wife which has assumed shapes and patterns he could never have foretold.

He hears his father-in-law moan in his sleep but sees a dry black pea rattling inside a brittle shell.

10

When the midday train pulled out the Proprietor and his father-in-law were aboard, but the Proprietor's eyes were still seeing what they had seen at the showroom before they left.

What he had seen should have made him happy, but it only served to deepen his depression.

Walking through the showroom he had seen, framed by the glass window of his office, the back of the Reverend Abrams' head. Hubby Lloyd sat on the other side of the desk from the Reverend Abrams who, according to everything the Proprietor had ever learned, should not be sitting there at all. But Hubby was calculating a Hire Purchase contract that the Proprietor had known would never be calculated. He came closer to the window, fascinated, as if he would see something, some detail, which would explain the workings of the Reverend Abrams' mind.

As he approached the window Hubby caught sight of him and waved; the Reverend Abrams, seeing the wave, turned and having seen the Proprietor smirked one more impossible time.

The Proprietor stared at the Reverend Abrams who was making

some sign to him, and then, rather than disrupt what was, in a business sense, a desirable process, waved and left the showroom.

And now as the train rocked and jolted on its locally famous square wheels, the Proprietor felt, once more, that he no longer understood anything, that he was losing that gut feeling for people that had guided him unfailingly from one sale to the next for over forty years.

Unlike Hubby who always retained the details of people's lives without in any way gaining a feeling for the way those people would react, the Proprietor forgot all the little scraps of personal information which were offered to him by his customers and operated instead by some seventh, almost psychic, sense which told him when to talk, when to shut-up, when to hide his drunkenness, when to accentuate it, when to play the fool, when to be serious, when to listen to a husband and ignore his wife, when to court the wife and forget the husband, when to be disrespectful and when to be polite. Some combination of the Reverend Abrams' respectability and dishonesty had so confused the seventh sense that he was unable to receive anything but an irritating static. The Proprietor was flying blind with faulty instruments. All he could see was a smirk suspended in space and the smirk, this one clear signal, danced around the Proprietor who clung to the wire and tried to keep his balance.

The train lurched sideways and the Proprietor knocked his head against the window.

The old man, after a lot of rummaging around in the big pockets of his trousers and the smaller pockets of his cardigan, had found his glasses. There were two pairs – his 'reading glasses' and his 'distance glasses'.

He fumbled around with the two pairs, putting on one pair and staring at his driver's licence which he held in his outstretched hand, moving the licence towards and then away from his eyes. Then, deciding that these were the wrong glasses, he repeated the operation with the other pair.

The Proprietor sat watching him and wondering why he had taken out his licence. Had the old man mistaken it for his ticket? Or was it some message for the Proprietor, a hint that the old man would like to drive the Fairlane back from the plant? He hoped it wasn't that.

But now the old man tapped the Proprietor on the knee and leaned across from the bench where he was sitting. He pointed to the date of birth which was shown on the licence. He laughed, which was his way of remarking on how old he was and how things had changed.

The Proprietor, searching for some way to continue this conversation, said, 'What car did you learn to drive in?'

'What's that?' The old man leaned forward a little more and the Proprietor noticed that he was still wearing the tie with the elastic loop. The old man loved to show off that elastic loop to his grandchildren, snapping it off from around his neck until the children were nearly sick with laughter. He had developed a kind of neck-tie language, a method of talking to children at least. 'What's that, Race?' The old man began to fiddle with his hearing aid. There was no one else in the carriage.

The Proprietor shouted, 'What car did you learn to drive in?'

The old man smiled deprecatingly and shrugged. 'Oh . . .' he said, and the Proprietor knew he couldn't remember.

The Proprietor smiled, feeling the fondness he might have felt for a difficult child in its less difficult moments.

'Are you feeling better today?' he asked.

'That's good,' said the old man, 'that stuff's no good for you, Race.'

It took a moment for the Proprietor to understand what the old man was saying. And when he understood the misunderstanding he said, 'Fuck you.' He didn't care if the old man had heard or not.

A few minutes later, looking out the window, he received a hard kick in the shins. He yelped with pain.

Looking across at the old man who appeared to be dozing, he was almost convinced that he had made a mistake. The pain, however, was real enough. As he rubbed his shin the old man opened his eyes and asked him the time. The Proprietor showed him his watch and the old man said, 'Oh well, won't be long now.'

Looking at his weathered face, the white fringe of hair around the bald freckled head, and most of all those eyes which were, at the moment, a sharp clear blue, the Proprietor wondered what the old man thought. He wondered if he loved his daughter, or if he even remembered her as being his daughter. He wondered if he thought of the Proprietor, if he hated him, liked him, pitied him, or, unlikely as it might seem, feared him.

As he watched, the Proprietor saw the old man slip a sweet into his mouth surreptitiously. Sweets were forbidden him, because of his diabetes, but the Proprietor said nothing. He rubbed his shin and wondered what the old man saw with his grey-blue eyes.

11

'When I come sixty fucking miles to pick up an Aztec White Fairlane I expect it to be a bloody Aztec White Fairlane and not some fucking Monza Gold thing. I've got *two* Monza Golds and I can't shift the bastards. That's why I came sixty miles to get an Aztec White. I didn't come sixty miles to get another Monza Gold, for Christ's sake,' said the Proprietor who stood red-faced, with his clenched fists held firmly down his side, inside the Ford Sales Manager's office. He had known the Sales Manager when he was an allocations clerk, but now he sat behind his big desk in his carpeted office, a large smooth-fleshed man who wore a sincere smile and very large cufflinks, who stroked the back of one hand with the palm of another as if this might, somehow, soothe the hoarse-voiced country dealer who stood in front of him.

The old man stood behind the Proprietor in the doorway and took off his hat to the secretaries who walked past in the corridor outside.

The Sales Manager made a church and then a steeple with his manicured hands. 'We all make mistakes, Race, if there *has* been a mistake. But anyway, according to this,' he dismantled the church and waved a piece of pink paper at the Proprietor, 'according to this, you're way over your allocation for the month anyway. So . . .'

'You bastards,' said the Proprietor, 'are impossible. Now you're complaining because I sell too many cars.'

'I didn't say that, Race.' The manicured hands put the pink slip back into a file which bore the Proprietor's name.

'You've got bullshit on your chin,' the Proprietor offered a handkerchief. 'Wipe it off.'

The Proprietor knew that if he kept talking loudly enough, foully enough and long enough, he would get, somehow, his Aztec White Fairlane. He would shout until he knew his voice had penetrated the walls of the office, until everyone could hear the shit that the Sales Manager was taking from a country dealer who was too good to be replaced. Ford executives were easily embarrassed by such unsophisticated anger.

'Listen to me.' The Proprietor leaned across the desk and jabbed a stubby finger at the Sales Manager who was at least twice his size and who, on the floor of the circus, would have strangled the Proprietor with his large white hands. 'Listen to me, I'm staying right here until you tell me I can get that vehicle. Who'd you give it to? Jack Ferris Motors or some cunt like that?'

'Race, you always over-react.'

Yes, thought the Proprietor, but it always works.

'If you'll stop shouting, Race, I'll try and see what I can do for you. Now why don't you bring in the old man and give him a seat.'

The Proprietor had forgotten the old man who may or may not have been shocked by it. He brought him into the office and indicated a large leather chair. The old man seated himself slowly and placed his hat carefully on the padded arm.

The Sales Manager was putting the pressure on someone else. 'You tell him I asked so,' he told the telephone, 'and get the forms round to Dealer Credit in ten minutes. Yes, the *new* forms. OK? You're right? Good.' He placed the receiver quietly in its cradle and said, 'Fixed.'

The Proprietor nodded and introduced his father-in-law.

'You weren't in the business yourself?' the Sales Manager asked.

'What's that?'

'You weren't in the car game?'

The old man said, 'General Gordon Gordon was one of my scholars. I still hear from him from time to time.' He took out his wallet and looked for a letter which, the Proprietor knew, he had lost long ago.

The Sales Manager looked at the wallet with smiling expectation but the old man put the wallet back in his pocket.

'So you were a school teacher,' he said. 'My boy is going to . . .'

'A headmaster.'

'Oh a headmaster. Where would that have been?' The old man counted the towns off on his fingers. And the Proprietor, who was sitting on the edge of the Sales Manager's desk, saw the old man in the way the Sales Manager was seeing him, like a grand old man walking through the cover of an old copy of the *Saturday Evening*

Post, raking autumn leaves, or simply standing in front of a white clapboard house in a small country town. He saw a courteous old man, proud, a little formal, but with warm eyes and a pleasant smile. It surprised the Proprietor to realize that he had seen his father-in-law in exactly the same way only five years before, although he had perhaps also seen a rigidity, a severity that the Sales Manager would be unaware of. Still, he had respected the old man's integrity and he had probably looked at him in the same respectful way that the Sales Manager was looking at him now.

But now all the stories seemed like fragments of a life, bricks, cornices and broken chimneys from a building that had long ago collapsed. He wondered if the old man could remember the shape of the building or recall the life that had gone on inside it. Later, as they walked over to Dealer Credit, the Sales Manager said, 'It's incredible, a man of that age, and sharp as a tack.'

12

Before the Proprietor drove the Aztec White Fairlane from the plant he rolled up the leg of his trousers and found a large red mark. It was sore to touch. He was convinced that the old man had not kicked him. He had somehow knocked his leg doing – something or other.

Peter Carey grew up in Bacchus Marsh, Victoria, and was educated at Geelong Grammar School 'where the children of Australia's Best Families all spoke with English accents'. He read Science at Monash University and then worked in advertising. He now lives in mountainous rain forest country near Yandina, Queensland, where many of his stories, such as *Exotic Pleasures* (Faber, 1980), were written.

The Borden Family Murders
by Angela Carter

Still the little children skipping rope chant:

> Lizzie Borden with an axe
> Gave her mother forty whacks
> When she saw what she had done
> She gave her father forty-one
> ONE . . . two . . . three . . . four . . . and etc.

Then you go on skipping rope for as long as you are able, until you trip over the rope, or tangle it; it is a counting rhyme, it is a counting *out* rhyme.

Although a jury of twelve good men and true found Lizzie Borden innocent of making such a clean sweep of her parents, the little children of Fall River and the world found her guilty, and the macabre jingle commemorating their verdict will last for just as long as skipping ropes because, of course, the little children understand her motives completely since they, too, want to kill us.

All our children want to kill us. Naturally! It is a fact of life, you have to put up with it, you have to learn to live with it and, then again, our children rarely get around to actually doing it; they are not strong enough, yet, and, besides, they, too, acknowledge the power of taboo. The forbidden thing forbids; that is why it is forbidden.

But surely you must have noticed how, in their favourite books, it is *orphans* who go off and have such marvellous adventures? Tom Sawyer had neither Mama nor stern Papa to stop him. Alice is as if sprung newborn from the head of pure logic. Louisa May Alcott sent Old Man March off to the Civil War although Marmee remained behind to stunt her four girls' growth, to shrink them like Chinese feet into 'little women' although even Louisa May cannot forebear, if

47

not to kill, then at least to pitch Old Man March to the brink of the grave for a few brief, intoxicating chapters and ship Marmee well away from home to care for him.

Did Louisa feel no obscure compulsion fret her pen, when she got so far, to wipe them both out forever with, say, yellow fever, or with dysentry, while they were both off stage, to see what the little Marches would do with themselves, then? I am sure she did!

But, oh! she loved her father, loved him so, truly loved old Bronson Alcott, the Bore of Concord, and truly loved her mother, too – so she reprieved them, as Lizzie A. Borden, of Fall River, who also loved her father, did not. But then Louisa, out of guilt at, however unconsciously, having allowed the malign shadow of parricide to darken her page, offered up a spotless child for sacrifice as substitute for the forbidden thing.

The frequent and heart-rending deaths of little children with which Victorian fiction abounds suggests a socially acceptable transformation of the slaughter of the parents. Indeed, in certain Oedipal respects, infanticide might almost be seen as no more than a preemptive strike, in the terrified expectation of parricide. Fathers only exist because they have children, after all. Parricide is impossible where no children are.

On the other hand, don't run away with the notion that the hostility in the eyes of the little children looking at us is implacable, or irreversible. That, because they want to do it, sometimes, they want to do it *all* the time, or that they *will* do it, one day. No. There is nothing personal in what they feel, you understand; it is not you nor me nor their fathers whom they dislike so much, only the idea of us; that they know they need us so is just what breeds so much resentment. In their hearts they know they cannot do without us and they may be easily bought off with a few crumbs of the cake of mixed emotions we call 'love'. All the same, since we dole out to them every last penny, wash them, put them to bed, teach them their manners, train them up to be like us and never ask them if that is how they want to be, is it any wonder they engage in vengeful fantasies of the orphaned, unhoused state? Are they not rational beings, after all?

ONE . . . two . . . three . . . four . . . and etc. Having successfully eliminated Mother, the first term of the syllogism of the self, and

48

suffered no harm from it, the logic of the child at play dictates that Father, the second term, should be the next to go.

Now, you must remember that little boys do *not* skip rope; it is a play only for little girls. It is a pliable game, you can play it by yourself, turning your own rope, or with several others – with one at either end, turning the rope for you; or, with one, two, three in the middle, but it will always be little girls skipping away with their guileless pigtails bouncing on their narrow backs. When their braces catch the light and glint they look as though their bites were made of steel. The crime of Oedipus is man against man; the little girls, negotiating the recurring arcs of the revolving rope, have chosen a hero of their own sex.

All the same – consider her name. Lizzie A. Borden.

For the lack of a son, Andrew Jackson Borden named his younger and better-loved daughter after himself. Andrew, most virile of names, since it is derived from the Greek 'andros' which means 'man'. From this same root is derived 'anthropophagi', as in 'the anthropophagi that do each other eat'.

ONE . . . two . . . three . . . four . . .

And when we have put away both Mother and Father, then – then! we can skip rope as much as we please, play whatever games we want, we shall be at perfect liberty; especially if we have a quarter of a million dollars in our pocketbook.

Lizzie and her big sister, Emma, shared out between them a cool half million once the trial was over and Lizzie was a free woman. Parricide in the service of enlightened self-interest, perhaps?

However, the rhyme is incorrect in two respects. First, in the court at New Bedford, Massachusetts, it was alleged that Lizzie gave her mother not forty but twenty strokes with the said axe and her father only nineteen; secondly Abby Borden was *not* Lizzie's mother. She was the second wife of Andrew Borden, while Lizzie and Emma were the children of his first wife. Lizzie Borden briskly corrected the judge at her trial when he made the same mistake: 'She is not my mother, sir; she is my stepmother: my mother died when I was a child.' Mr Borden brought his new bride home the same year Lizzie was five.

The clear stream of myth muddies here, with the introduction of the folkloric element of the stepmother, whose fate is always to be rolled down a hill in a barrel of flaming tar by a child whom she deceived when she pretended to be blood kin although she was nothing of the kind. Yet I don't believe blood is *that* much thicker than water; if 'Mother' is good enough for the little children skipping rope, then one must bow to their judgement and Lizzie had always called Abby Borden 'Mother', until, one day, only a few years before the cruel events of August 4, 1892, after a mean, ugly quarrel about money, Lizzie ceased to do so.

Lizzie suffered from 'peculiar spells'

The Indians cursed the land with madness and death.

Even on the sunniest days you could not say the landscape smiled; the ragged woodland, the ocean beaten out of steel, not much, here, to cheer the heart, and all beneath the avenging light – that light of the first cruel day of creation that illuminates the New World and gives to its inhabitants the emblematic quality that makes the rest of us watch their every moment to find out what human beings in that unprecedented country will do in order to enlighten us.

Cursing the land with death and madness the Indians departed, after they stuck a few flints of their hard-cornered language onto the map, those names like meals of stone, Massachusetts, Pawtucket, Woonsocket, names with blades. Connecticut. And there are certain fruits of the region, such as the corn – epecially those strange ears of crimson corn, some of the kernels are black, you cannot eat them, they dry out and then they rattle, but people in our times like to hang them on their doors in the fall as if to appease spirits – that strange, archaic-looking corn; and various squashes, the long-necked, pale yellow butternut, and the squat, whorled acorn squash, pine green with a splash of orange on one cheek, squash and pumpkin that look and feel like votive objects carved from wood, edible only after long boiling and then they taste flattish, insipid . . . alien. Not to *our* taste. These fruits retain the ineradicable sombreness of the aborigines.

From puberty she had been troubled by peculiar spells that often, though not always, coincided with her menses; at these times, everyday things appeared to her with a piercing, appalling clarity that rendered them mysterious beyond words, so that the harsh, serrated leaves knocking against the windows were those of a tree whose name she did not know in which sat birds whose names were not yet invented, whirring, clucking, chucking as no birds had before, while a sputtering radiance emanated from everything. All the familiar things, then, seemed not only unknown but unknowable, always unknowable.

So, helplessly strange, must the Saints and Strangers have felt after they watched the boat that brought them there slide away from them over the horizon, and then, abandoned, turned their faces inland, towards the wilderness. That anguish, anguish of the new-born confronted with infinite space; how can it be rendered ours?

Surely Adam, confronted with the task of naming names, panicked.

Time opened in two. Suddenly she was not continuous any more. In this gap of existence she might be something other than she was, but she had no language in which to describe what she might become.

Dull headaches announced the approaches of these seeming trances, of which she retained not one shred of memory and from which she returned as from an electric elsewhere. She would quiver with exhaustion; her sister would bathe her temples with a handker-chief moistened with eau-de-Cologne, she lying on her bedroom sofa.

She kept the knowledge she was discontinuous to herself. Or, rather, she steadfastly ignored the knowledge that she was discrete, because the notion had no meaning to her, or perhaps, too much meaning for her to assimilate. She believed that either a person was, or else was not; but don't think, because she believed this, that she believed it *in so many words* . . . she believed it in the same way that she believed she lived in Fall River, Massachusetts, and in the same way that she believed the second Mrs Borden had married her father for his money. She did not believe she believed in these things; she thought she *knew* them. Therefore these intermittent lapses in day-to-day consciousness, in which she was and was not at the same time, were unaccountable in every way and she did not dare to think of them once she came back to herself. So she remained a stranger to herself.

A trap rattled by in the street outside. A child burst out crying across the way. Emma hovered with the acrid cologne. Lizzie

experienced the departure of vision as though it were the clearing of a
haze; again, to her relief, she saw as through a glass, darkly, and
listened with a stony face while Emma told her what, during her
ensorcelled absence, she had done *this* time.

But, in those lapses of over-clarity, she would think it was the end
that was beginning, and then be overcome by joy.

The sisters lived on in their father's house. They and his wife lived
on together. Impossible to conceive of the stagnant stillness of their
lives.

They kept a good table

Refrigeration is, perhaps, the only unmitigated blessing that the Age
of Technology has given us, a blessing that has brought no bane in
tow, a wholly positive good that can be welcomed wthout reluctance
or qualification. The white-enamelled refrigerator is the modern
genius of every home, the friendly chill of whose breath has banished
summer sickness and the runs for good! How often, nowadays, in
summer, does your milk turn into a sour jelly, or your butter separate
itself out into the liquid fat and the corrupt-smelling whey? When did
you last see the waxy clusters of the blowfly's seed-pearl eggs
materialize on the left-over joint? Perhaps, perfect child of the
Frigidaire, you've known none of all this, none!

But, in those days, great-grandmother's days, the butt end of the
nineteenth century, dysentery and daisies, summer and salmonella,
came in together.

Mr Borden and his wife were murdered on the Thursday morning.
They had been out of sorts and poorly all week.

On Saturday, for dinner, at twelve, they had a big joint of roast
mutton, hot. Bridget, the Irish servant girl, cooked it. They must have
had potatoes with it. Mashed, probably. With flour gravy. I don't
know if they had greens or not. The records don't say. But we know
the main items of the Bordens' diet during their last week because the
police thoroughly investigated the rumour they had been poisoned
before they were butchered.

On Saturday they had more mutton, cold for supper. They ate
their roast on Saturdays because they were Sabbatarians and did not

believe work should be done on Sundays, so Bridget had Sundays off, to go to church.

Because Bridget had Sundays off they ate more cold mutton for Sunday dinner, with bread and butter, I daresay, and, perhaps, pickles.

On Monday they had mutton for midday dinner. I don't know how Bridget fixed the mutton; perhaps she warmed it up in left-over gravy, to make a change from having it cold. They had mutton for breakfast on Tuesday, too. It must have been a veritably gargantuan joint of mutton – or else none of them ate much.

Old Borden must have carved thin as paper money and laid the slice on your plate with as great a disinclination as if he'd been paying back a loan.

There was a wooden ice-box of the old-fashioned kind, the doors of which you must keep tight shut at all times or else the ice melts and everything inside goes rotten. Every morning Bridget put out the pan for the ice-man and filled up the dripping ice-compartment.

In this ice-box she lodged the remains of the mutton.

In and out of the ice-box went the joint of mutton.

On Tuesday it was time for a change; they had swordfish for midday dinner. Bridget bought the thick steaks of swordfish in a fish-market that smelled like a brothel after a busy night. She put the swordfish in the ice-box until it was time to grill it. Then the left-over swordfish went back into the ice-box until supper time, when she warmed it up.

That summer, the summer of the murders, was the hottest summer ever recorded in the city of Fall River, Massachusetts. It was July, the dog days.

Borden and his wife vomited all that night. According to her testimony at the trial, Lizzie felt unwell but did not vomit. Bridget did not start vomiting until the Thursday.

Bridget had kept back the knuckle from the leg of mutton in order to make broth. They had the broth for Wednesday dinner, followed by mutton, again. (Was that warmed-over, too?) They had mutton for supper, on Wednesday.

What Bridget served up for breakfast on the morning of the fatal Thursday was this: warmed-up broth and cold mutton; bread and butter; cookies; a bowl of bananas; coffee; and Abby asked Bridget to make johnnycakes to add to the spread. A hearty New England breakfast. At seven o'clock, the mercury halted momentarily at eighty-five on its rapid dash up the glass. Mr and Mrs Borden shared out this feast between them; Lizzie absented herself from the breakfast table and, later, having nibbled on a cookie, laid it aside.

Mrs Borden has already planned the menu for the Thursday dinner she and her husband will not eat; mutton broth, refreshed by the addition of potatoes, and mutton, once more.

Perhaps on Saturday mornings Bridget was always sent out to buy a joint big enough to last the week. Perhaps that was the custom of the time, of the town, of these Balzacian households ruled by pinchmouth misers.

There is nothing quite like cold mutton. The sinewy grey lean and the veined lumps of congealed fat, varicosed with clotted blood; the sheep's Pyrrhic vengeance on the carnivore! Considering what it was she had on her plate Mrs Borden's habitual gluttony takes on almost a heroic quality. Undeterred by the vileness of the table, still she pigs valiantly away while the girls look on, feel nauseous already, wince to see the grease on her chin.

Oh, how she loves to eat! She is Mrs Jack Spratt in person, round as a ball, fat as butter . . . the heavy fare of New England, the chowders, the cornmeal puddings, the boiled dinners, has shaped her, and continues to shape her. Her husband's vice is avarice; hers is gluttony, and so they balance one another out.

See her rub her bread round her plate.

'Is there a little bit more gravy, Bridget, just to finish up my bread?' She pours cold gravy, lumpy with flour, into her plate, so much gravy she's forced, in the end, to cut herself just another little corner of bread with which to finish up the gravy . . . She is a promiscuous eater; food is food. She eats it. She is the nymphomaniac of the pig-bin.

The sisters think, she eats and eats and eats; she eats everything; she will eat up every single thing, crunch up the plate from which she eats when no more gravy is forthcoming, munch through the greenbacks in father's safe for a salad, polish off the gingerbread house in which they live, for dessert . . . .

If the old woman thought to deceive them as to her true nature by affecting to confine her voracity only to comestibles, Lizzie knew

54

better; her guzzling stepmother's appetite terrified and appalled her, for it was the only thing within the strait and narrow Borden home that was not kept strict in confinement.

There had never been any conversation at table; that was not their style. Their stiff lips would part to request the salt, the bread, the butter, yes; but, apart from that, only the raucous squawk of knife on plate and private sounds of chewing and swallowing amplified and publicized and rendered over-intimate, obscene, by the unutterable silence of the narrow dining-room. A strip of sticky paper hung from a nail over the table, bearing upon it a mourning band of dead flies. A stopped clock of black marble, shaped like a Greek mausoleum, stood on the sideboard, becalmed. Father sat at the head of the table and shaved the meat. Mrs Borden sat at the foot and ate it.

'I won't eat with her; I won't,' said Lizzie. 'I refuse to sit at the trough with that sow.'

After this little explosion of ill-temper, Bridget served the meal twice, once for Mr and Mrs Borden, then kept all warm and brought it out again for Lizzie and Emma, since Emma knew it was her duty to take the part of her little sister, her little dearest, the tender and difficult one. After this interruption calm returned to the household; calm continued to dominate the household. Empty days. Oppressive afternoons. Nights stalled in calm.

Saturday, Sunday, Monday, Tuesday, Wednesday, Thursday morning; in and out the ice-box went the slowly dwindling leg of mutton, until Thursday dinner was cancelled because, when dinner-time came round, corpses and not places were laid out on the table, as if the eaters had become the meal.

Angela Carter was born in 1940 and has published seven novels, of which the most recent was *Nights at the Circus* (1984), besides three collections of short stories, and much miscellaneous prose, besides.

Costigan by Dennis Silk

Note

Christopher Costigan, a young Irish traveller, sounded the Dead Sea in 1835. He died of exposure. He has a ghostly link with Thomas Molyneux, an English naval officer who died of fever after an attempt on The Dead Sea in 1847.

Very little is known about them. I give them a religion they would dislike, I suppose.

Six sentences of Costigan's log-book come from the Maltese sailor's account of the voyage, given to J. L. Stephens in Beirut. The first seven words of the August 3rd entry are taken from Solomon Alkabets' spiritual diary (translated by Zvi Werblowsky). The first line of *Molyneux: Nightmare* was taken from Lynch's *Expedition To The Dead Sea*, the Palestinian English – Pinglish – of Heim Wiseman's hotel-register is lifted from Lynch, and *Bedouin* is a paraphrase and in part a parody of the same source.

The spiral is the conventional shape of the eye of the goddess. In earlier megalithic temples in Malta, it is severely geometrized in stone. In the underground temple at Hal Saflieni – 'many layers' – after a thousand years of development the spiral lashes out wildly in red ochre coils.

Clearly, it is maze-like, with a way out and back.

PART ONE

Christopher Costigan landed at Malta in 1835. He didn't please Garrison Society. He took with his hat, to Government House and the dead messes of the regiments, a genuinely funereal Dublin: a mother he'd buried, a vocation he'd abandoned. But Malta didn't signify, was a dropping-off place on his way to the Dead Sea. He was an excellent sailor, he hoped to sound it. He would sail a boat, there, in Palestine. In the meantime he loitered.

Glass

Glassy Valletta! Grand Harbour looked like an engraving of itself. At Scicluna's the Ecclesiastical Tailors *Monsignors* dedicated themselves to glass. Ladies fed cake to themselves on Strade Reale. They polished their children's glass skin.

He heard splinters of glass tinkle in his coat-lining. He cut his fingers on them at the levée of Queen Adelaide and at the English sermon of the Jesuits. His fingers didn't bleed. Everyone knew a gentleman's handshake when it was offered.

There were so many bay-windows for every house in town. More windows than doors in Valletta.

More Glass

He lay in bed listening to the harbour-hoots. Why does sound lodge in someone's ear? What did the hoots hope for? He remembered the family doctor in Dublin, a forlorn man talking about communication. He'd demonstrated with ears, tongue, mouth, eyes, he'd been made for communication. Costigan remembered ineffectual Dr Stephens, a kind of flounder behind glass. The blankets were made of earth and spades, a third skin between himself and a girl in Dublin. What did she do with her undeclarable love, in her house at night?

He didn't understand what he was, alone or with her. Sometimes, going out toward her, he was pushed back terribly. (For she was scared of making him her confidant, maybe on that he would build high towers.) Then he wasn't with her or himself. Sometimes, three times, he'd gone out toward her, and she met him. Then he wasn't what he was when he set out but hadn't lost in this, he was so much more than he'd hoped. Sometimes he was with himself, not glassy-isolate, and this was good too, though not so good as when they met. Most of the time he was in lumber-limbo. Having gone out toward her, could he bear to rub his glass against others, a universe of glass? Only cowardice, or a bad memory, would allow that.

He was thinking of himself but what did she do all day with her love, her thoughts? How did she climb her stair at night? He quickly got up and dressed, and walked around town, voluble, eating, drinking.

The English Tea-Room

He mourned but didn't show the town his earth. Didn't pour grief into a cup in the English Tea-Room. He fitted himself to the shape of a grieving boat. Where was it pointed? Palestine and nowhere.

The Temple At Gozo

It was the English fool, he was standing there with his cocked hat. From the 73rd Regiment, Costigan decided, judging from that regiment's menu as it expressed itself in his face.

'Excuse me, Sir, did you hear of this gentlemen in Gozo who found the windings?'

'Windings?'

'Yes, Sir, windings in Gozo. I thought one could take a trip there, Sir, have a picnic.'

'What kind of menu do you contemplate in Gozo?'

'Yes, I'm extremely interested in temples. A little champagne, snakes and mothers, that would be very agreeable.'

The Death-Bed

The death-bed is steered by the mother, she ferries her son a little further, comes back to quieten. To be laughed away by the microscope but not by him. Queen of the room. She tried on a new dress, laughed, went away.

Boat-Houses

There were death-flecks everywhere in the city. Not all the regiments assigned to their stations could hide them. Streets and houses the boat-houses where a million boats push off.

Brockdorff

Brockdorff had a megalith-model to show Costigan. It was from Ggantiya at Gozo, he'd been sketching among the ruins. He showed it to Costigan guiltily, it was scarcely his to have in his studio.

A few trial-pieces patched together with Brockdorff's plaster. He remembered his toy-boat in the Dublin nursery. Built very modestly, it got larger underground. Its sails were smeared with ochre, with dead Malta.

The Wine-Label

'Cheerio', the Gozo man said. Costigan stared at the Gozo label as though it gave him the key to Eleusis. Wine poured by an austere man.

'Have you been in Gozo a long time?'

His daughter laughed. 'Mr Loretto has been in Gozo a lot, I would say he has been there a good number.'

The Temple At Gozo

He needed a new coat. It would have to be a severe one, to fit him now. His hat went through the dolmen-door. Boots in the centre of a myth. Costigan looked at his feet. Could they dance out a labyrinth? Laces were untied, clerical feet clumsy.

The fields whirled like a water-wheel. They dizzied Costigan. He gingerly tried out the dancing-ground. Brockdorff danced, too, escaped from his genre. The guide hid in ochre.

The Temple At Gozo

A huntsman stalked the labyrinth of the Queen. Dolmen-death of a rabbit scut. The huntsman held it between his fingers. Costigan stared at Ggantiya the temple. A little blood was seemly.

Brockdorff and his easel were impervious. That rabbit didn't help him with the temple: it was too small to give it scale, too recent to be historical. But he'd lost a colour. Costigan had hidden the true north of ochre in his hat, his gait, his killing courtesy to Brockdorff. The hunter went home with his scut. The Queen waited.

A Field-Day

He'd womanized with caves and dolmens. He'd been Costigan enough. In a Gozo bar he looked at memories of Nelson on the wall. Fingers of the Gozo women made that cobwebby stuff in frames. All that lace, he thought, the trousseau of a death-goddess.

Moon

The moon shone all night. Children travelled into her, seed of churches, moon food. She'd sown them. A scared line of popes went into the moon.

The Recital

Loneliness like the old Maltese. In Strade Reale he pierced the dolmen-world. He was on his way to the Manoel Theatre, there was to be a recital by Camilla Darbois, the celebrated soprano. All that fiction and suction. He had attended the levée of Queen Adelaide, the English sermon of the Jesuits, the Admiral of the Fleet had greeted him kindly. The priest raised his knife (who was linked to the bull-blood, to the Lady of Malta). Costigan paused at the door of the Manoel Theatre. Everything is done by the daemon, or is it?

Camilla Darbois

She was the Fairy Queen for Her Majesty's ships in port. Clumsy impersonation, thought Costigan, a Maltese confection. Her wand did not transform him. He remained the ironical Irishman, part wit, part dolmen-man, collecting her false notes, her abortive runs and little defeated sallies. This was the town-soprano, the bird-in-a-cage of a hundred shops.

The Blur

The staircase girl was a long way off. It appeared to Costigan he'd fallen into his own hands. Maybe he'd always been misdirected. Two people look at one another but each has a small machine inside, a blurring machine to wipe out that look. Going back couldn't remove that blur. Going down might.

Going down. You loiter at the forecourt, pour libations. Everyone goes down, fascinated, frightened. Costigan loitered. He was the English fool, playing. And if there are no more sheep, or bulls. Then where's the blood for the libation?

Costigan was going down. All his truants sat at the supper-table. He looked back through the dolmen-door. 'Don't loiter', they said. He loitered.

PART TWO

The Poultry-Boy

The puppeteer was Roberto Mallia, an eight-year-old poet in Maltese and English. Jesuits had shown Costigan his poems. They were in the lingua franca of eight-year-old poets. Then, the puppet-play.

The puppets were excellent, made apparently by the servants of that great house in Mdina. A poultry-boy loves the egg-seller's daughter, plucks poultry for her, all this graphically done by the servants, Roberto declaiming for both figures. But the daughter loves the water-seller, who pours water on the poultry-boy's head. Enter an old priest on a donkey, under a sun-shade held by a fawning negro.

'An egg
I beg

New-laid
Of the maid'

chants the poultry-boy. The priest sprinkles water and a *pater noster*
on the scene, intones:

'With holy water
Under my umbreller
I sprinkle the feller
Who loves the egg-seller's only daughter.'

And then some concluding lines, from Samuel Rogers or *Cymbeline*
said a Jesuit, and the play was over. Roberto made Costigan take the
poultry-boy.

The Bird-Catcher

A little oval wall the lobe of the Lady. There the bird-catcher hides,
with net and guile. Bird-cages sadden a field. The caged sirens inside
sing to the migrations from Africa. Then the free ones, the sailors,
come down, to be fetched back through the lady-lobe. The bird-
catcher of Malta entangles them, there.

Festa

Originals were devising their petards and rockets, their *kaxxa infernal*
for the Virgin. Wives, half-afraid, half-pleased, carried meals to their
firework-makers. They worked behind closed doors. Occasionally
someone would die for the sake of a new species. They were
injudicious saints working for that sky a child likes.

The Fairy Queen

It was a festa, her earth flared everywhere, smelt of incense and
gunpowder. He heard the harbour-hoots, the fireworks. He steered
through Valletta, he was her partisan in the grave. The Fairy Queen

was smiling at Valletta, bobbing kisses, nostrils never frightened by
gunpowder. Catherine-wheels set off from the Auberge; she waved
them good-bye.

The Pope

The stilt-boy came in through the window. All the stilt-people were
higher than Valletta. The King's float was advancing along Strade
Mercanti, the King surrounded by papier-mâché courtiers, staring.
They must have been looking for the Fairy Queen, to tell her man,
who looked a little anxious, held up an empty cup, as though refusing
to fill it till he'd news of his Queen. She was still two corners away at
Strade Christoforo, delayed by her crowd, but generous, smiling at
everyone and at limestone. Costigan helped the stilt-boy into the
room. He sat there looking back at Costigan, his stilts dangling over
the sill. He wiggled them for Costigan to help take them off. He was
dressed as a cardinal, spoke to Costigan in sign-language, pointed at
wine. Costigan poured him some and he took off his mask. Costigan
had helped a Pope Joan into the room, who laughed at the deception
and offered her face. Costigan got involved in her religious rouge.
The Pope wandered around, stopped at the poultry-boy hanging on
the wall, took him off his nail, held him to her, singing wildly in
Italian, clearly a parody of Camilla Darbois.

Strait Street

She was silent when they got to Strait Street. She had the poultry-boy
and he her stilts. A small girl came laughing up to them and *Phwt* she
whistled through her teeth, guying the advances of the Strait Street
girls.

The throb of the Gut could be heard downstairs. Her friends were
launching into small talk for the sailors. She sat there by the window
and played with the poultry-boy. Light reflected his control-strings
on the wall. To Costigan, he was the boy at the end of that string. She
wound him back into some mazy place. She held the control-strings,
under Gozo, under Valletta, conducting.

PART THREE

Mgarr

At the police station, asking for the key of the temple he felt strange. The mother was under lock and key. Strange to walk round her humble trefoil, to sit with a family of stones. There were wasps as he went deeper down. He kept company with snails in limestone. Their spirals called him home.

Hal Saflieni

A tomb-like temple. She'd taken it underground to intensify it. All the dead, thought Costigan, the real congregation. He touched the ochre spirals on the wall, the oculus spirals of the Lady of Malta. He rubbed a finger against the red ochre, found it came off damp. He wanted to rub it against his forehead but a surprising fear prevented. He wiped off the ochre against the wall. Yet he didn't matter: this mattered. Fascination of Hal Saflieni.

It was a severe town where the dead lived. All the pastry-cooks of Malta lived here in the spiral boat of the grave. Children and priests at benches in school, they watched the lesson on the ceiling, the coiling sums of the Lady. Everyone was separate, no one knew anyone else, shared their room with anyone else, their bed with anyone else. Only the spirals linked.

The coils came down a long way into the room. Sometimes they gathered themselves into circles, and then the Lady spiralled home, wiped out her way down. Then she'd tire of her walled garden, the secure fruit, and lash down in coils. This was for the children of Hal Saflieni, not to leave them alone with each other, school of many languages.

The little family goes into the other world, is extended there. First one goes, looking back, waving, and no one waves back. She establishes the bridge, the first to die is there, in the walled garden. But no one wants to know, everyone is such a trial-self, apprentice-self, not with anyone else for long or only in memory. Only the spirals are good neighbours. The first to die looks down. You have other things to do, she says. I'm here.

The Cart

Suppliant goitres, pendulous breasts, twisted spines, all going to Hal Saflieni. The goitrous sleep a night in a cubicle, hope for an oracle, a healing dream. How lonely to be tucked away in a cubicle, in the society of ochre and the dead! To dream back, through long sweeps of corridor, dank falls of pit, to the mother. Everyone wants to go back: the puzzled, the querulous, the divided, the long-memoried, all going back like a cartful of sick parts of the body to the whole one. A cart of spiral wheels to carry them back.

All the *ex votos* are going back, the little clay images of sickness to the mother. Heal me here, make me well there, lift my breast, magick the goitre. All the *ex votos*, and even the Virgin and Son, are going home, travelling back in the one cart with the old Maltese, to the seed, the mother.

The Staircase

He was going up the staircase in Dublin, going very much deeper into the spirals. Here was the ochre girl going up, also.

Bored

He was the petitioner of spirals. He was there, sometimes, at the landing-place, when they sailed in. But Valletta was that boring baroque town he walked through, cut to the lines in a soldier's head. He shared it with the 45th, 57th and 73rd Regiments. Costigan was bored with his hope. He hadn't seen it for a week. He'd been carrying his own image around, in a little Lenten procession of one, an image, it turned out, of a fat Mediterranean lady, tucked away in some niche by the labyrinth-men. Madame Spaghetti.

The Tea-Shop

Two ladies and a little girl sat before three plates of pastries. They were grooming her, Costigan supposed, for a hand-maiden, showing her the way, pushing cake down.

The Loft

His mother called to him from the loft. He ran toward her but she drew the curtain. She was rowing away, carrying her household with her, figureheads and virgins. She was talking Gaelic, wearing curlers underground, shining.

Two

The big face and the little one. One moon or another. Two women, knitting.

Back

The moon was lying on the death-bed at Hal Saflieni. Her face was going back. Then she was taken out of the room.

Covering Her Tracks

He'd had a month's mind of her, trailed her around Valletta. Now the family was being whittled away, built up elsewhere. She was dieting, going away.

Boat

'What for you come up?' He'd gone back, very diligent, to settle a bill. His grocer laughed. What for he steered his clerical boat? Under the pavement the Lady laughed. Her boat went every which way. Spiral boat of the grave, it arrived, departed, its crew of dead children waved good-bye, white faces of old Malta, coming up to eat cake in Strade Reale.

Dead Sea Dreams

In the first dream a sea had become its own bad critic, didn't want to know itself any more. A mountain accepted its salt. Costigan was climbing this mountain, he was the dead boatman going up. His oars went into the mineral. Whether it was a frozen boat, or a drifting mountain, he didn't know. His hand bled, holding on to a forelock of the mother.

In the other dream he herded bulls and calves along a strip between two stretches of the Dead Sea. The inexperienced calves were sniffing at the water. Some of the bulls were already drowning. They couldn't find the way back. The bulls of Malta were drowning in the Dead Sea.

Good-bye

Pallor of journey leaving the ochre house! All the tribe of spirals said good-bye. Malta was a mother, and the name of bars. Good-bye then, Near You, Crossroads, Reborn, Calypso, Maybe, Jane, good-bye.

Valletta/Jerusalem 1967

Dennis Silk was born in London in 1928, educated at several private schools, read manuscripts for John Lane and The Bodley Head and settled in Jerusalem in 1955. His books include: *Hold Fast* (poems) published by Viking Penguin and Elisabeth Sifton Books, New York in 1984; *The Punished Land* (poems) by Viking Penguin and Viking, New York in 1980; *Retrievements: A Jerusalem Anthology* by Keter, Jerusalem in 1977; *Fourteen Israeli Poets: A Selection of Modern Hebrew Poetry* (together with Harold Schimmel) by André Deutsch in 1976. 'Costigan' belongs to a sequence of fantastic stories about travel in 19th Century Malta and the Levant. A number of his plays for actors, thing-actors and puppets have been performed in Israel, in either English or Hebrew.

The West Midland Underground
by Michael Wilding

The West Midland Underground goes from   to   . Or should I say went? Should I have said went? Should I be saying went? Or even will go? May go? Could go? Could have gone? Was to have gone? Is to go? Is to have gone? Is it possible to say is to have gone? Are there certain tenses that do not exist, may not, cannot, will not, did not; though now do? Perhaps the impossible tenses are needed for the impossible underground. Perhaps the hitherto impossible tense will bring into being the hitherto imposs-ible West Midland Underground.

Henry James! Papua New Guinea has everything you could ever need. A brief example from a Papuan language of average com-plexity, Gadsup of the East New Guinea Highlands Phylum, may be given here to show the structure of the verbs occurring at the end of sentences – these are simpler verbal forms than the so-called medial forms. These sentence final verb forms consist of a verb stem plus a number of elements suffixed to it. All these, linked together in a single word, constitute the sentence final verb forms, and such a verb form will show the following composition: verb stem+benefactor marker (that is, the action is carried out for the benefit of somebody)+potential marker+ability marker+statement marker+interrogative marker+completion marker+subject marker+two emphasis markers (i.e. kùmù-ánk-àdád-òn-ték-áp-ón-ì-nó-bé). Thus the full shades of meaning of this elaborate verb form given above can be expressed in English only inadequately and may best be rendered by a sentence like 'Had he indeed wanted to go down for him?' Had she indeed wanted to go down for them? The nun. I recur remorselessly to the nun's tunnel. Like a movie of memory and compulsion, cutting back and back to those same frames. In the Gaumont, Worcester, I see *The Private Life of Sherlock Holmes* and *Underground*. *Underground* is about an officer parachuted behind the German lines who works with the Maquis, shoots people, blows up bridges. Our truer underground runs still beneath. Sometimes buildings would collapse along the high street, and we always believed they fell into the nun's tunnel.

> She trailed along behind the others as they returned along the underground corridor from the cathedral. At least having Mass there once a week was a change from the other six days when it was held in the nunnery. A change – but to what effect? She suddenly realized in all fulness how barren her life was, when she could call the difference between pious faces in the priory and the same pious faces in the cathedral a change.
>
> She jumped up suddenly. All the stored up misery had burst out, overwhelmed her. But she had sat there crying far too long. The door at the end of the passage would be closed, barred, bolted. She ran. She ran through the blackness of the corridor, on, on.

In 1959 I was writing about the nun's tunnel in the school magazine. In 1972 I add her into a story about cats in London. Why do I return to the nun's tunnel? The door was bolted. She died in the tunnel between the Cathedral and the Nunnery and her ghost still walks.

Was that the West Midland Underground? Does the West Midland Underground, alone of all undergrounds, have a ghost to parade along it? The White Lady of Worcester, patron saint of the underground. We could make a million, casting medallions of her for every freak's neck.

As for the dimensions, they are no more certain than the tenses.

Does		historically	
Did		topographically	
Will	the West Midland	geographically	
May	Underground go	bibliographically	from
Can		chronologically	
Should		adjectivally	

the Anglo-Saxons		the Industrial Revolution
hills		valleys
limestone	to	marl
Feckenham		Wyre Piddle
1100 hrs		2300 hrs
bad		worse

Where would we look for direction?

During the war the signposts were all taken down so parachuted spies wouldn't be able to find their way around. The land was without identity. When had the signposts first been put up, when had the land first been named for those who did not know the names? For those who grew from it, the names were always there, each lane and hill, track and cluster of buildings. With merely an odd milestone for the aspirant Dick Whittingtons. And then came the century that broke the secrecies, that labelled the intimacies for anyone to see. The mysteries were revealed and the strangers spread over the land.

But with the war the labels and arrows were all erased; the surfaces were cleansed, and places existed only in themselves, their names accessible only for those who were at them, not for those who would only point. Perhaps it was then that the arrows to the West Midland Underground were removed. And after the war, never re-erected. Perhaps they had got mislaid. Perhaps the men who had pulled down the signs had died, or lost their memories, and nothing had been written down for fear the enemy might gain access to the records. So that there was nothing from which to rediscover the underground. Yet archaeologists could find traces of the old post holes if they looked. Though could they deduce the direction of the arrows from the post holes? The station entrances must lie there for discovery, beneath their thickets of brambles, their landslides of shale. Moles and ferrets and dormice scuttling into hiding there, bats hanging from the tunnel roofs to issue out at twilight.

Another possibility is that of deliberate closure by the overground; as with the canals. In my days of searching through the countryside I stalked the clues of this other possibility. I often crossed the canal, which canal it needs no more to answer than to question, exquisite brevity. And on the soft worn red-brick bridges over-arching the dried-up canal bed, were rusted iron plaques, asserting ownership by the London and West Midland, or some such combination, steam locomotive company, taking us back to those days when the overground had bought the canal companies to close down their cheap competition. And could it be that the Overground had also bought out the Underground, and affixed iron plaques of ownership to stations and arches and tunnels and platforms; and closed it down. And as the canals silted up and the lock gates rotted and crumbled and the reeds took over, resuming the deep cut of the navvies back to the contours of the brambly hills, unseen, the tunnels collapsed behind their boarded entrances, the air chimneys piercing up through the hills were fenced off and bricked over and the briars and hawthorn spread across them, and within the bricks fell from the lining one by one, as tree roots and incautious moles pushed and encountered no resistance. The underground filled with the hollow bones of small animals and stale air; the heavy drapes of cobwebs closed off passages and fell into disuse. While the overground roared above crushing the bed of granite chips beneath its steel tracks and creosoted sleepers.

Research Service Bibliographies. Series 4. No. 61. Underground Radio Communication. Compiled by I. Boleszny. Adelaide. Public Library of South Australia, January 1966.

At last our network of underground radio communication spreads the counter culture through our global ether, underground nomadic transmitter caravans sending out new writing and revolution on accessible frequencies at the underground hours. What k/Ms will find them, what is the West Midland Underground Transmitter's call signal? 'Articles prefixed by x are to the best of our knowledge not available in South Australia. Photocopies of these references can usually be obtained from libraries in other states and overseas. While this may sometimes be expensive, we have found that on most occasions the cost is about 2/- (20 cents) per page.'
1963.
3. x *Funktechnik und Elektroakustik sowie Sonderanlagen der Drahtnachrichtentechnik im Bergbau.* H. Jahn. BERGBAUTECH-NIK 13: 82–91, February 1963; 13:131–45, March 1963.

4. New traducers for communicating by seismic waves. il diag K. Ikrath *and* W. Schneider. ELECTRONICS 36:51–5, April 12, 1963.
5. Investigation of the design of underground communication systems. L. M. Valles *and others*. IEEE INTERNATIONAL CONVENTION RECORD 11, pt. 8:234–41, 1963.
6. Modes in lossy stratified media with application to underground propagation of radio waves. M. E. Viggh. IEEE TRANSACTIONS ON ANTENNAS AND PROPAGATION AP–11:318–23, May 1963.
7. x Electronic equipment for mine communications. R. E. Havener. MECHANIZATION 27:52–4, March 1963.
8. Communications in mining industry. R. Lee. MINING JOURNAL 261:30–3, July 12, 1963.

From about 3 am there isn't much happening on the cab radio, we'll broadcast stories then. They'll be picked up by every cab operating. When the service gets known people will start taking cabs in order to hear the stories. Then we can extend to other times; eventually we'll broadcast twenty-four hours a day; we can have breaks for commercials, we can stop the story and give the cab calls, Bondi Road, Bondi to Darling Street, Balmain, Newcastle Hotel, George Street to St Vincent's Hospital; and then back to the story. We can even fit the messages into the story; we have people phoning a cab in the story and we hear the operator calling the cab for them and when they're in the cab they listen idly to the cab radio calling Steyne Hotel, Manley to Sylvania Hotel, Sylvania and so on and they listen idly to the cab radio as long as there are messages to be transmitted; and if there aren't any messages to be transmitted they can be written into the story to create cab bookings. In the end the entire population of the city would be taking cabs in order to hear the stories. Different companies will run different programmes. It will be impossible to get a cab to travel in; people will be going into bookshops to buy short story collections in order to travel home. 'Have you got the volume of short stories *Seaforth Crescent, Seaforth to Mort Street, Balmain*?' 'This is the last one sir.' 'Do I get a 10 per cent discount as a university teacher?' 'Not on paperbacks under a total of 23 miles, sir.' The biggest boom in the short story known to history will eventuate. The presses will be pouring volumes out, daily newspapers featuring them, special stories printed on cornflakes packets and passiona bottles; fragments of stories: 'Collect the entire story from the ends of ten packets of meat pies.' New visitors to the city will have to discover the dead hour, in between the afternoon and evening story shifts; it will be as impossible to buy a short story between three and four pm as in the past it had been to travel by cab.

Gadsup was at college with me before he joined the East New Guinea Highlands Phylum. Even as an undergraduate, without the range of verbal forms that later was indeed to have become his, he had a knack of memorable expression. I remember one vacation entering The Cellars, a basement coffee lounge in which the youth of the West Midlands gathered in their motor-cycling jackets and tattoos.

'I say,' he said as we sipped our coffee, his voice reverberating through the underground rooms, 'don't these marble topped tables remind you of altars in a Greek temple, Diana at Ephesus or something?'

In the cellars the youth of the West Midlands sat and looked.

'Just waiting for a human sacrifice.'

The coffee very hot.

Likewise he once boomed out, entering a country pub, 'I'm thinking of writing a novel about someone who turns to Catholicism from excessive masturbation.'

The 'excessive' was a note characteristic of Gadsup, the shade of meaning he strode unerringly towards.

I wouldn't think the Salwarpe has trout. Don't trout streams have to be through limestone or something? Clear water? The Salwarpe wasn't clear; but ran slowly and muddily through clay, sandstone; trundled along. I used to canoe up it and that took about eight times as long as just walking because it meandered so much. It didn't really want to get to the Severn and lose its identity. So it kept winding from side to side. And didn't flow too fast. And then all the way along were these mills, that had been there for centuries, damming up its hardly forceful flow, and letting what wasn't dammed up rush away through some narrow hurtling mill race, which as soon as it got round past the mill settled into the old comfortable sluggishness. Hawford Mill, Bill's Mill, Porter's Mill. Porter put up Queen Elizabeth when she went through, at one of his houses. I don't know who Bill was. But none of the mills work now; they just dam up water and the soft drink bottles and the twigs and the old boots, and let some of the other water hurtle down the mill race, which it probably likes doing, once in a while.

And then alongside the Salwarpe is the Wych Canal; straight as a die. They ran together like two cops or two comedians, the straight one and the funny one, the nice one and the heavy one. There's a fable in it too, sermons in stones and something in running brooks. Well, the canal isn't running any more. Back in the end of the eighteenth century it was Brindley's most beautiful canal, he said it was, and it ran as straight as a die from the Severn to Droitwich, to take the salt away. And all the way it ran straight, the Salwarpe wriggled along beside it, making all these sinuous, concertina'd curves, like Marilyn Monroe alongside John Wayne. But then there wasn't too much use for the straight canal and it silted up; there wasn't too much use for the winding Salwarpe either, but it had always been there and had its own sources of water and current and so just kept on flowing, not worrying any too much about use.

But just on the offchance of trout I thought it might lead to the underground so I walked along, not exactly beside it since in that rainy winter everything had become pretty waterlogged, and between the old canal and the river, often a distance of only three or four yards or so, it tended to get a bit swampy; but I walked near it, along roads and paths that crossed over it or ran beside it and crossed back over it again. Till I came to this bare cleared patch of ground, and this high wire fence, and these new concrete buildings, and a label: Ladywood Pollution Control Unit. And down below the Ladywood Pollution Control Unit ran the Salwarpe. Maybe the West Midland Underground is a Dostoevskian underground.

The Salwarpe may have outlived John Wayne but technology gets its revenge in the end. Now they pour shit on the river I used to canoe along. And for certain there wouldn't be any trout there. And as the winter went on men with tractors and power saws went along the winding curling organic edge of the Salwarpe and cut down all the willows that hung over it, all the hawthorn and elder and bramble that ran down from the bank to the water's edge; they cut away everything that might ever collapse and hold up the flow of shit into the Severn. They razed the edges of the Salwarpe flat like an airfield. Because if an old willow tree that had grown on the edge there for fishermen to sit under and kingfishers to fish under and mayflies to mill beneath, decided to lay itself down in the river that had undermined its roots all its years, decided just to surrender itself to the flow, then it would hold up all the shit, and they had to get the shit from the Ladywood Pollution Control Centre as quickly as ever possible into the Severn where it would be washed down with the fuller flow and eventually out to the Bristol Channel and America.

I guess next they'll cut off all the corners of the old meandering Salwarpe which Brindley would've done if he could've done only he didn't have the technology but he thought of it, so the shit will just shoot down straight into the Severn without having to wind round at all; and then they'll concrete the whole top of the river over, with semi-circular pre-cast concrete culverts, and pump through double the volume; then they'll concrete over the Severn. Every river in the country will be arched over with pre-cast concrete culverts, arteries of shit being pumped along the old waterways, to form a solid, coagulate ring round the British Isles.

What are the advantages of looking for the West Midland Underground?
1. Health: daily walks through the clear air, good for the circulation, leg muscles, lungs, digestion.
2. Mental ease: the state of mental relaxation induced by walking through the country lanes, numbness.
3. Architectural: to explore the varieties of half-timbering, the black and white domestic architecture of the district. There is a barn built of stone, rare in this district, which a countryman who lives in the cruck cottage next to it said was stone left over from the church. That would be round about 500 years ago. The corrugated iron roof was added later.
4. Historical: Warwick the Kingmaker was born in a half-timbered huge manor house beside the Salwarpe. On the skyline you can

see Woodbury Hill where Caractacus made his famous last stand against the Roman invader.

5. Geographical: the way hills roll and rivers wind.

6. Botanical: flowers and plants and things, most of them not in flower yet. I can only tell their names when they're in flower.

7. Natural fauna: dormice, water rats, moles – but they stay underground and you can only see the mole hills; there are badgers underground too, I know where a badger sett is, tunnelling into a ridge beside the old canal. Perhaps the fauna are there before us.

8. To talk to oneself watched only by cattle.

9. Fantasy: a long straight road, must be a Roman road running to Droitwich to get salt. Flat fields each side. Distantly, the clip clop of a horse. I walk, my breath white in the cold air. I am a dragon and behind a gentle knight is pricking on the plain. A lady with a headscarf, riding jacket, jodhpurs; she turns to smile down on me. I turn to smile up to her, we wish each other good day. She rides on, along the straight road between the flat fields. She rides out of sight. At the crossroads I look for horseshoe marks in the mud at the roadside. There are horseshoe marks in all the mud, at every roadside, in every direction. For weeks I walk along the old Roman road, salt-free, lady-less.

10. Hope: somewhere, over the rainbow, the crock of gold, the gates of Eden, the doors of bliss.

Michael Wilding is the author of four volumes of stories: *Aspects of the Dying Process* (1972), *The West Midland Underground* (1975), *The Phallic Forest* (1978), *Reading the Signs* (1984); a volume of selected stories, *The Man of Slow Feeling* (1985), and five novels, *Living Together* (1974), *The Short Story Embassy* (1975), *Scenic Drive* (1976), *Pacific Highway* (1982) and *The Paraguayan Experiment* (1985). He was born in the West Midlands in 1942 and is Reader in English at Sydney University. In 1987 he was visiting professor at the University of California at Santa Barbara. His critical studies include *Political Fictions* (1980) and *Dragons' Teeth: Literature in the English Revolution* (1987).

Everyone Knows Somebody Who's Dead
by B. S. Johnson

So you like the title? That is the first thing, they say here, the *Title*.

Conflict, they say, as well. I should engage my reader in a *Conflict*. That is easy. What I have in mind is the conflict between understanding and what does not appear to be understandable. Few subjects could be more interesting. Surely you must see that? I trust you, not knowing you.

It is also the partialness in the *Soul* (not a word I have ever used before I think) *of Conflict* that concerns me here.

There is *Resolution* at the end, I see, skipping ahead. Be calm. I have written before. Trust me, not knowing me.

This is the difference between doing it and teaching it. Perhaps. Who am I to presume? I am (like you) everyone to presume, there is no one else.

Conflict, it says here. *Of three kinds, viz: within the self; without the self, with other humans; without the self, with non-human forces.* Gross simplification, but what else is there?

One conflict is within me, certainly. Many, rather. But what I have to write of is not a conflict within him: indeed it is rather of that moment of perfect non-conflict, in the end, of unity, unison, when his self was absolutely at one with his non-self, when the will and the act itself were in accord, at peace, were the same.

One should also start at the *Beginning*, it says here. That I could have done, easily.

I first met him at the evening college of London University, Birkbeck College. We must have sat next to one another at some lecture or another. English and Latin were what we had in common, History and I think Economics were points of divergence. Everyone had to do Latin. He was tall, angular is unfortunately the only word, smart: I was none of these. He introduced me to the *New Statesman* and his fiancée, a dumpy, curly blonde quite unlike him in almost everything, unsuited, I thought. Or perhaps think now, with hindsight. I introduced him to me, I was all I had. We joined the college rowing club together, Saturday afternoons for that spring we would imagine the exercise did us good. I may still have a key to their locker half a generation later, they may still have in it my heavy white wool sweater. He worked in an office quite near mine, both in Kingsway. Occasionally we would meet for lunch, too. Shell was his company, Standard-Vacuum mine, oil was another thing we had coincidentally in common. His job I cannot remember, mine is

. . . Irrelevant.

A Plot is . . .

There were other things. Bengs and Joyce were also friends, at this time. We each passed our examinations. He and I went separate ways, then. We left Birkbeck, the evening lectures and steady jobs, both managed to become possessed of grants to go full-time to different colleges, though still of London University. I chose mine because I thought well of the name, he his because he admired the staff. We were both five years mature. The Registrar warned me, objecting to my full-time going, that I at twenty-three would be amongst a lot of eighteen-year-old girls. That is probably also amongst the things which are not relevant.

. . . a Conflictful Situation . . .

There was a party for Birkbeck friends, he and I met the curls at the Albert Hall (built as a rendezvous), the rain was heavy in a way not common in July. Probably that summer too I went once and never again to the family home, Churchill Gardens, tall flats aligned north and south so that the sun set garishly on the supper table. The conversation centred, so I remember, Bengs was there, on the way the place was warmed by surplus heat generated across the river at mighty Battersea power station, piped presumably. They were very early postwar reconstruction or development.

. . . Exacerbated by Additional Circumstances of Increasing Difficulty . . .

He bought an identifying scarf for his new college. I obtusely wanted nothing of such symbols, it was more than enough that I was

80

admitted. Though they looked warm, and the winter might be coming.

That summer also I was best man at his wedding to the unlikely curls. I was brought in late, a kind of locum, second-best man. I do not know why the first choice man was not available. I did wonder then and later that he should have so few friends that I, little more than an acquaintance, and recent, too, should be honoured. But that is speculation. I am allowed a little speculation?

> . . . *Proceeding to one or more Abortive Efforts to overcome the Situation.*

The marriage was at a church overlooking Brighton. The spire was said to be a blessing to mariners, as well. It was a modern church. I produced the ring without any of the mishaps celebrated in tradition. Afterwards in the vestry, is it called, I paid the gentleman vicar. He kept what the other functionaries were owed and pressed back on me his own share, saying, 'It is something I do for young couples, I love weddings you see.' You see.

At the reception I stole an epigram from Oscar Wilde, something about a spade. My punishment was that it fell flatter than discus. And they probably thought I was bent, too, all those relatives, to boot. This occasion represents my only appearance as a best man. At another wedding, where the best man's name was Fat Gerald, the bride's father asked me to make a speech because I was a writer and writers were good at speeches. But one of the reasons I am a writer is because I am no giver of speeches at weddings or anywhere else, I explained to him. I do not think he understood, he remained disappointed.

You would not be forgiven for thinking my life one long round of weddings, the like.

The first (or Oscar) wedding reception was at a hotel on the front. Very pleasurable, being at the seaside with something proper to do, with a purpose, and with friends, like Bengs, in this case. But the epigram, and reading the telegrams, too, were almost distressing. And so was the bill. My duties as best (available) man, it seems, included paying for the reception. Not out of my own money, the father of the bride footed. I cast the bill carefully and quickly, being at that time more an accounts clerk than a student. It seemed the least I could do following the pagan flatness of my speech. Mine was nothing approximate to the *maitre*'s total, differing by some fourteen pounds if I remember as accurately as I cast. A considerable sum, even more considerable (as ever) then. The difference was in the favour of the *maitre*, no surprise, or of those who employed him. His apologies were certainly profuse, though practised and just not conceal-ing a challenge to my sharpness. The bride's father was noticeably grateful to me. The *maitre* must have hoped we were all too drunk by then. Perhaps more often than not that is the usual state at the end of these functions. I hardly remember the bride and groom during this wedding: only her on the church path after, him in the church as we awaited the delegation. Perhaps that is as it should have been.

Abortive is shortly a good word in context.

Three years for our respective degrees, ha, and we hardly saw each other. One occasion though I remember with some clearness: a Fireworks Day, one of three, by deduction. A dinner or supper with him and the curls, me and my moll, what a metonym. The streets, afterwards, of Pimlico – ('Have at thee, then, my merrie boyes and hey for old Ben Pimlicos nut browne' – as it occurs first written down in *News from Hogsdon*, 1598. But no doubt they would frown on such a scholium as having no place.) There were fireworks in the streets, we threw them, a bonfire on a bombsite, St George's something the road was called, in Pimlico, where one may be catered for but hardly satisfied.

Then when we had both just finished we met in the coffee bar in Torrington Place next to Dillons, on purpose. We were able to tell each other what we had done in between. The marriage had just become or was becoming a divorce. My moll had cast me off in favour of a sterile epileptic of variable temperament. But yes! Now I remember exactly, ha! We had not just finished, but were beginning finals. One of the days we met in the Rooms, I feel they called them, the first day probably, arranged to meet afterwards downstairs. And thence to the coffee bar. On our way, talking at a junction, waiting, just before Euston Road, to the south, I could look it up, gazetteers are at hand, but why should I? Am I not allowed to be lazy too? Or reckless? But as we stood talking at this junction, she who was once my moll appeared in the long distance, walked the long way towards us, crossed the other wide diagonal, went the long way away. And all that while I tried to talk as though I were unaware of her, of all that she had meant to me, of all those things I have exorcised elsewhere. Ah.

After the coffee we made an evening of it, did the thing most opposite to degree finals we could think of at such notice: front row of the royal circle at the Victoria Palace. The Crazy Gang were then tailing off, we could have sat anywhere, at any price, they would have had us. No doubt there were other funny things, we were raucous with relief, but now I remember only a game they played with a fat lady, throwing old pennies so they landed flatly on her bare mottled wet chest, stuck briefly, then dropped into her cleavage. There were things like that, then. No doubt we also caught up more at the time, he and I, though since I was without any direction, where was he?

Robin (now I have to name him) had taken up with a student, a girl in the year below him (before, during or after the divorce was unclear), a Swiss who was having an affair also with a much older man with money, and all that went with it, a car. The curls, he told me, had had an abortion, arranged with confounding liberality (for this was in what was thought of as the heyday of the backstreet abortionist) by his tutor, to whom he had gone for help in this matter. The marriage was virtually broken, after less than a year, and satisfaction at having foreseen their short incompatibility was not absent from my remarks at the death on this occasion. But I could not have acted otherwise, in marrying her, I am sure, emotionally, he insisted. But there had been hints, heard over the telephone not long before Finals, that they had parted. I was put off, easily, working all that afternoon by indecision as to ringing her and taking sexual advantage of the state she might or might not have been in. I did not know about the heyday then, and after all I had been more or less best man.

It occurs to me now because of this and other things that I could not and cannot call myself his friend. Was he capable of friendship? I do not think so. Am I? It was more a working relationship, he was like a colleague though we had no common enterprise or ambition beyond both being working-class boys bent on an education, the illusion that that was the key to —

Extension is always achieved by the Insertion of one or more Abortive Efforts.

There was another occasion. Bengs and I went to a Wandsworth hill road, in the curls' time. Of more I have no recollection.

Their *Comprehensive Scheme* should deal with this *Common Problem*. But it does not.

It was another flat in which I remember him next, as it may be, in Old Brompton Road, the corner of Drayton Gardens, near the powerhouse of the literary trade union movement. Though I was then of course unaware of its militancy. And now I am quaintly aware of one of those loops in time where . . . but you do not need me to explain that cliché of the twenties. What has happened is more important, of certain interest to me, and what has happened is that I have remembered that the girl I took to this Old Brompton Road flat Robin had was in fact the very same girl whose marriage I attended all those years later and whose father I disappointed! This can be no coincidence: a real loop in time has happened.

I think I did not want to marry her myself. I was at that time between girls I wanted to marry. But it is a curious loop, though I have not wanted for more curious. And while describing it the one thing I remember is that we four (the Swiss being there too) discussed a topical tragedy in the world of politics, Sharpeville. The reason I remember what he said is that he was shortly proved to be right: in that the Sharpeville massacre, far from being the spark which would ignite a conflagration to consume the old repressive system, was on the contrary more likely to be the flame which would harden into steel the iron resolve of the oppressors. I do not know that his imagery was as elegantly contrived as mine is, but he had written an unpublished article about the incident, for (I think) a serious weekly. But he was remarkably right! I am myself never right for anyone else but me, and not too often do I achieve that small victory. How many times have you yourself been right for other people, then? Ah.

He was at this time teaching at some South London secondary school, his writing was towards another job. If ever you want to make a lot of money, he told me, open a sweetshop next to a school, the kids are in and out all day long. As we left I told the Swiss privately I thought that what he had read to us of his writing had . . . saleability! As though I knew, it was mere politeness!

The Solution Stage . . .

Perhaps it was this perceptive rightness which led him inevitably to a post on the *Evening Standard*, at the City Desk.

*. . . involves the character in either (a) overcoming his
problems . . .*

How full everyone's life is! Why, I hardly knew him and here I am
well past two thousand words already!

. . . or (b) succumbing to them.

Later in this stage they visited me. I cannot avoid the thought that he
was showing me that he had arrived in the world of affairs before I
had. That is, he had a car and after eating curry out he bought a whole
bottle of whisky to take back to the flat I had then. I think he even told
me how much he was earning; it seemed at that time I was managing
adequately on about a quarter of his salary. I think he wanted not only
to show me he was doing well but that his way of doing well was better
than mine. My way then was simply to try to write as well as those
exemplars from the past I had chosen to set up whilst at college.
Neither did it escape my notice that he was ahead in the matter of a
mistress, too, and a glamorous foreigner at that. All I had to show was
a bound set of page-proofs of my first novel: high hopes as I had of it,
I do not remember it as being sufficient to set against the car, the
whisky, and the Swiss mistress.

What other news from Hogsdon?

A finished copy before publication I took around to dinner at their
flat, still in Pimlico, some (presumably short) while later. I do not
remember what Robin said about the book on this occasion: at some
time previously he had expressed great scepticism about what it was
trying to do. He was right if the amount of money garnered was his
criterion. Perhaps it was; or was not. Present was a very pleasant,
charming and witty man of about our age called Charles, who was by
the way of being a printer and an actor, though not necessarily in that
order. I think Robin had meanwhile made a daring leap from the
Standard to a young, vital organ which was highly relevant and called
Topic. Robin became either its business manager or writer on
business affairs, business editor: I think the latter. Much talk of a
world I did not know, very high-powered, men who were coming or
all the go at the time, have since gone even further, some of them, his
colleagues in print.

Have I finished with the *Abortive Effort(s)* yet?

I have recently become aware that an uncomfortable number of my contemporaries are dying before what I had imagined to be their times, simply jacking it all in, for one reason or another.

There was another, hardly remembered. The landlady of a friend with the same forename as myself. Her daughter came up to attend to the disposition of the remains and remnants. She was married to a naval officer, the daughter. My friend made (he convinced me) steamy love with her, unexpectedly, in some sort of consolatory reaction to the mother's death. She had drunk a bottle of gin and sealed the drawing-room cracks and turned the gas on. Probably for her a comfortable, euphoric occasion, making herself comfy: I imagine her not desperate. The day after, the daughter and my friend were alone in the house, the naval officer as if nowhere. She had to stay the night, it was only nature, my friend was sure. My friend was also a colleague at work in a sweet factory, and he was remarkable amongst my acquaintance in that each morning after an evening on the beer he would wake up to find the plimsolls he used as slippers seeping with urine. It could clearly be no one else's but his own, though at the same time he could never remember having risen in the night to perform. He would relate each occasion to me, baffled, whenever we ... but I digress, and the *XLCR Plotfinder* leaves me unclear as to whether digressions are permitted.

Oh, I look forward to my own deathbed scene: the thing I shall have to say which I could not say before!

The *Topic* job was a great success but the magazine collapsed, ahead of its time in some respects, I seem to remember. Robin went (though there may have been a hiatus) back to the *Standard* as full-blown City Editor. We were proud of him, Bengs and I, and others, too.

I meant to tear it out, I was in a foreign country, I never did.

My wife and I, newly married, visited Robin and the Swiss girl, Vivienne, something like as newly-married, now, I think, at their new small house in Maida Vale, very demure, *bijou*. We had a meal, supper or dinner as usual. He showed me the room that he intended to fill with his files. A comprehensive filing system, he informed me, was a major factor in the success of any journalist: one simply collected facts together from many sources, filed them under subjects, and regurgitated them in new combinations as one's own articles.

Soon we must arrive at the *Resolution* or *Point of Solution* . . .

Not long afterwards we took him up on the offer of the gift of a large wardrobe he had made himself from battens and hardboard, collected it in the old navy blue banger of a van which was the first four-wheeled vehicle I had ever owned. He described how the wardrobe was the first thing he had made for the home in the palmy days of the curls, how it was constructed over-elaborately and uneconomically due to his lack of craftsmanlike experience. He had, unexpectedly and soon, an opportunity to demonstrate its methods of construction since it became stuck on the third flight of stairs up to our second-floor flat and we had to take it to pieces there to move it any higher. They had decently followed us in their car, a bigger car, and helped us carry the wardrobe. But there we were, unsocially stuck, we above having access to our flat, they below; it was hardly possible to pass even refreshments between. I have taken it to pieces myself since then, on moving out five years later. I reassembled it for lodgers, and then on another advent I had it in bits again, roughly, crudely, with the children. It had served us well, I burnt it in the yard. Except for one piece I shall keep, have before me for this piece, having cut a foot specially with his writing on it, in pencil, curious things that confirm how he said he made it: OSSPIECE, it says, cut off by the removal necessary for a tee-halving joint, TOP BACK. Yes, the point is in. SCREW TOP ONTO XI PIECE. IT WILL HAVE TO BE SHORTENED BY TWICE THE WIDTH OF THIS. What writing! It was always rickety, was unsightly from the first, too, we accepted it only because we had no money for a proper one.

. . . which can

admit of a Surprise Ending.

Mostly professional things. They must have visited us in that flat when we had straightened it; I was very careful about reciprocating hospitality in those days. We learnt at one point he had been demoted to Assistant through the return of a former City Editor, a star; this was an uncomfortable arrangement but we understood he accepted it. Not so very much later he was promoted again when the star ascended ever higher. One anecdote he told us concerned travelling in a taxi with the superstar and Vivienne: a carefree cyclist overtook them, dodging in and out, glorying in his mobility amongst the impacted cars in Regent Street, until some minutes later near the

Vigo Street junction he was involved in a jam of his own causing which he was unable to avoid since his brain was now distributed hither and thither.

All that time, and the only exact words of his I remember are some of those spoken in the Malet Street coffee bar on that one occasion: 'Life is a series of clichés, each more banal than the last.'

I certainly do not feel up to inventing dialogue for your sake, going into oratio recta and all that. These reconstructed things can never be managed exactly right, anyway. I suppose I could curry a dialogue in which Robin and I argued the rights and wrongs of his *Conflictful Situation*, but it would be only me arguing with myself: which would be even more absurd than trying to write of someone else's life.

The last I think I saw of him was at the home of a smart lawyer to whom I had originally introduced him. I remember feeling resentful that they now knew each other better than I knew either of them. We have diverged, I thought, arrogantly, geometrical progression cannot be unwelcome.

It must have been perhaps two years later that I attended some quiet function and met again the charming Charles. He said he was very relieved to be able to tell me that our mutual friend Robin appeared to have sorted himself out at last, after his trouble. I had not heard of any trouble, I told him apologetically. With genuine sorrow, Charles explained that Robin had become involved with another girl and Vivienne had as a result successfully gassed herself. I was equally genuinely shocked, and guilty, too, that I had not been in touch with him for the period within which this had happened. Then I shared his relief that Robin had recovered to the extent that he was living with another girl: whether this was the same another girl I do not remember Charles telling me. No doubt I could find out by ringing him now and perhaps inviting him round for supper, dinner, or a drink.

Patience: we are about to reach the *Solution Point*. I was for three months in Paris at the time, and nervously keeping in touch by purchasing the airmail edition of *The Times* perhaps every third day. Thus I was again genuinely shocked to read of his death only by a one-in-three chance. I cannot at this stage remember if I read a news story and the obituary, or only the latter. I seem to know that he too employed the good offices of the North Thames Gas Board, but whether this was from the newspaper or later from the splendid Charles, or some other source, I cannot ascertain. I meant to tear it out, the way one does, and never does. It cannot happen with North Sea Gas, I am assured. But certainly I read the obituary, which was without a photograph, I think. It was not very long. After some facts, the only opinion expressed as to how he might be remembered, or had been in any way remarkable, concerned the way in which he had helped to find out what was in the minds of businessmen by organizing a luncheon club at which they were invited to meet the press. There was more than that, but that is all it said, all there was to say, his life summed up, the obituary, full point.

There. I have fully satisfied the *XLCR* rules, I think. Popular acclaim must surely follow.

B. S. Johnson (Bryan Stanley William Johnson) was born in 1933 in Hammersmith, and apart from the war, during which time he was an evacuee, lived in London all his life. He read English at King's College London at the late age of 23. He published six novels, *Travelling People* (1963) which won the Gregory Award of 1962, *Albert Angelo* (1964), *Trawl* (1966) which won the Somerset Maugham Award of 1967, *The Unfortunates* (1969), *House Mother Normal* (1971) and *Christie Malry's Own Double-Entry* (1973). He was also a poet and worked as a writer and director in television, radio, cinema and theatre. B. S. Johnson died in 1973.

The NRACP by George P. Elliott

(*The* NRACP *is the National Relocation Authority: Coloured Persons.*
The CPR *is the Coloured Persons Reserve.*
PR *is Public Relations.*)

March 3

Dear Herb,

Your first letter meant more to me than I can say, but the one I
received yesterday has at last aroused me from my depression. I will
try to answer both of them at once. You sensed my state of mind; I
could tell it from little phrases in your letter – 'open your heart,
though it be only to a sunset', 'try reading *Finnegans Wake*; if you ever
get *into* it you won't be able to fight your way out again for months'. I
cherish your drolleries. They are little oases of half-light and quiet in
this rasping, blinding landscape.

How I hate it! Nothing but the salary keeps me here. Nothing. I
have been driven into myself in a very unhealthy way. Long hours,
communal eating, the choice between a badly lighted reading-room
full of people and my own cell with one cot and two chairs and a table,
a swim in a chlorinated pool, walks in this violent, seasonless, arid
land – what is there? There seem to be only two varieties of people
here: those who 'have culture', and talk about the latest *New Yorker*
cartoons, listen to imitation folksongs and subscribe to one of the less
popular book clubs; and those who play poker, talk sports and sex,
and drink too much. I prefer the latter type as people, but
unfortunately I do not enjoy their activities, except drinking; and
since I know the language and mores of the former type, and have
more inclination toward them, I am thrown in with people whom I
dislike intensely. In this muddle I find myself wishing, selfishly, that
you were here; your companionship would mean so much to me now.

But you knew better than I what the CPR would mean – you were most wise to stay in Washington, most wise. You will be missing something by staying there – but I assure you it is something well worth missing.

I must mention the two universal topics of conversation. Everyone from the filing clerks to my division chief say they haven't much preference in mysteries, but the folksongers to a man prefer the tony, phoney Dorothy Sayers–S. S. Van Dine type of pseudo-literary snobbish product, and the horsey folk prefer the Dashiell Hammett romantic-cum-violent realism; there is one fellow – a big-domed Irishman named O'Doone who wears those heavy-rimmed, owlish glasses that were so popular some years ago – who does nothing but read and reread Sherlock Holmes, and he has won everyone's respect, in some strange way, by this quaint loyalty. He's quite shy, in a talkative, brittle way, but I think I could grow fond of him. – Yet everyone finds a strong need to read the damnable things, so strong that we prefer the absolute nausea of reading three in one day – I did it once myself, for three days on end – to not reading any. What is it actually that we prefer not to do? I can only think of Auden's lines, 'The situation of our time/Surrounds us like a baffling crime.' Of our time, and of this job.

What are we doing here? – that is the other subject none of us can let alone. We are paid fantastic salaries – the secretary whom I share with another writer gets $325 a month, tell Mary *that* one – and for one whole month we have done nothing while on the job except to read all the provisions and addenda to the Relocation Act as interpreted by the Authority, or to browse at will in the large library of literature by and about Negroes, from sociological studies to newspaper poetry in dialect. You will know the Act generally of course; but I hope you are never for any reason subjected to this Ph.D.-candidate torture of reading to exhaustion about a subject in which you have only a general interest. But the *why* of this strange and expensive indoctrination is totally beyond me. I thought that I was going to do much the same sort of PR work here on the spot as we had been doing in the State Department; I thought the salary differential was just a compensation for living in this hell-hole. That's what everyone here had thought too. It appears, however, that there is something more important brewing. In the whole month I have been here – I swear it – I have turned out only a couple of articles describing the physical charms of this desiccated cesspool; they appeared in Negro publications which I hope you have not even heard of. And beyond that I have done nothing but bore myself to death by reading Negro novels and poetry.

They are a different tribe altogether; their primeval culture is wonderful enough to merit study – I would be the last to deny it. But not by me. I have enough trouble trying to understand the rudiments of my own culture without having this one pushed off onto me.

I have been stifled and confused for so long that all my pent-up emotions have found their worthiest outlet in this letter to you, my dear friend. I have been vowing (as we used to vow to quit smoking, remember?) to stop reading mysteries but my vows seldom survive the day. Now I do solemnly swear and proclaim that each time I have the urge to read a mystery, I will instead write a letter to you. If these epistles become dull and repetitious, just throw them away without reading them. I'll put a mark – say an M – on the envelope of these counter-mystery letters, so you needn't even open them if you wish. I'm sure there will be a lot of them.

Does this sound silly? I suppose it does. But I am in a strange state of mind. There's too much sunlight and the countryside frightens me and I don't understand anything.

Bless you,

ANDY

March 14

Dear Herb,

It wasn't as bad as I had feared, being without mysteries. We get up at seven and go to work at eight. Between five and six in the afternoon, there's time for a couple of highballs. From seven or so, when dinner is over, till ten or eleven – that's the time to watch out for. After you have seen the movie of the week and read *Time* and the *New Yorker*, then you discover yourself, with that automatic gesture with which one reaches for a cigarette, wandering toward the mystery shelf and trying to choose between Carter Dickson and John Dickson Carr (two names for the same writer, as I hope you don't know). On Sundays there's tennis in the early morning and bowling in the afternoon. But then those gaping rents in each tightly woven, just tolerable day remain no matter what you do. At first I thought I should have to tell myself bedtime stories. One evening I got half-drunk in the clubrooms and absolutely potted alone in my own room afterwards. First time in my life. Another time, O'Doone and I sat up till midnight composing an 'Epitaph for a Mongoose'. I can't tell you how dreary some of our endeavours were; O'Doone still quotes one of mine occasionally. He's a strange fellow, I can't exactly figure him out but I like him in an oblique sort of way. We neither one fit into any of three or four possible schemes of things here and we share a good deal in general outlook. But he can amuse himself with a cerebral horseplay which only makes me uneasy. O'Doone has a French book – God knows where he got it – on Senegalese dialects so he goes around slapping stuffy people on the back and mumbling 'Your grandmother on your father's side was a pig-faced gorilla' or else a phrase which in Senegalese has something to do with transplanting date trees but which in English sounds obscene, and then he laughs uproariously. In any event, he's better off than I, who am amused by almost nothing.

Now that you have been spared the threatened dejection of my counter-mystery letters, I must confess to the secret vice which I have taken up in the past week. It grows upon me too, it promises to become a habit which only age and infirmity will break. I had thought it a vice of middle age (and perhaps it is – are we not 38, Herb? When does middle age commence?). I *take walks*. I take long walks alone. If I cannot say that I enjoy them exactly, yet I look forward to them with that eagerness with which an adolescent will sometimes go to bed in order to continue the dream which waking has interrupted. Not that my walks are in any way dreamlike. They are perfectly real. But they take place in a context so different from any of the social or intellectual contexts of the CPR day, and they afford such a strong emotional relief to it, that I think these walks may be justly compared to a continued dream. My walks, however, have a worth of their own such as dreams can never have, for instead of taking me from an ugly world to a realm of unexplained symbols, they have driven me toward two realities, about which I must confess I have had a certain ignorance: myself, and the natural world. And standing, as I feel I do, at the starting point of high adventure, I feel the explorer's excitement, and awe, and no self-pity at all.

I have recaptured – and I am not embarrassed to say it – the childhood delight in stars. That's a great thing to happen to a man, Herb – to be able to leave the smoke and spite-laden atmosphere of bureaucracy, walk a few miles out into the huge, silent desert and look at the stars with a delight whose purity needs no apology and whose expansiveness need find no words for description. I am astonished by the sight of a Joshua tree against the light blue twilight sky, I am entranced by the vicious innocence of one of the kinds of cactus that abound hereabouts, I enjoy these garish sunsets with a fervour that I once considered indecent. I cannot say I like this desert – certainly not enough to live in it permanently – but it has affected me, very deeply. I think that much of my trouble during my first month here was resisting the force of the desert. Now, I no longer resist it, yet I have not submitted to it; rather I have developed a largeness of spirit, a feeling of calm magnificence. Which I am sure is in part lightheadedness at having such a weight of nasty care removed all at once, but which is wonderful while it lasts.

But it's not *just* lightheadedness. Some obstruction of spirit, an obstruction of whose existence I was not even aware, has been removed within me, so that now I can and dare observe the complexities of that catalogued, indifferent, unaccountable natural world which I had always shrugged at. One saw it from train windows, one dealt with it on picnics; one admired the nasturtiums and peonies of one's more domesticated friends, one approved of lawns and shade trees. What then? What did one know of the rigidity of nature's order or of the prodigality with which she wastes and destroys and errs? I came here furnished only with the ordinary generic names of things – snake, lizard, toad, rabbit, bug, cactus, sage-brush, flower, weed – but already I have watched a road-runner kill a rattlesnake, and I am proud that I know how rabbits drink. Do you know how rabbits drink? If you ask what difference it makes to know this, I can happily reply, 'None at all, but it gives me pleasure.' A pleasure which does not attempt to deny mortality, but accepts it and doesn't care – that is a true pleasure and one worth cherishing.

11 pm
I owe it to you, I know, to give a somewhat less personal, less inward

95

account of this place. But a calculated, itemized description of anything, much less of so monstrous a thing as a desert, that is beyond me. Instead I'll try to give you an idea of what effect such physical bigness can have upon one.

Our buildings are situated at the head of a very long valley – the Tehuala River Valley – which is partially arable and which, in both the upper and lower regions, is good for grazing purposes. The highway into the valley, that is, the highway that leads to the east, as well as the railroad, runs not far from our settlement. Being Public Relations, we are located just within the fence (it is a huge, barbarous fence with guards). We have had a rather surprising number of visitors already, and hundreds more are expected during the summer. Our eight buildings are flat-roofed, grey, of a horizontal design, and air-conditioned. But our view of the valley is cut off by a sharp bend about four or five miles below us. The tourists, in other words, can see almost nothing of the valley, and just as little of the Reserve stretching for 800 miles to the southwest, for this is the only public entrance to the Reserve, and no airplanes are permitted over any part of it. Around the turn in the upper valley is yet another even more barbarous, even better guarded fence, past which no one goes except certain Congressmen, the top officials (four, I believe) in the NRACP, and SSE (Special Service Employees, who, once they have gone past that gate, do not return and do not communicate with the outside world even by letter). All this secrecy – you can fill in details to suit yourself – is probably unnecessary, but it does succeed in arousing an acute sense of mystery and speculation about the Reserve. Well, being no more than human I walked the five miles to the bend, climbed a considerable hill nearby, and looked out over the main sweep of the valley for the first time. I was hot and tired when I reached the foot of the hill, so I sat down – it was around 5.30 – and ate the lunch I had brought. When I reached the top of the hill the sun was about to set; the long shadows of the western hills lay over the floor of the valley and in some places they extended halfway up the hills to the east. Far, far to the west, just to the north of the setting sun, was a snow-capped mountain; and immediately in front of me, that is, a mile and a half or so away, stretched the longest building I have ever seen in my life. It had a shed roof rising away from me; there were no windows on my side of the building; nothing whatsoever broke the line of its continuous grey back; and it was at least a mile long, probably longer. Beyond it, lay dozens of buildings exactly like this one except for their length; some of them ran, as the long one did, east and west, some ran north and south, some aslant. I could not estimate to my satisfaction how large most of them were; they seemed to be roughly about the size of small factories. The effect which their planner had deliberately calculated and achieved was that of a rigidly patterned, unsymmetrical (useless?) articulation of a restricted flat area. Nothing broke the effect, and for a reason which I cannot define, these buildings in the foreground gave a focus and order to the widening scene that lay before me such that I stood for the better part of an hour experiencing a pure joy – a joy only heightened by my grateful knowledge that these Intake buildings were designed to introduce an entire people to the new and better world beyond (and I must confess I felt the better that I myself was, albeit humbly, connected with the project). The fine farms and ranches and industries and communities which would arise from these undeveloped regions took shape in the twilight scene before me, shimmering in the heat waves rising from the earth. But presently it was quite dark – the twilights are very brief here – and I was awakened from my reverie by the lights going on in one of the buildings before me. I returned to the PR settlement, and to my solitary room, in a state of exaltation which has not yet deserted me.

For an hour, the Universe and History co-extended before me; and they did not exclude me; for while I am but a grain on the shore of events, yet only within my consciousness did this co-extending take place and have any meaning. For that long moment, mine was the power.

I will write again soon.

ANDY

March 20

Dear Herb,

You complain that I didn't say anything directly about my voyage of discovery into myself, as I had promised in my last letter. And that the internal high pressures of urban life are blowing me up like a balloon in this rarefied atmosphere.

Maybe so. I'll try to explain what has been going on. But I forgot to take a cartographer on my voyage, so that my account may resemble, in crudeness, that of an Elizabethan freebooter in Caribbean waters. (If I had the energy, I'd try to synthesize these balloon-voyage metaphors; but I haven't.)

It all began when I asked myself, on one of my walks, why I was here, why I had taken this job. 8,000 a year – yes. The social importance of the project – maybe (but not my personal importance to the project). Excitement at being in on the beginning of a great experiment in planning – yes. The hope of escaping from the pressures of Washington life – yes. These are valid reasons all of them, but in the other balance – why I should want *not* to come here – are better reasons altogether. An utter absence of urban life. No friends. No chance of seeing Betty. The loss of permanent position (this one you pointed out most forcefully) in State for a better paid but temporary job here. Loss of friends. Too inadequate a knowledge of my duties, or of the whole NRACP for that matter, to permit me to have made a decision wisely. And an overpowering hatred of restrictions (never once, Herb, for three years to be allowed to leave this Reserve! I've been sweating here for seven weeks, but that is 156 weeks. Christ!). Now I had known, more or less, all these factors before I came here, all these nice rational, statistical factors. But when I asked myself the other night, in the false clarity of the desert moonlight, why I had chosen to come, why really, I still could not answer myself satisfactorily. For of one thing I was still certain, that none of the logical reasons, none of my recognized impulses, would have brought me here singly or combined.

I also, being in the mood, asked myself why I had continued to live with Clarice for five years after I had known quite consciously that I did not love her but felt a positive contempt for her. Betty accounted for part of it, and the usual fear of casting out again on one's own. But I would not have been on my own in any obvious sense: I am sure you know of my love affairs during those five years; I could have married any of three or four worthy women. And I ask myself why it was that the moment Clarice decided once and for all to divorce me – she did the deciding, not me; I don't think you knew that – from that time on I lost my taste for my current inamorata and have not had a real affair since. These questions I was unable to answer; but at least I was seriously asking them of myself. I was willing and able to face the answers.

The key to the answer came from my long-limbed, mildly pretty, efficient, but (I had originally thought) frivolous and banal secretary – Ruth. She is one of those women who, because they do not have an 'intellectual' idea in their noodles, are too frequently dismissed as conveniently decorative but not very valuable. And perhaps Ruth really is that. But she has made two or three remarks recently which seem to me to display an intuitive intelligence of a considerable order. Yet they may be merely aptly chosen, conventional observations. It is hard to tell. She interests me. She has a maxim which I resent but cannot refute: 'There are those who get it and those who dish it out; I intend to be on the side of the dishers.' (Is this the post-Christian golden rule? It has its own power, you know.) In any case, the other day I was sitting in my cubicle of an office, in front of which Ruth's desk is placed – she services two of us. I had my feet up on the desk in a rather indecorous fashion, and I had laid the book I was reading on my lap while I smoked a cigarette. I suppose I was daydreaming a little. Suddenly Ruth opened the door and entered. I started, picked up the book and took my feet off the table-top. Ruth cocked an eye at me and said, 'You like to feel guilty, don't you? All I wanted to know was whether you could spare time for a cup of coffee.' So we went to the café and had coffee, and didn't even mention her statement or its cause.

But it set me thinking; and the longer I thought about it, the better I liked it. I had always discounted wild, Dostoevskian notions like that as being too perverse to be true. But now I am not at all sure that frivolous, red-nailed Ruth wasn't right. So long as Clarice had been there to reprove me for my infidelities, I had had them. When her censorship was removed, the infidelities, or any love affairs at all, lost their spice – the spice which was the guilt that she made me feel about them. And then, having divorced Clarice, I took this job. This job is a sop to my sense of guilt at being white and middle class, that is to say, one of Ruth's 'dishers', a sop because I am participating in an enterprise whose purpose is social justice; at the same time it is a punishment, because of the deprivations I am undergoing; yet the actual luxury of my life and my actual status in the bureaucracy – high but not orthodox, privileged yet not normally restricted – nourishes the guilt which supports it. What it is that causes the sense of guilt in the first place, I suppose Freud could tell me, but I am not going to bother to find out. There are certain indecencies about which one ought not to inquire unless one has to. Social guilt – that is to say, a sense of responsibility toward society – is a good thing to have, and I intend to exploit it in myself. I intend to satisfy it by doing as fine a job as I possibly can; and furthermore I intend to find a worthy European family, say Italian, who are impoverished, and to support them out of my salary. I must confess that the CARE packages we used to send to Europe after the war made me feel better than all the fine sentiments I ever gave words to.

I am grateful that I came here. I have been thrown back upon myself in a way that has only benefited me.

We begin work soon. The first trainload of Negroes arrived today, 500 of them. They are going through Intake (the buildings I described in my last letter) and the work we are to do will commence within a few days. Exactly what we are to do, we will be told tomorrow. I look forward to it eagerly.

ANDY

I read this letter over before putting it in the envelope. That was a mistake. All the excitement about myself which I had felt so keenly sounds rather flat as I have put it. There must be a great deal for me yet to discover. As you know, I have never spent much of my energy in intimacies, either with myself or with other people. One gets a facsimile of it when talking about the universal stereotypes of love with a woman. But this desert has thrown me back upon myself; and from your letter I take it you would find my explorations of interest. However, you must not expect many more letters in so tiresome a vein. I will seal and mail this one tonight lest I repent in the morning.

April 10

Dear Herb,

I have not known how to write this letter, though I've tried two or three times in the past week to do it. I'm going to put it in the form of a homily, with illustrations, on the text, 'There are those who get it and those who dish it out; I intend to be on the side of the dishers.'

First, in what context did it occur? It is the motto of a charming young woman (any doubts I may have expressed about her are withdrawn as of now; she is all one could ask for) who is not malicious and does not in the least want to impose her beliefs or herself upon other people. She sends $100 a month to her mother, who is dying of cancer in a county hospital in Pennsylvania. When she told me she was sending the money, I asked her why. 'Why?' said Ruth. 'I'm disappointed in you to ask me such a thing.' 'All right, be disappointed, but tell me why.' She shrugged a little in a humorous way. 'She's my mother. And anyway,' she added, 'we're all dying, aren't we?' The important thing to note about Ruth is – she means it but she doesn't care. Just as she doesn't really care whether you like her clothes or her lovely hair; she does, and you ought to; the loss is yours if you don't. She was reared in a perfectly usual American city, and she has chosen from its unconscious culture the best in custom and attitude.

But she said it here, in the Public Relations division of the Coloured Persons Reserve, here where there is as much getting and dishing out as anywhere in the world, where the most important Negro in the Reserve, the President of it, may be in a very real sense considered inferior to our window-washer. The first time O'Doone heard her say it – he had dropped by to talk a while, and Ruth had joined us – he made the sign of the cross in the air between himself and Ruth and backed clear out of the room. He didn't return either. I'm sure he's not religious. I don't know why he did that.

Now what does the statement imply? Primarily, it makes no judgement and does not urge to action. It is unmoral. 'There is a condition such that some people must inflict pain and others must receive it; since it is impossible to be neutral in this regard and since I like neither to give nor to take injury, I shall choose the path of least resistance – ally myself with the inflictors, not because I like their side and certainly not because I dislike the other side, but only because I myself am least interfered with that way.' No regret. No self deception (*it is impossible to be neutral*). A clear conscience (*I like neither to give nor to take injury*). In other words, true resignation – this circumstance is as it is, and it will not and should not be otherwise. There is a certain intensity of joy possible after resignation of this order, greater than we frustrated hopers know. (Where do I fit into this scheme? I think I have discovered one thing about myself from contemplating Ruth's maxim: that is, I want profoundly to be a disher, but my training has been such, or perhaps I am only so weak, that I am incapable of being one with a clear conscience. Consequently I find myself in a halfway position – dishing it out, yes, but at the behest of people I have never seen, and to people I will never know.) Ruth took a job with the NRACP for the only right reason – not for any of my complicated ones nor for the general greed, but because she saw quite clearly that here was one of the very pure instances of getting it and dishing it out. She left a job as secretary to an executive in General Electric for this. I think she gets a certain pleasure from seeing her philosophy so exquisitely borne out by events. Ruth is 27. I think I am in love with her. I am sure she is not in love with me.

Tell me, Herb, does not this maxim ring a bell in you? Can you not recognize, as I do, the rightness of it? This girl has had the courage to put into deliberate words her sense of the inevitable. Do you not admire her for it? And is she not right? She is right enough. If you doubt it, let me tell you what our job here is.

The authorities consider the situation potentially explosive enough to warrant the most elaborate system of censorship I have ever heard of. To begin with, there is a rule that during his first week in the Reserve every Negro may write three letters to persons on the outside. After that period is over, only one letter a month is permitted. Now all letters leaving here during the first week are sent to PR where they are censored and typed in the correct form (on NRACP letterhead); the typed copies are sent on and the originals are filed. The reason for this elaborate system is interesting enough, and probably sound; every endeavour is to be made to discourage any leaking out of adverse reports on conditions in the CPR. There are some fourteen million Negroes in the nation, not all of whom are entirely pleased with the prospect of being relocated; and there are an indeterminate number of Caucasian sympathizers – civil liberties fanatics for the most part – who could cause trouble if any confirmation of their suspicions about the CPR should leak out. We have put out a staggering amount of data on the climatic, agricultural, power production and mining conditions of the region; and we have propagandized with every device in the book. Yet we know well enough how long it takes for propaganda to counteract prejudice, and sometimes how deceptive an apparent propaganda success can be.

We are more than grateful that almost the entire news outlet system of the nation is on our side.

Well then, after the three letters of the first week have been typed and sent, the writer's job begins. Every effort is made to discourage the interned Negroes from writing to the outside. For one thing, we keep in our files all personal letters incoming during the first month. Anyone who continues to write to an internee after this month needs to be answered. The filing clerks keep track of the dates, and forward all personal letters to us. (The clerks think we send the letters on to the internees.) We then write appropriate responses to the letters, in the style of the internee as we estimate it from his three letters. We try to be as impersonal as possible, conveying the idea that everything is all right. Why do we not forward the letters to the internees to answer? First of all we do – if the internees request it. They are told they will receive letters only from those persons whose letters they request to see, and such a request involves yards of red tape. Very few are expected to use the cumbersome mechanism at all. Then, we write the letters for them simply to save ourselves time and trouble. We would have a lot of rewriting to do anyway; this method assures us of complete control and an efficient *modus operandi*. Any outsider Negro who writes too many insistent letters will be, at our request, relocated within a month; we do not want any unnecessary unhappiness to result from the necessarily painful programme. Friends and relatives are to be reunited as fast as possible. Whole communities are to be relocated together, to avoid whatever wrenches in personal relationships we can avoid.

Is not this getting it and dishing it out on a fine scale? All for very good reasons, I know. But then, is it not conceivable that there are always good reasons for the old crapperoo? Sometimes I feel absolutist enough to say – if it's this bad, for any ultimate reason whatsoever, then to hell with it. After which sentiment, comes the gun at the head. But then reason reinstates my sense of the relativity of values, and on I go writing a letter to Hector Jackson of South Carolina explaining that I've been so busy putting up a chicken-house and ploughing that I haven't had a chance to write but I hope to see you soon. (I doubt if I will.)

ANDY

I forgot to mention – I have a special job, which is to censor the letters of all the clerical personnel in PR. One of my duties is to censor any reference to the censorship! A strange state of affairs. None of them know that this job is mine; most think the censor must be some Mail Department employee. I must say you look at some people with new eyes after reading their correspondence.

I need hardly say, but if there is any doubt I will say, that this letter is absolutely confidential. How much of our system will become publicly known, I cannot guess; but naturally I don't want to jump the official gun in this regard.

April 12

Dear Herb,

Let me tell you about the strange adventure I had last evening. I am still not quite sure what to make of it.

Immediately after work I picked up a few sandwiches and a pint of whisky, and walked out into the desert on one of my hikes. One more meal with the jabber of the café and one more of those good but always good in the same way dinners, and I felt I should come apart at the seams. (Another thing I have learned about myself – I am ill adapted to prison life.) I had no goal in view. I intended to stroll.

But I found myself heading generally in the direction of the hill from which I had looked over the Tehuala Valley and the city of CPR Intake buildings. I came across nothing particularly interesting in a natural history way, so that by early dusk I was near to the hill; I decided to climb it again and see what I could see.

The first thing I saw, in the difficult light of dusk, was a soldier with a gun standing at the foot of the hill. I came around a large clump of cactus, and there he was, leaning on his rifle. He immediately pointed it at me, and told me to go back where I belonged. I objected that I had climbed this hill before and I could see no reason why I shouldn't do it again. He replied that he didn't see any reason either, but I couldn't just the same; they were going to put up another fence to keep people like me away. I cursed at the whole situation; if I had dared I would have cursed him too, for he had been rude as only a guard with a gun can be. Then, before I left, I pulled out my pint and took a slug of it. The guard was a changed man.

'Christ,' he said, 'give me a pull.'

'I should give you a pull?'

'Come on,' he said, 'I ain't had a drop since I came to this hole. They won't even give us beer.'

'All right,' I replied, 'if you'll tell me what the hell's going on around here.'

He made me crouch behind a Joshua tree, and he himself would not look at me while he talked. I asked him why all the precautions.

'They got a searchlight up top the hill, with machine guns. They sweep the whole hill all the time. They can see plain as day in the dark. They keep an eye on us fellows down here. I know. I used to run the light.'

'I haven't seen any light,' I said.

He glanced at me with scorn.

'It's black,' he said. 'They cut down all the bushes all around the top part of that hill. Anybody comes up in the bare place – pttt! *Any*body. Even a guard.'

'I still don't see any light.'

'Man, its black light. You wear glasses and shine this thing and you can see better than you can with a regular light searchlight. It's the stuff. We used to shoot rabbits with it. The little bastards never knew what hit them!'

I didn't want to appear simple, so I didn't ask any more questions about the black light. He was an irascible fellow, with a gun and a knife, and he had drunk most of the bottle already.

'Why do you let me stay at all?' I asked.

'Can't see good in the dusk. Not even them can't.'

I couldn't think of anything more to say. I felt overwhelmed.

'I used to be a guard on the railroad they got inside. Say, have they got a system. Trains from the outside go through an automatic gate. All the trainmen get on the engine and drive out. Then we come up through another automatic gate and hook on and drag it in. Always in the daytime. Anybody tried to hop train, inside or out, pttt! Air-conditioned boxcars made out of steel. Two deep they come. Never come in at night.'

'Are you married?' I asked.

'Ain't nobody married up front, huh?' I didn't answer. 'There ain't, ain't there?'

'No, but there could be if anybody felt like it.'

'Well, there ain't even a woman inside. Not a damn one. They let us have all the nigger women we want. Some ain't so bad. Most of them fight a lot.'

He smashed the pint bottle on a rock nearby.

'Why didn't you bring some real liquor, God damn you?' he said in a low voice full of violence. 'Get the hell back home where you belong. Get out of here. It's getting dark. I'll shoot the guts out of you too. Bring me something I can use next time, huh? Get going. Stay under cover,' he shouted after me. 'They're likely to get you if they spot you. They can't miss if it's dark enough.'

The last I heard of him he was coughing and spitting and swearing. I was as disgusted as scared, and I must confess I was scared stiff.

I walked homeward bound, slowly recovering my emotional balance, trying to understand what had happened to me with the guard, the meaning of what he had told me. For some absurd reason the tune 'In the Gloaming, O, My Darling' kept running through my head in the idiotic way tunes will, so that I was unable to concentrate intelligently upon the situation. (I wonder why that tune business happens.)

I heard a sound at some distance to my left. I stopped, suddenly and inexplicably alarmed to the point of throbbing temples and clenched fists. I saw a slim figure in brown among the cactus; and then, as the figure approached, I could see it was a young woman. She did not see me, but her path brought her directly to where I was standing. I did not know whether to accost her at a distance or to let her come upon me where I stood. By the time I had decided not to accost her, I could see it was Ruth.

'Why, Ruth!' I cried, with all the emotion of relief and gratified surprise in my voice, and perhaps something more. 'What are you doing here?'

She started badly, then seeing who it was she hurried up to me and to my intense surprise took my arms and put them around her body.

'Andy,' she said, 'I am so glad to see you. Some good angel must have put you here for me.'

I squeezed her, we kissed, a friendly kiss, then she drew away and shook herself. She had almost always called me Mr Dixon before; there was a real affection in her 'Andy'.

'What's the matter?' I asked her. 'Where have you been?'

'I didn't know you took walks too.'

'Oh, yes. It's one way to keep from going nuts.'

She laughed a little, and squeezed my arm. I could not refrain from kissing her again, and this time it was not just a friendly kiss.

'Where did you go?' I asked again.

'To that hill. I went up there a couple of times before. There was a guard there wanted to lay me.'

We didn't speak for a few moments.

'I think he almost shot me for giving him the brush-off. I didn't look back when I left, but I heard him click his gun. You don't know how glad I was to see you.'

So we kissed again, and this time it was serious.

'Wait a minute,' she said, 'wait a minute.'

She unlocked her arm from mine, and we continued on our way not touching.

'I had some trouble with a guard too,' I said. 'I wonder why they're so damned careful to keep us away.'

'Mine told me they didn't want us to get any funny ideas. He said things aren't what they seem to be in there.'

'Didn't you ask him what he meant?'

'Sure. That's when he said I'd better shut up and let him lay me, or else he'd shoot me. So I walked off. I'm not going to call on *him* again.'

I put my arm around her – I can't tell you how fond I was of her at that moment, of her trim, poised body, her courage, her good humour, her delightful rich voice and laughter – but she only kissed me gently and withdrew.

'I want to keep my head for a while, darling,' she said.

I knew what she meant. We walked on in silence, hand in hand. It was moonlight. This time if I was lightheaded I knew why.

When we were about half a mile from our buildings, we came across O'Doone also returning from a walk.

'Well,' he said brightly, 'it *is* a nice moon, isn't it?'

It wouldn't do to say that we had met by accident; I was embarrassed, but Ruth's fine laugh cleared the air for me.

'Nicest I ever saw,' she said.

'Did you ever walk up that hill,' I asked him, 'where you can see out over the valley?'

'Once,' he said in a surprisingly harsh voice. 'I'd rather play chess.'

So we went into one of the recreation rooms, and O'Doone beat me at three games of chess. Ruth sat by, knitting – a sweater for a cousin's baby. We talked little, but comfortably. It would have been a domestic scene, if it had not been for the fifty or sixty other people in the room.

Herb, what does it all mean?

ANDY

April 20

Dear Herb,

(This is a *Prior* Script. If all goes well you will receive this letter from Ruth's cousin, who will be informed by O'Doone's sister to forward it to you. O'Doone's sister will also send you instructions on how to make the invisible ink visible. When I wrote the letter, I was in a self-destructive frame of mind; I was prepared to take all the certainly drastic consequences that would come from its being read by someone of authority. But O'Doone's invisible ink (what a strange fellow to have brought a quart of it here! He said he had brought it only to play mysterious letter-games with his nephew – I wonder) and Ruth's baby sweater, upon the wrapping of which I write this, combined to save me. If the authorities catch *this*, I don't care what happens. It takes so long to write lightly enough in invisible ink for no pen mark to show on the paper, that I doubt if I will have the patience to use it often. Most of my letters will be innocuous in regular ink. I may add an invisible note or two, between the lines, in the margin, at the end. O'Doone says it's not any of the ordinary kinds and if we're careful the authorities are not likely to catch us. O'Doone is strange. He refused to take this whole ink matter for anything more than a big joke – as though we were digging a tunnel under a house, O'Doone pretending we are just tunnelling in a straw-stack to hide our marbles, myself trying to protest (but being laughed at for my lapse in taste) that we are really undermining a house in order to blow it up. Which perhaps we are. In any event, I don't have the energy left to rewrite this letter; I'll merely copy it off, invisibly.)

I cannot tell you how shocked I was to discover the familiar, black censor's ink over five lines in your last letter. The censor censored! I had not thought of that. In my innocence I had thought that we writers in the higher brackets could be trusted to be discreet. One would think I was still a loyal subscriber to the *Nation*, I was so naive. But no – I am trusted to censor the letters of inferiors (I suspect my censorship is sample-checked by someone), but my own letters are themselves inspected and their dangerous sentiments excised. And – irony of ironies! – your own references to the fact that my letters were censored were themselves blacked out.

Who is it that does this? The head of PR here? That's a strange way to make him waste his time. One of his assistants? Then the head must censor the assistant's letters. And the chief board of the NRACP censors the head's letters? And the President theirs? And God his? And—?

Which is the more imprisoned – the jailer who thinks he is free and is not, or the prisoner who knows the precise boundaries of his liberty and accepting them explores and uses all the world he has?

I am a jailer who knows he is not free. I am a prisoner who does not know the limits of his freedom. And all this I voluntarily submitted to in the name of a higher freedom. Ever since my adolescence, when the New Deal was a faith, liberty has been one of the always repeated, never examined articles of my creed. Well, I have been examining liberty recently, and she's a pure fraud.

One thing I have learned – you don't just quietly put yourself on the side of Ruth's dishers you become one of them yourself; and a disher *has* to dish it out, he cannot help it at all; and he pays for it. Or maybe I am only paying for my guilt-making desire to be a more important disher than I am.

Ruth was surprised at my distress upon receiving your censored letter. She only shrugged. What had I expected, after all? It was inevitable, it was a necessity. That's the key word, Herb – Necessity. Not liberty, Necessity. True liberty is what the prisoner has, because he accepts Necessity. That's the great thing, Herb, to recognize and accept Necessity.

I've slowly been working toward a realization of this. I think my decision to work in the NRACP came from recognizing the social necessity of it. The Negro problem in America was acute and was insoluble by any liberal formula; this solution gives dignity and independence to the Negroes; it staves off the Depression by the huge demand for manufactured products, for transportation, for the operations of the NRACP itself; but perhaps most important of all, it establishes irrevocably in the American people's mind the wisdom and rightness of the government; for if capitalism must go (as it must) it should be replaced peaceably by a strong and wise planned state. Such a state we are proving ourselves to be. Very well. I accepted this. But what I forgot was that *I*, I the individual, I Andrew Dixon, must personally submit to the stringencies of Necessity. The relics of the New Deal faith remained to clutter up my new attitude. This experience, coming when and as it did, particularly coming when Ruth's courageous wisdom was nearby to support me, has liberated me (I hope) into the greater freedom of the Prisoner of Necessity.

Such are my pious prayers at least. I cannot say I am sure I fully understand all the strictures of Necessity. I *can* say I do not enjoy those I understand. But pious I will remain.

Remember the days when we thought we could *change* Necessity? Democracy and all that? How much older I feel!

ANDY

May 1

Mary, my dear,

Please let me apologize – sincerely too, Mary – for having neglected you so cruelly for the past months. Herb tells me you are quite put out, and well you might be. I can find no excuses for it, but this I will stoutly maintain – it was not a question of hostility or indifference to you, my dear. Actually I have been going through something of a crisis, as Herb may have been telling you. It has something to do with the desert, and something to do with the NRACP, and a lot to do with the charming young woman whose picture I enclose. She is Ruth Cone. We are getting married in a couple of Sundays – Mother's Day. Why Mother's Day, I really don't know. But she wants it, so there's no help. The details of our plighting troth might amuse you.

A couple of evenings ago I was playing chess in the recreation room with a man named O'Doone, my only friend here. Ruth was sitting beside us knitting some rompers for a cousin's baby. From time to time we would chat a little; it was all very comfortable and unromantic. O'Doone, between games, went to the toilet. When he had left, Ruth said to me with a twinkle in her eye, 'Andy, darling, don't you see what I am doing?' I replied, 'Why yes, my sweet, knitting tiny garments. Is it –?' And we both laughed heartily. It was a joke, you see, a mild comfortable little joke, and no one would have thought of it a second time except that when we had finished laughing it was no longer a joke. Her face became very sober, and I am sure mine did too. I said, 'Do you want children, Ruth?' 'Yes,' she replied. 'Do you want to have my children?' 'Yes,' she said again, without looking at me. Then with the most charming conquest of modesty that you can imagine, she turned her serious little face to me, and we very lightly kissed. O'Doone had returned by then. 'Well,' he said in a bright way, 'do I interrupt?' 'Not at all,' I answered; 'we have just decided to get married.' He burbled a little, in caricature of the overwhelmed, congratulating friend, pumped our hands, and asked us when we were marrying. 'I don't know,' I said. 'Why not tomorrow?' 'Oh no,' said Ruth severely, 'how can I assemble my trousseau?' At which O'Doone went off into a braying laugh, and we set up the chess pieces. 'Bet you five to one,' he said, 'I win this game in less than sixty moves.' I wouldn't take his bet. It took him about forty moves to beat me.

And thus did Dixon and Cone solemnly vow to share their fortunes.

It's the first marriage in PR. Everybody will attend. The chief promised me Monday off and temporary quarters in one of the guest suites. We are to get a two-room apartment in the new dormitory that is nearly completed. Such privacy and spaciousness will make us the envy of the whole community. I'm sure there will be a spate of marriages as soon as the dormitory is completed. We will not be married by a holy man, partly because neither of us believes in it and partly because there isn't one of any kind on the premises. (I wondered why there were those detailed questions about religious beliefs on our application forms.) There was a little trouble at first about who was authorized to marry people here. The PR chief, as the only person permitted to leave the place, went out and got himself authorized to do it legally. I think he rather fancies himself in the capacity of marrier. He runs to paternalism.

Ruth urges me, Mary – she assumes, quite rightly, that I have not done it already – to tell you some of the homely details of life here. Of our sleeping rooms, the less said the better. The beds are comfortable, period. We live quite communally, but very well. There's a fine gymnasium, with swimming pool and playing fields attached – tennis, baseball, squash, fencing, everything but golf. There's the best library (surely the best!) in the world on American Negro affairs, and a reasonably good one of modern literature. We have comfortable working quarters – with long enough hours to be sure. There is a fine desert for us to walk around in, and I have come to need an occasional stroll in the desert for spiritual refreshment. And we eat handsomely, except for vegetables. In fact, the only complaint that I have of the cooking is the monotony of its excellence – roast, steak, chop, stew. Never, or seldom, liver and kidneys and omelettes and casseroles. And always frozen vegetables. Well, probably the Negroes will be producing plenty of vegetables within a few weeks. There's lots of liquor of every kind. There is a sort of department store where one can buy everything one needs and most of the luxuries one could want in this restricted life. There's a movie a week – double-feature with news and cartoon – and bridge or poker every day. A microscopic plenitude.

Well, as for the rest of our routine life here, I can think of nothing interesting enough to mention. We work and avoid work, backbite, confide, suspect. It's a bureaucratic existence, no doubt of that.

Will this epistle persuade you to forgive me?

Now you must write to me – soon.

Devotedly yours,

ANDY

(In invisible ink)

O'Doone, who sometimes gives his opinions very obliquely, came to me today with some disturbing figures. He wasn't in the least jaunty about them, and I must confess that I am not either.

According to *Time*, which seems to know more about the CPR than we do, there have been about 50,000 Negroes interned already, and these 50,000 include nearly all the wealthy and politically powerful Negroes in the nation (including an objectionable white-supremacy Senator one of whose great-great grandmothers turns out to have been black). The leaders were interned first, reasonably enough, to provide the skeleton of government and system in the new State which they are to erect. *But*, O'Doone points out, we have yet to receive from them a request for letters from an outsider; and if any

Negroes at all are going to make such requests, it must surely be these, the most important, the least afraid of red tape. (He also pointed out that not one of the entertainers or athletes of prominence has been interned. That, I'm afraid, is all too easily explained.) You see, says O'Doone, you see? But he didn't say Why? to me, and I'm glad he didn't for I can't even guess why.

Another statistic he had concerned the CPR itself. We all know that the figures on natural resources in the CPR are exaggerated. Grossly. Fourteen million people cannot possibly live well in this area, and O'Doone demonstrated that fact to me convincingly. The Negro problem, economically, in the US has been that they provided a larger cheap labour market than consumer market. Now the false stimulus of capitalizing their beginnings here will keep American industry on an even keel for years and years, but after that what? O'Doone bowed out at that point, but I think I can press the point a little further. They will provide a market for surplus commodities, great enough to keep the pressures of capitalism from blowing us sky-high, meanwhile permitting the transition to a planned State to take place. Very astute, I think, very astute indeed.

June 12

Dear Herb,

Why I have not written, you ought to be able to guess. I will not pretend to any false ardours about Ruth. She is wise and winning as a woman, and everything one could ask for as a wife. I love her dearly. She has not read very widely or profoundly, but I think she is going to do something about that, soon. We are very happy together and I think we shall continue to be happy during the difficult years to come. What more can I say?

Why are happiness and contentment and the sense of fulfilment so hard to write about? I can think of nothing to say, and besides Ruth is just coming in from tennis (it's 9.30 Sunday morning).

10 p.m.

Ruth has gone to bed, so I will continue in another vein.

I have been discovering that the wells of pity, which have lain so long locked and frozen in my eyes, are thawed in me now. I am

113

enclosing a letter which came in from a Negress in Chicago to her lover, in the CPR, and his response. It is the first letter from inside, except for the usual three during the first week, that I have read. Apparently a few have been coming out now and then, but this is my first one. I cannot tell you how I pitied both these unhappy people. When Ruth read them, she said, 'My, what a mean man! I hope he has to collect garbage all his life.' I cannot agree with her. I think his little note betrays an unhappiness as great as the woman's, and even more pitiable for being unrecognized, unappreciated. Judge for yourself. I can think of nothing to add.

ANDY

Honey dear child, why don't you write to me? Don't you even remember all those things you told me you'd do no matter what? And you're not even in jail, you just in that place where we all going to go to sooner or later. O I sure hope they take me there with you. I can't live without you. But I don't even know who to ask to go there with you. I went to the policeman and they said they didn't know nothing about it. I don't know what to do. You don't know how I ache for you honey. It's just like I got a tooth pulled out but it ain't no tooth it's worse, and there is no dentist for it neither. There's a fellow at the store keeps bothering me now and again, but I assure him I don't want him I got a man. I thought I had a man, you, but I don't hear nothing from you. Maybe you got something there, I don't see how you could do it not after those things you said, but if you have tell me so I can go off in some hole and die. I don't want this Lee Lawson, he's no good, it's you I want, sweetheart, you tell me it's all right. I *got* to hear from you or I'll just die.

Dear ———,

I've been so busy baby, you wouldn't believe how busy I've been. You'll be coming here pretty soon and then you'll feel better too. It's nice here. We'll get along fine then. You tell that guy to leave you be. You're my gal. Tell him I said so.

Yours truly,

(In invisible ink)

I didn't include these letters because I thought they were in the

Heloise-Abelard class, but because I wanted to say something about them, and also because they gave me more invisible space.

The man's response came to us already typed. That very much astonished me, and O'Doone, when I told him, let fly a nasty one. 'I suppose,' he said, 'they have a couple of writers in there writing a few letters in place of the Negroes, which we then relay. Complicated, isn't it?' Not complicated, upsetting. Devastating. What if it were true? And I must say this letter has an air more like the PR rewrite-formula than like a real letter. Then *none* of the Negroes would have even a filtered connection with the outside world. Why? Why fool even us? Is there no end to the deception and doubt of this place?

O'Doone posed another of his puzzles yesterday. He read in the current PR weekly bulletin that the CPR has been shipping whole trainloads of leather goods and canned meats to China and Europe for relief purposes, under the government's supervision of course. O'Doone came into my office at once, waving the bulletin and chortling. 'How do you like it?' he cried. 'Before we get a carrot out of them the Chinese get tons of meat.' Then a sudden light seemed to dawn on his face. 'Where did all the cattle come from?'

A strange thing happened: O'Doone's intelligent, sensitive face collapsed. The great domed forehead remained almost unwrinkled, but his features looked somehow like one of those children's rubber faces which collapse when you squeeze them. No anguish, no anxiety. Only collapse. He left without a word. I wish he had never come here with that news.

Last night I lay awake till three or four o'clock. I could hear trucks and trains rumbling occasionally through the night – entering and leaving the Reserve. But that guard I met at the foot of the hill told me that they only bring internees in the daytime. Are those shipments? How can it be? Sometimes I am sick at heart with doubt and uncertainty.

I dreamt last night that I was a Gulliver, lying unbound and unresisting on the ground while a thousand Lilliputians, all of them black, ate at me. I would not write the details of that dream even in invisible ink. Not even in plain water.

Dear Herb,

Hail Independence Day! Some of the overgrown kids around here are shooting off firecrackers. No one is working. It is all very pleasant. I suppose March 20 will be the Independence Day of the new Negro nation – the day when the first trainload arrived. How long ago that seems already. I do not think I have ever been through so much in so short a time. And now for the real news.

Ruth is pregnant! Amazing woman, she remains outwardly as humorous and self-contained as ever. No one else knows her condition, because she wants to avoid as much as possible of the female chatter that goes with pregnancy. She insists upon playing tennis still. Yet she is not all calmness and coolness; when we are lying in bed together before going to sleep, she croons little nonsense hymns to pregnancy in my ear, and yesterday afternoon at the office she walked into my cubicle, up to where I was sitting very solemnly, and placed my hand over her womb. Then she kissed me with a sort of unviolent passion such as I have never known before in my life. I tell you, she's a wonderful woman.

How miraculous is conception and growth! I no more understand such things than I really understand about the stars and their rushings. One event follows another, but I'm sure I don't know why. You get back to an archaic awe, if you permit yourself to, realizing that you yourself have started off a chain of miracles. I never had a sense of littleness when observing the naked heavens, of man's puniness, of my own nothingness. Perhaps it was a fear of that feeling which for so long prevented me from looking upwards at all. I mentioned my reaction to O'Doone on one of the first occasions of our meeting; he nodded and said, 'But is not a man more complex than a star, and in every way but one that we know of, more valuable?' What he said remains with me yet; and when I am presented with the vastness of the stars and the forces which operate within them, I am impressed and excited enough but I am not depressed by the imagined spectacle. Their bigness does not make me little. My own complexity does not make them simple. Man is no longer the centre of the universe perhaps, but neither is anything else. That I have learned.

But when I am presented with the proof of the powers that men (and myself) possess, then I still feel a little off balance. When Clarice was pregnant with Betty, I had no such feeling. I felt annoyed chiefly. But now, in this desert, in the CPR, I have been sent back at last to fundamentals, to the sources of things; and I realize fully how unaccountable is birth of life. Ruth, who never departed far from the sources, is less embarrassed in admitting her sense of mystery.

One thing I am going to teach this child, if it can be taught anything: that the humane tradition has been tried and found wanting. It's over, finished, kaput. A new era of civilization commences. Kindness and freedom – once they were good for something, but no more. *Put yourself in his place* – never. Rather, fight to stay where you are. I think we are entering upon an age of reason and mystery. Reason which accepts and understands the uttermost heights and depths of human power, man's depravity and his nobility; and, understanding these, dares use them toward a great and future goal, the goal of that stern order which is indispensable to the fullest development of man. Mystery toward all that is not explainable, which is a very great deal. Rationalism failed, for it asserted that everything was ultimately explainable. We know better. We know that to destroy a man's sense of mystery is to cut him off at one of the sources of life. Awe, acceptance, faith – these are wonderful sources of power and fulfilment. I have discovered them. My child shall never forget them.

ANDY

(In invisible ink)

I have put the gun to my temple, Herb, I have pointed the knife at my heart. But my nerve failed me. There were a few days when I was nearly distracted. My division chief told me to stay home till I looked better, but I dared not. I think it was only Ruth's pregnancy that saved me. My newly awakened sense of mystery, plus my powers of reason, have saved me. This is the third letter I have written you in a week, but I knew the others were wild and broken, and I was not sure at all that I was physically able to write in such a manner as to avoid detection.

It came to a head, for me, two weeks ago. O'Doone entered my office, his face looking bright and blasted. He dropped a booklet on my desk and left after a few comments of no importance. The booklet was an anthropologist's preliminary report on certain taboos among American Negroes. The fellow had been interviewing them in Intake. There was nothing of special interest about it that I could see, except that it was written in the past tense.

I expected O'Doone to reclaim the booklet any day. For some reason he had always done the visiting to me, not I to him. He was very restless, and I am slothful. But a week passed, and no O'Doone. I did not meet him in the café nor in the recreation room. I went to his own room, but he did not answer. The next day I went to his office, and his secretary told me he had not shown up for two days. I returned to his room. It was locked. The janitor unlocked it for me. When I entered I saw him lying dead on his bed. 'Well, old boy,' I said to drive the janitor away, I don't know why, 'feeling poorly?' He had drunk something. There was a glass on the table by his bed. There was no note. His face was repulsive. (That is a mystery I have learned to respect, how hideous death is.) He was cold, and somehow a little sticky to the touch. I covered his face with a towel, and sat down. I knew I should call someone, but I did not want to. I knew the janitor would remember letting me in, and my staying too long. Yet I felt that there was something I must do. What it was I could not remember, something important. It took me an eternity to remember – the invisible ink. I knew where he had kept it. It was not there. I looked throughout his room, and it was simply gone. I left the room.

I still did not notify anyone of his suicide. I was not asking myself why he had done it. Or perhaps I was only shouting Where's the ink? in a loud voice to cover up the little question Why? I went to our rooms and straight to the liquor shelf. I took down the Scotch and poured myself a stiff one, and drank. It was horrible. I spat it out, cursing; then I recognized the odor. O'Doone had come over, poured out the Scotch (I hope he enjoyed it himself) and filled the bottle with the invisible ink. At that, I broke down in the most womanish way, and cried on the bed (never ask Why? Why? Why?).

Ruth found me there some time later. I told her everything that had happened, and she immediately pulled me together. She had the sense to know I had been acting more oddly than was wise. She notified the right people, and O'Doone was disposed of. No one asked me any embarrassing questions, and no official mention of O'Doone's end was made anywhere.

I must continue this on a birthday card.

(In invisible ink, on a large, plain Happy Birthday card to Mary)

I had still not allowed myself to ask why he had done it, but Ruth put the thing in a short sentence. 'He was too soft-hearted to stand it here.' She was right; he was a Christian relic. He knew more than he could bear. I resolved to go that very evening again to the hill where the black searchlight threatened the night.

Some sandwiches. Four half-pints of whisky. A hunting-knife (a foolish gesture, I know). Plain drab clothes. The long walk in the still hot, late-afternoon sun. Sunset. The huge, sudden twilight. And I was within sight of a guard (not the same one I had seen before) standing by the new fence at the foot of the hill.

I crept up toward him under cover of brush and cactus, till I was close enough to toss a half-pint of whisky in his direction. His bored, stupid face immediately became animated by the most savage emotions. He levelled his gun and pointed it in my general direction. He could not see me, however, and rather than look for me he crouched, eyes still searching the underbrush, to reach for the bottle. He drained it in five minutes.

'Throw me some more,' he whispered loudly.

'Put the gun down.'

I aimed my voice away from him, hoping that he would not spot me. I was lying flat beneath a large clump of sagebrush. There was a Joshua tree nearby, and several cactus plants. He pointed the gun at one of the stalks of cactus, and crept up toward it. Then he suddenly stopped, I don't know why, and walked back to his post.

'What yer want?' he asked.

I tossed out another bottle. He jumped again; then he got it and drank it.

'What's going on in there?' I asked him.

'They're fixing up the niggers,' he said. 'You know as much about it as I do.'

He began to sing 'O Susannah' in a sentimental voice. It was beginning to get too dark for my safety. I was desperate.

I tossed out another bottle, only not so far this time. When he leaned for it, I said very clearly, 'You look like a butcher.'

He deliberately opened the bottle and drank off half of it.

'Butcher, huh? Butcher?' he laid down his gun and took his villainous knife out. 'I'm no butcher. I won't have nothing to do with the whole slimy mess. I won't eat them. No, sir, you can do that for me. But I can do a little carving, I think. No butcher, you son of a bitch. You dirty prying nigger-eating son of a bitch. I'll learn you to call me a butcher.'

He was stalking the cactus again. He lunged forward at it, and with much monotonous cursing and grunting dealt with it murderously. Meanwhile I crawled out on the other side of the sagebrush and ran for it. He never shot at me. Nothing happened, except that I too ran full tilt into a cactus, and had to walk hours in agony of flesh as well as of spirit. I vomited and retched till I thought I would be unable to walk further.

I must continue this letter some other way.

ANDY

(In invisible ink, on the papers wrapping another sweater for Ruth's cousin's baby)

I told Ruth nothing of what I had learned. Not even *her* great sense of the inevitable could survive such a shock, I think. Yet sometimes it seems to me that she must surely know it all. I do not want to know whether she knows. Could I support it if she did?

It was more painful pulling the cactus needles out than it had been acquiring them. But she removed them all, bathed the little wounds with alcohol and put me to bed. The next morning I awoke at seven and insisted upon going to work. I sat all day in my office, eating crackers and drinking milk. I didn't accomplish a thing. It was that day my chief told me to take it easy for a while. I was in a sort of stupor for a couple of days; yet I insisted, to everyone's consternation, on going to work. I accomplished nothing, and I intended to accomplish nothing. It was just that I could not tolerate being alone. In fact, today was the first day I have been alone for more than five minutes since I returned from the walk. But today I have regained a kind of composure, or seeming of composure, which for a time I despaired of ever possessing again. And I know that by the time I have given shape enough to my thoughts to put them on this paper for you to read, I shall have gained again a peace of mind. To have you to write to, Herb, that is the great thing at this point. Without you there, I do not know what I would have done.

So much for my emotions. My thinking, my personal philosophy, has gone through at least as profound an upheaval as they.

In the chaos of my mind, in which huge invisible chunks of horror hit me unexpectedly from unexpected angles again and again, my first coherent and sensible idea came in the form of a question. 'Why did they make it possible for me to find out what has been going on?' For I finally realized that it was no fluke that I had discovered it. Or O'Doone either. Or anyone with the suspicions and the courage for it. When the atom bombs were being produced, the whole vast undertaking was carried off without a single leak to the outside. Therefore, if I had been able in so simple a way to find out what had been going on in the CPR, it was only because they didn't care. They could have stopped me.

Then I thought: invisible ink is scarcely new in the history of things. Perhaps they have been reading my correspondence with you all along and will smile at this letter as they have smiled at others; or perhaps they haven't taken the trouble to read it, because they simply don't care.

Perhaps the authorities not only did not care if we gradually found out, but wanted us to.

Why should they want us to? Why, if that were true, should they have put up so formidable a system of apparent preventives? Double fences, censorship, lies, etc, etc?

The only answer that makes sense is this. They want the news gradually and surreptitiously to sift out to the general population – illegally, in the form of hideous rumours to which people can begin to accustom themselves. After all, everyone knew generally that something like the atom bomb was being manufactured. Hiroshima was not the profound and absolute shock in 1945 that it would have been in 1935, and a good deal of the preparation for its general acceptance was rumour. It is in the people's interest that the CPR functions as it does function, and especially so that they can pretend that they have nothing to do with it. The experience of the Germans in the Jew-extermination camps demonstrated that clearly enough. It would do no good for me to go around crying out the truth about NRACP, because few would believe me in the first place and my suppression would only give strength to the rumours, which were required and planned for anyhow.

But I still had to set myself the task of answering Why? What drove them (whoever they are) to the decision to embark upon a course which was not only revolutionary but dangerous? I accepted the NRACP as inevitable, as Necessity; there remained only the task of trying to understand wherein lay the mystery of the Necessity and of adjusting myself to the situation. The individual, even the leader, has no significant choice to make in the current of event; that current is part of natural law; it is unmoral, cruel, wasteful, useless, and mysterious. The leader is he who sees and points out the course of history, that we may pursue that course with least pain. It is odd that we Americans have no such leader; what we have is committees and boards and bureau heads who collectively possess leadership and who direct our way almost impersonally. There is nothing whatsoever that I myself would like so much as to be one of those wise, courageous, anonymous planners. The wisdom I think that I possess. But in place of courage I have a set of moral scruples dating from an era when man was supposed to have a soul and when disease took care of overpopulation. The old vestigial values of Christianity must be excised in the people as they are being excised in me. The good and the lucky are assisting at the birth of a new age. The weak and unfit are perishing in the death of an old. Which shall it be for us?

For my own part, I think I am in a state of transition, from being one of the unfit to being one of the fit. I feel it. I will it. There are certain external evidences of it. For example, I was face to face with the truth at the end of April, but instead of acknowledging what I saw I turned to my love for Ruth. Yet that refusal to recognize the truth did not long survive the urgings of my sense of Necessity. And I remember, when being confronted with piecemeal evidences of the truth, that I was unable to explain a number of them. You know, Herb, how accomplished a rationalizer I can be; yet this time I did not even *try* to rationalize about many of the facts.

It is dawn outside. I cannot read this letter over, so I am not entirely sure how incoherent it is. I feel that I have said most of what I wanted to say. I am not very happy. I think I shall sleep the better for having written this. I eat nothing but bread and fruit and milk. A bird is singing outside; he is making the only sound in the world. I can see the hill which separates us from the Intake buildings. It's a pleasant hill, rather like an arm extending out from the valley sides, and I am glad it is there. I am cold now, but in three hours it will be warm and in five hours hot. I am rambling I know. But suddenly all my energy has leaked out. I walk to the door to see Ruth so happily sleeping, mysteriously replenishing life from this nightly portion of death, and I think of that baby she is bearing and will give birth to. If it were not for her and the baby, I am sure I should have gone mad. Is not that a mystery, Herb? Our child shall be fortunate; it is the first conscious generation of each new order in whom the greatest energy is released. There are splendid things ahead for our child.

It is not my fault. I did not know what I was doing. How could I have known? What can I do now?

I stare at the lightening sky, exhausted. I do not know why I do not say farewell, and go to bed. Perhaps it is because I do not want to hear that little lullaby that sings in my ears whenever I stop: I have eaten human flesh, my wife is going to have a baby; I have eaten human flesh, my wife is going to have a baby.

Remember, back in the simple days of the Spanish Civil War, when Guernica was bombed, we speculated all one evening what the worst thing in the world could be? This is the worst thing in the world, Herb. I tell you, the worst. After this, nothing.

Perhaps if I lay my head against Ruth's breast and put her hands over my ears I can go to sleep. Last night I recited Housman's 'Loveliest of trees, the cherry now', over and over till I went to sleep, not because I like it particularly but because I could think of nothing else at all to recite.

My wife is going to have a baby, my wife is going to have a baby, my wife is going to have a baby.

Bless you,

ANDY

George P. Elliott was born in Knightstown, Indiana in 1918. He was educated at the University of California and then went on to be Assistant Professor at St Mary's College, California. In 1963 he became Professor of English at Syracuse University, New York. He published four novels and two collections of short stories: *Among the Dangs* (1961) and *An Hour of Last Things and Other Stories* (1968). He also published four collections of verse. George P. Elliott died in 1980.

Aubades and Serenades by Igor Pomerantsev

translated by Frank Williams

I like this dog. Her skinny, elongated body, long muzzle, moist eyes. In the lift she gets agitated and even kisses near-strangers. Once, walking past in the corridor, I heard her say to our new colleague, 'Pop in and see us.' If she'd said it to me, I'd have said yes straight away. But she avoids me because she feels I've got something on her. Very occasionally, in passing, in the corridor, she'll bark hoarsely: 'Hi!' My eyes become moist, my ears go velvety and I rush whining into the toilet to give free rein to my tears behind the locked door of the cubicle.

When it's his turn to share out the meat, it always makes me depressed. It's a cosmic depression. I know: the pieces might all look the same, but he'll still get more than me. I don't begrudge it, it depresses me. I know, he's much older than we are, he's old enough to have run with the last packs in the forests. It's the lore of the forest. The main thing there was survival. And since he has survived, one of the few, that really does mean something. I'm depressed because I know I wouldn't have survived then. I suddenly hear my name, in its affectionate short form '. . . why haven't you taken my share?' How fortunate that I didn't live with them in the forest. I grab my ration, run without a backward glance to the lift, go up to our department, wrap the meat in a clean form and throw it into the rubbish bin.

I like the morning best of all. She flies into the office, her beak rose-pink, wings wet with rain. The narrow strip between beak and chin is beaded with sweat. I am overcome. These beads are a confession of love. Her breathing is still irregular – she is in my arms. I lick up her sweat, just as I caught rain-drops on my tongue when I

125

was little. The day has only just begun, but for me it has already passed.

Crash, tinkle, tinkle – glass is broken on the ground floor. Half an hour later the same sound – a little stronger this time – comes from the first floor. Everybody's working. I, too, am silent. Glass is breaking on the second floor, and I start calculating when it will happen to our windows as well. In four hours. Must do something. I go up to the squirrel and quietly, so as not to cause a panic, ask: 'Did you hear it?' The squirrel is bewildered. Follows me with a long stare. Over the next three hours the noise of breaking grows more and more. I can imagine what hell it must be downstairs: the wind blowing through the offices, forms and carbon paper flying about, everyone clinging to the walls, to the desks. And out on the street? A carpet of broken glass, the pavement cordoned off, idlers gawping from a distance. They must be looking at our floor now. But it's all quiet here. Typewriters clatter. The squirrel gnaws nuts. What is this – courage or unconcern? I feel sick and go to the toilet. I groom my fur with a damp paw, but it still sticks up. I go back and sit at my desk. We do not look each other in the eye. I press my rump into an armchair, throw back my head, swallow saliva. Here it comes.

The rat reeks of musk. She's got me up against the wall and talks and talks. The smell could drive you mad. A door slams at the end of the corridor. I recognize the rustle of the wings I love. If she flies past and the rat breathes on her, she is doomed. The rustle comes nearer. Oh my beloved, I shall save you! I suddenly sink my teeth into the rat's lips in a deadly kiss and my body becomes swollen with musk. I am soaring and do not see how my shoelaces, undone now, flutter in the wind.

By midday the fog had thickened and was pressing up against the windows. It even became necessary to switch on the light. Never in my life have I seen such fog: thick, a bluey colour, sticky probably. A racoon came into our office and stayed glued to the window. A dog came running in and also froze. Then others. Everybody, literally everybody, was there. To see I had to haul myself up on the coat rack. We didn't take our eyes off the fog. The glass trembled. You could hear it distinctly in the silence. The blue, almost violent on the other side of the glass, electric in the office; us, frozen still. Oh, how terrible, how unbearable!

I am jealous of her fondness for his voice. When the door is ajar we both hear his voice. She sits with the back of her head to the door, and the voice first of all nestles against her fur and kisses it soundlessly, then it reaches her mouth, her knees. But I must not betray myself, and so I sit motionless. Only when the racoon passes outside in the corridor do I ask, as if by chance, 'Be so kind as to shut the door to the office.' The door bangs shut, and I see the voice come swimming up to the glass in the door, gawp, flutter his fins and open his mouth convulsively. This is awful: now she will feel sorry for him and so, love him. Agitated, she gets up from her chair and almost runs from the room. I fix my eyes on a paper-clip.

Today is the last day. I can go to the park. They're making bonfires there now. My heart is sad. I'm sure the skunk felt this way this time last year. The week before he was going round with red eyes, and everybody even avoided standing next to him. On the penultimate day they drew lots. The skunk was there, though he didn't have to be. All this year I've remembered the look in his red eyes – the way he looked at me when I drew the lot. That day we were brothers, and the skunk said farewell to everybody except me: after all, we were parting for only a year.

They drew lots again yesterday. I didn't go. So I don't know who was next. It's not important. I now realize the skunk went out of weakness. But who said that it's bad or shameful to be weak? I'm strong. But is that good? I do not feel fear. I'm just sad at heart. I'll go to the park. I'll stand a while near a bonfire. The skunk probably cannot think of anything else except meeting me. The wind will carry the smoke away from the bonfire. If only it could carry away my sadness, too!

Today my attention was caught by the fact that the racoon was standing for ages near the aquarium in the canteen. I, too, was standing quite close, but the racoon didn't even see me – he was so absorbed. I watched the aquarium for a long time and came to understand something. The secret of oriental love. This was a harem. The rhythmic movements of the fish. Their finery trembled in time to their bodies. This was a dance. The water was thick and closeness difficult. Light draughts, was it? or a tabla provided the rhythm. One fish shamelessly rubbed her lips against the glass. The racoon was listener and viewer. My head was splitting and I, like a drunk, moved away. My mouth tasted sweet. The racoon came back from lunch absolutely shattered and could not start work again for a long time.

We were taken on an excursion. We two are walking along a canal. I do not like this town. It is the work of a glass-blower. I like a different sort of town, thrown by a potter. That kind, the other one, is warm, just right for my paws. This one is cold, sharp. Good to recall in a heatwave. The water is covered with mildew and lichen. We walk in silence. Suddenly she plunges into the canal. I shudder with disgust: how could she throw herself into the brown, green-tinged scabs? The swill washes into her ears, her mouth. I lean down from the low parapet and stretch out my paw to her. She catches hold. With my right paw I lift her slightly out of the water – her muzzle already green with slime, beak sharpened – and with my left strike hard and unexpectedly between the eyes.

They brought in boxes and began to unpack them right there in the office. By midday I suddenly saw we were crammed out with boxes. All was quiet, and I began to feel uneasy. I put my shoulder to what seemed to me to be the smallest box, but it was nothing of the sort. Then I heard whimpering. I recognized the polecat and for some reason it pleased me. My shoulder was itchy because bits of sawdust had got into the fur. I picked up a pair of scissors and began jabbing them into the wood. Then I set to with my two fangs, spitting out a continuous stream of wood chips. I called: 'Polecat, we have to chew a way through to the door.' The polecat, judging by the sound of gnawing, had also set to work.

A month ago we had a mole in our office. We could have done with him now! There were Christmas tree decorations in the box. You only had to prick them gently with the scissors and they literally gave up the ghost. A paper streamer was painfully wound round my neck. I was tired, my eyes were watering, my stomach was rumbling. I lay down to take a breather, sucking a sugar lump. Calculated how long it would take to get to the door. Three to four days. Do I have enough strength, determination and, ultimately, love of life? I don't know, don't know.

They loaded us into cages and took us for a check-up at the clinic. I saw snowflakes through the car window; my eyes watered from the cold and lack of air; the squirrel's breath was flavoured with a smell of rancid nuts. At the clinic we were given an X-ray. We had to get undressed in an office in pitch darkness. My skin was covered in pimples. The radiologist's fingers were electric. I got a shock. I thrashed about in the dark; the radiologist pinched me hard and I froze still. When I'd dressed they put the squirrel in the machine. While the radiologist was putting in a new plate the squirrel kicked and scratched and chattered her teeth. I'd got used to the dark and could make things out now. The white blob of a coat seared my eyes. The radiologist pressed a knob so as to restrain the squirrel from two sides. Something scrunched, like a nut, and a dead silence hung. I thought I would go mad. The radiologist dived towards the apparatus and, keeping his back to me, pulled something out, cursing and muttering. Then his back went out through the emergency exit. On the way home, the cage was empty. It was so, so easy to breathe.

Not long before his death, the badger took up learning Mararanian. At first we pulled his leg. 'Off to Mararania are you, me old MacBadger?' His table was quite covered with textbooks, dictionaries and children's books. The badger's lips were constantly in motion, as though he were praying or casting a spell. Little by little his mumbling began to form crystals of sounds. The badger went round all the departments declaiming, denouncing, praising, without paying any attention to anybody. We'd all almost stopped talking and were feeling somehow uneasy. The screech, thunder, roar of Mararanian filled the rooms. One day the badger was called to the telephone and we could tell by his excited tirade that the caller was his Mararanian girl-friend. Somehow at midday the din had stopped and each of us guessed what had happened. I now realize why the badger finally took up a foreign language; those who make a beginning are far from the end. Since then, I have only to chance to hear the screech of Mararanian and I recall how desperately the badger clung to life.

There are four lifts in our building. They all move simultaneously: up-down, down-up. When you use the stairs you always hear their squeak, rattle, rasp. These noises are all simply obscene. If I happen to be on the stairs with the marten or the weasel, I always blush. The plaited steel cables are taut. The lifts brush against the air, and I haven't the strength to stand next to the marten. Even when you're sitting in your office you can hear a muffled rustling that's even worse than their rasping. The whole building is eaten away by rustling noises: paper, carbon paper, the trees outside the tightly shut windows. We, too, are beginning to speak in whispers. The weasel bends to my ear and whispers something. Her lip rustles against the lobe of my ear. I swallow and hear the saliva slipping slowly down my throat. It's a good thing I've only got one throat. The weasel keeps on whispering while I stare fixedly at a piece of fluff shivering under my gaze.

Mystery and horror just happened. The eider duck, always so neat and tidy, rushed down the corridor looking dishevelled and half-crazed, and on her white downy breast two red wine stains, quite fresh. You felt ashamed if you looked at her, but not to look at her was impossible. It was not the eider duck that was obscene, but ourselves, the fact that we found ourselves by chance in the corridor. Now each of us sits at his desk and pretends to be absorbed in his work. But those two red stains! I even managed to catch a whiff of ascerbic, stupefying grape. Oh, to lick it with the tip of my tongue. But what am I saying – lick? No! Drink it in, suck onto it, choke on it.

Oh, foxawolf! Could any of us forget your leap through the glass? It shattered, splintered, tinkled down, while you flew smoothly and your paws trembled like springs. Oh, how you ran over the squares of the city! Launched out, landed, and between times soared: your body floated slowly through the air, and this soaring was inexpressibly beautiful. What can I say about our feelings, even of those of us who until then had not loved you? In the office a television flickered. They were filming your dash from a helicopter. We could see what was hidden from your eyes. All roads out of the city had already been blocked. The roar of motorcycles, the perfect co-ordination of the foot patrols, the howl of the ambulances, the precision of telescopic sights. All this seemed empty hustle in comparison with your dash, with your body, now convex, now concave. You ran, you rushed, you flew towards freedom, love – we, fixed to the screen, knew towards what.

Igor Pomerantsev was born in Saratov in 1948. After spending his early childhood in Siberia he moved with his family to the Western Ukranian city of Chernovtsy. His poetry was published in the mass-circulation magazine *Smena*. In 1978 he emigrated, and now lives in London, working as a translator and journalist. His stories have appeared in the major Russian-language literary journals published in the West, and in English translation in the magazine *2PLUS2* and on Radio 3.

Frank Williams is a translator specializing in contemporary Russian writing. His translations of Igor Pomerantsev, Zinovy Zinik, Vladimir Voinovich, Andrey Sinyavsky and Yevgeny Popov have appeared in *The Listener*, *Index on Censorship* and have been broadcast on Radio 3.

Enemy Territory by Emanuel Litvinoff

Mr James, the trade school master, had a square, freckled, open-air face with a cleft chin like Johnny Weismuller. The look of a good sport. 'Sit down anywhere,' he said in a jolly voice as we shuffled into the class-room and sniffed the unfamiliar air. Some deep racial memory stirred the sediment of disquiet: fear of the uncircumcised. 'We'll sort out the sheep from the goats later,' he threatened, grinning matily.

The animal metaphor was unfortunate. A strong carnivorous smell filtered in from neighbouring Smithfield Market which I'd seen for the first time as I walked to school that morning past rows of refrigerated pigs, agony frozen in their tiny slitted eyes. Worse still, the stench of an evil brew permeated the playground from an adjoining building where cauldrons bubbled with offal ripped from the flesh of slaughtered beasts. It was a disquieting place for one convinced of his own goatishness to begin a new education.

The Headmaster came striding in on short fat legs.

'All together, boys,' Mr James said, lifting his arm with the flourish of an orchestral conductor.

'Good morning – Sir!'

The face of a rosy, bald-headed schoolboy of sixty ballooned over the Headmaster's wing collar. He cleared his throat, spat daintily into a large clean handkerchief and examined the result before folding it away. 'As 'Ead of this College, it's my privilege and duty to greet you with a few words of welcome.' He paused to ensure he was receiving full attention. 'What we hexpect of our pupils is hobedience and guts. Hobedience means when you're told to do something, do it, don't lark about. Guts is don't go moaning to your mums when you get whacked across the posterior because you didn't.'

Folding his short arms behind his back, he strode up and down the dais for a few moments, chin meditatively resting on his chest. 'I'm stressing that point,' he went on, confronting us again, 'because you 'ave been selected to learn a honourable and hancient craft – practised, if I might say so, by one of the holdest Guilds in the kingdom. The British boot, like the British hinfantryman, is the finest in the world. And that's something to remember with pride. We marched to victory on British leather!' The recollection of patriotism stiffened the Headmaster's podgy frame and made us all sit up straighter. 'Righto!' he said, threateningly, 'we'll now call the register. When you 'ears your name jump hup smartly and reply "Present".' He opened a large book, bending back the covers till the spine cracked, and unscrewed a thick fountain pen. The roll call in alphabetical order proceeded briskly. Each boy stood up as commanded, was duly scrutinized, and resumed his seat. The first interruption occurred when the name Leoni, G. was read out. A sallow boy with close-cropped black hair stood up. He had a long thin nose and hairy wrists protruding from the short sleeves of his jacket. The Headmaster examined him for several painful seconds.

'What's the G. stand for, lad?' he asked eventually.

'Giuliano, sir.'

'Dad an ice-cream merchant, his 'e?'

'No, sir.' Leoni's dark eyes flinched. 'My father's a waiter.'

The Headmaster exchanged an amused glance with Mr James and said, 'Righto, sit down. Lester, R.'

My own name seemed a long time coming and I prepared for the shock of it by pressing my knees together to control their trembling. I knew with hopeless certainty that I should never have come to this school. When the official letter from the London County Council offered me a place at Cordwainers' Technical College it seemed a reprieve. Otherwise at fourteen, like any other unsuccessful boy, I'd be dressed up like a man of forty sawn off at the knees and pitched into the turbulent labour market. The choices were few and gruesome. I could boil a glue-pot and sweep up wood shavings, carry a tailor's sack from workshop to retailer, learn to baste a hem, press out a seam, nail a fur, lather a chin, weigh sugar into one-pound bags, or diss a stick of lead type with average competence. During my first week I'd be sent on errands for pigeon's milk, rubber nails and elbow grease, be ordered to take my hands out of my pockets and stop playing pocket billiards and might well be held down while bootblacking was smeared on my penis. At the end of the week I'd buy my first packet of fags and have nothing to hope for but the Revolution.

In contrast, college was Greyfriars, Harry Wharton, the jolly heroes of the Remove and comic masters in tasselled mortar-boards. Then I discovered that a cordwainer was someone who made boots and shoes. *A boot and shoe college yet.* But somehow, in a manner unforeseen, I retained a desperate hope that Cordwainers' might still lead to the cloisters of the elect.

The Headmaster adjusted his glasses to peer more closely at the register. He was having trouble in pronouncing the next name. 'Lit-in-totinoff?' His head rotated in its starched collar as he surveyed the class. 'Did I get it wrong?' He tried once more. 'Lit-pot-sky-off, E.'

No one answered.

'Well,' he said in a tone of surprise, examining the register yet again. 'We are 'aving difficulties. Hi wonder, now, could it be that fine hold Hanglo-Saxon name Levinskinoff?'

I had the sensation of taking up a role I'd long rehearsed, a disagreeable but not unrewarding feeling. It happened to all of us. I was thirteen years and ten months old: time already. My brother Abie once refused to read the part of Shylock, explaining that it insulted his people. Six times he was caned on the palm of his hands, six times he refused. And Abie, then only twelve, became the hero of the neighbourhood for a week. Here I was, facing my own test, surrounded by strangers and a long way from home. It was a stern and lonely prospect. With what seemed extraordinary patience, everybody watched and waited. My bladder suddenly filled with the strain of it.

'Please, sir,' I blurted out, 'can I leave the room?'

Mr James coughed disapprovingly and glanced at his superior. 'What's *your* name, lad?' the latter asked with an innocent stare.

'Me, sir?' I had to swallow to get it out. 'Litvinoff, sir.'

'You're not 'ard of 'earing, har you?'

'No, sir.'

'Then why didn't you speak hup when you were called?'

'Hi-I . . . wasn't, sir. Called.'

The Headmaster looked round the class in a puzzled way. 'Did the rest of you 'ear his name read hout?' They said they had. 'Did you, Mr James?'

'I did, sir. Very plainly.'

'There, lad, you must a been daydreaming. Hit won't do, you know. Not in Cordwainers'.' The tone was mild, tolerant and amused. 'Hand another thing. Any boy worth 'is salt hought ter be able ter control 'is hanimal functions till break. Ain't that so?'

What defeated me was not so much timidity as bad timing. The mutilation of my name could hardly be made an issue now that the subject had been changed to one so embarrassing and unheroic. Besides, I wasn't going to be able to hold it in much longer.

'Yessir,' I groaned. *For Christ's sake hurry up!*

Two dimples appeared in the Headmaster's fat, red-veined cheeks and his eyes had a pigly twinkle. 'Righto, young feller,' he said cheerily. 'Lavatory-offsky.'

The laughter eructed like a great fart, and an extraordinary thing happened. The Lord stood at my right hand. He anointeth my head with oil and the need to pee miraculously vanished. I stood up slowly and searched for the annihilating phrase as David must have searched for the pebble that struck down Goliath. Pow!!!

. . . But nothing came; not a single coherent word except balls. 'Balls!' I yelled and made a dash for the door.

'Grab 'im, Mr James!' the Headmaster ejaculated. He caught me with a flying tackle as I sprinted down the hall and marched me to a room. The walls were lined with cryptic trophies. A glassed mahogany case held a display of slender-ankled boots and the place smelled punishingly of greased leather. 'You got off to a good start, old son,' Mr James remarked, sitting on the edge of the desk and swinging his leg. He jumped up hurriedly when the Headmaster entered. 'I'll go back to the class, sir, shall I?' he asked deferentially.

The Head rubbed his palms together. 'You do that. They're all sitting nice and quiet.' When we were alone, he said: 'Do you suffer from a weak 'eart or any hother physical weakness that could be hacerbated by corporal punishment?'

'N-no, sir.'

'Very good, stand over 'ere.' He pointed to a spot on the carpet well-worn by the feet of the guilty.

The lecture was severe and brief. I'd behaved shocking. Insubordination wouldn't be stood for. In his school things had got to

136

be done the British way. It was either make or break and the choice was up to me.

'Hi don't enjoy this, yer know,' Mr Sloper concluded. 'Hit don't gimme no pleasure to chastise a lad.'

Several canes stood in an umbrella stand. He selected one of suitable thickness and flicked it a few times to test its flexibility – wheesh . . . ! wheesh . . . ! wheesh . . . ! Satisfied, he ordered me to bend down, keep my knees straight and touch my toes.

His face glistened rosily from exertion. With every stroke our grunts mingled. It really did sound as if it hurt him more than me. It was over at last and I limped to the bog. I did a long pee high up on the wall. My rear felt as if it had been seared with a red-hot poker. Locking the door of a lavatory stall, I pulled down my trousers and fanned the inflammation, swearing a secret revenge. Then I washed the tears from my face under the cold tap.

And back to the battlefield.

Cordwainers' taught me the painful lesson that whenever they start separating sheep from goats they're searching the flock for the scapegoat. I bent to touch my toes on average about twice a week. Mr James whacked me for having filthy habits (a squashed sardine was found on the floor under my desk), for losing tools (a one-and-six-penny clicking knife), for dumb insolence, talking back, sucking bull's eyes in class, creating a disturbance by getting my ear in the way of an ink-pellet, and for other cardinal infractions.

A Headmaster's flogging was an occasion as ceremonious as Trooping the Colour and hence less frequent. To achieve one on the very first day was something of a record. But I most resented the punishment he gave me for cheating from a dimwitted chap named Sagger. Specifically it was for copying Sagger's composition on 'Footwear in Work and Play'. Protesting my innocence apparently made it worse: it wasn't True Blue. Retribution included segregation at the back of the class as well as the stick. Leper Litvinoff.

Venturing into the playground was a fearful undertaking. It was a lucky day if I escaped without being tripped, shoved, pummelled or having itching powder forced down my neck. During games, Grindle, a fast bowler, pitched yorkers at my head and once raised an iridescent lump as big as a pigeon's egg. When I dropped the bat to mop my streaming eyes, Mr James cast doubts on my sex. But the crowning humiliation, the thing that injected hatred drop by drop into my soul, was the odious nickname they fastened on me. Pissoffsky.

It was raining one day. An oily suck of viscous liquids sounded in gutters as if London was bleeding into the sewers. Everyone huddled under the inadequate roof of an open shed, but I stood in an exposed doorway alone, moisture trickling under my collar. It was sodding cold! As unobtrusively as possible, I squeezed into the crowd under the shed. 'Pissoffsky – out!' someone said. The cry was taken up: it was a chance for a bit of fun.

My temper went off like a bomb. In a rapture of kicking, punching, screaming violence, I exploded into the soft mass of bodies. The surprise and momentum of this attack caused a stampede and boys fell over each other in a wriggling heap on the ground, hitting out in aimless panic. One of the masters came on the scene and seized four of us at random. With my luck, it was inevitable I would be included. So was Grindle. We were all caned. Grindle rubbed his smarting backside and said in a low voice: 'I'll getcha for this, Ikey boy! I'll nail you to the bloody wall, God 'elp me!'

I would not like to suggest that every single boy – or even master – joined in this persecution. Some of the lads went out of their way to be discreetly friendly. But the school was a frightening place. One passed through the gates and entered a zone of danger. Class-rooms were unnaturally quiet and orderly. In the workshop too no unnecessary words were spoken, partly because you couldn't talk with a mouthful of tacks. Instruction was given in the cold level tones prison-warders might use to read regulations to convicts, and the work seemed no more useful than oakum-picking. In the short while I was there, I never did more than practise skiving scraps of waste leather, and nobody ever made a real shoe. Each day was a curious disconnected experience. I would escape from the pervading misery into a grey stupor, returning as if from a long journey; there were times when I had the feeling that the place only existed in my perverse imagination.

Another lonely boy was 'Okey-Pokey' Leoni. The nickname came from an old street-cry of Italian ice-cream vendors: 'Okey-Pokey, penny a lump!' No one associated with him, but neither did anyone molest him. He owed this immunity to the popular idea that Eyeties were quick to stick a knife in your gizzard when aroused, being very hot-blooded. It was the period of cigar-chewing Chicago gangsters with enormous padded shoulders who made love to the broads with a wisecrack and buried their massacred rivals in sumptuous wreaths of flowers. Some of that romantic violence rubbed off on all the spaghetti fraternity, although no one could be less like Al Capone than skinny four-eyed Leoni, who was quiet and rather old for his age, the sort of boy who looks as if he's worked out his whole life in advance.

During the first couple of weeks, Leoni and I passed each other as if we lived on different planets. Then one lunchtime I went into a cafe to get a cup of tea to drink with my sandwiches and he was sitting at the only table with a vacant chair. Between us, a meat porter in a bloody smock hacked away at a plateful of steak and chips. Leoni unwrapped a piece of salami, cut it into slices with a penknife, unscrewed a small jar of olives and proceeded to eat with neat composure. After finishing this meal, he lit up a fag and inhaled expertly.

'Do you smoke, already?' I asked, highly impressed.

He flicked some ash in my direction and said, lifting the corner of his mouth in a cynical smile: ''Course I do. I'm over fourteen.'

The meat-porter grinned. 'What about wimmin? 'Ad your under yet?' Leoni's sallow face reddened but he kept silent. 'I 'ad my 'and on it all night,' the man said. 'Wanna smell?'

Still silent, Leoni carefully nipped the glowing end off his cigarette and left. So did I. We walked side by side along Farringdon Road. Lunchtime crowds browsed at the second-hand bookstalls. A group of factory girls with plucked eyebrows and broad scarlet mouths sat on a low wall pretending not to hear the coarse flatteries of their unshaven fellow workmen. There was the cheerful rattle of trains shunting on the nearby railway. Soprano noises came from a junk-stall gramophone, giving a lilt to the sunny afternoon. It was spring: there was companionship: I felt pretty good.

'Do you like the English?' Leoni asked, frowning.

I looked up in surprise. 'I am English.'

'Then why you got a Polish name?'

'It's not Polish. It's a world-famous Russian name. Everybody knows that.'

Leoni walked in silence for several paces, hands thrust deep into his pockets and shoulders hunched, thinking it over.

'You don't look English to me,' he said. 'Old Grindle was telling everyone you're a Jew from Whitechapel.'

'Sod Grindle!' My ears began to roar. 'Whitechapel's not in a foreign country, is it? It's in London, the capital of England. And plenty of Jews are English.' A superior kind of English, I could have added. Cleaner, cleverer, soberer, harder-working, friendlier, nicer to live with – altogether better class. 'Some of the leading English people are Jewish people,' I added heatedly, trying to think of a suitable example. 'Did you ever hear of Colonel Kisch?'

'Colonel who?'

'He was only one of the biggest heroes of the war!'

'Okay, no need to shout,' Leoni protested mildly, and dropped the subject.

When we got to know one another better I discovered that although Leoni was born in London, in the Italian colony of Saffron Hill, he thought of Firenze – where his family originated – as his native city. He despised the English because Italians were cleaner, cleverer, more sober, harder-working, friendlier and more religious. Until the Roman Italians came under Caesar, the English couldn't read or write, had no laws and roamed about in animal skins slaughtering one another. As soon as Leoni was old enough he intended to return to the Firenze he'd never seen and set up as high-class shoemaker. The Italians made better shoes.

Once he took me to his home, a dark and airless apartment in an ugly block of flats on the main Clerkenwell Road, muffled from the din of traffic by dusty curtains. His father, who worked late, was asleep in a screened alcove. The place was full of swarthy moustached women with black braided hair and big hanging breasts who gabbled fiercely in their strange language as if engaged in an interminable quarrel. Although there was a tribal resemblance to my own world, this was distanced by pictures of saints and crucifixes and, most of all, by the pervading smell of foreign cooking. It made it easier to understand why Leoni was not English like me.

So now I had a friend and, in a way, it meant I'd begun to settle in. Every morning I left home and stole rides to school on the backs of lorries. I'd learned to smoke and money saved on bus-fares went to buy Woodbines. The smell of the meat market no longer bothered me. An inner toughening had taken place. I walked into class like the Lone Ranger entering a hostile bar room, eyes narrowed, hands resting loosely on the holsters of my invisible six-shooters. There was even something flattering about my notoriety and I played up to it. Whenever Mr James asked some simple question I gave an insolent display of knowledge, having acquired a fund of curious information from Bethnal Green public library.

'Let's ask old Clever Dick,' he would say, and the boys grinned in pleasant anticipation. 'You up there at the back, why did Lancashire become the centre of the cotton industry?'

'The problem with cotton-spinning,' I'd reply with relish, 'is it's hard to stop the fibres breaking except in a very humid atmosphere. Lancashire has a high rainfall, and is therefore an ideal place for cotton-weaving. Besides, sir, in the Industrial Revolution much use was made of child labour. Now, according to Karl Marx –'

'All right, we'll have none of that,' Mr James would growl, and I'd sit down smirking.

So the weeks passed and it looked as if I'd get through term alive and chipper. But on the grave occasion of my fourteenth birthday I tried to look beyond this limited horizon. No anniversary would be more momentous. If the Head should pick on me again I could, with glorious impunity, snap my fingers in his face and exit from Cordwainers' forever with a careless laugh. And then – what? Although I had an inner conviction that an exceptional destiny awaited me somewhere out there like a made-to-measure suit, as a class-conscious boy who read the *Daily Worker* I also knew that fourteen-year-olds were glutting the labour-market and being ruthlessly thrown on the scrap-heap. On the other hand, if I sold out to the System by staying on after the term was over I'd qualify for a modest grant. And, perhaps – who knew? – an influential School Inspector would enter the room just as I was skilfully expounding Einstein's Theory of Relativity and, summoning the Headmaster, declare: 'Who is this erudite scholar? I demand to know why he is wasting his time here instead of being prepared for a brilliant future at Oxford University.'

The importance of becoming fourteen led me to scrutinize myself more closely than usual in my mother's full-length fitting mirror. It showed a tallish boy at an unfair disadvantage because he'd outgrown the sleeves of his threadbare jacket and his skinny trousers exposed more shank than was dignified. Seen from the front the nose was not too long and roughly in the right place, but he had thick negroid lips, big square teeth with a gap in the middle, and one hinge of his nickel-framed glasses was tied with cotton. Discouraged, I retreated a few paces and turned swiftly to catch the reflection by surprise, the way it might be seen by a stranger. It hesitated and shambled towards me with an agonized look. It didn't have the appearance of a successful boy.

'I think I ought to leave school and make a career,' I said despondently that evening over supper.

My stepfather stretched his pale eyes in mocking amazement. 'Career?' Laughter gurgled in his throat like phlegm. 'What in, banking?'

When the usual recrimination subsided, he said he might be able to get me a job in the tailoring. My mother handed me an extra thick slice of cheese with an expression of moist tenderness that said she wished it could be everything – health, wealth and happiness. Abie had seen an advert in a Brick Lane grocer's window for a tricycle delivery boy and, with his usual crude humour, suggested I'd soon work my way down to chief floor-sweeper. We kicked one another under the table and started another row. Grimly rolling a shag cigarette, Solly announced that I'd soon find out life was no bed of roses.

'Must you put a curse on the child?' my mother shouted, cutting furiously into a loaf of bread.

But my real curse is indecision, and when I act at all it is impulsively, in most cases at the wrong moment. I started behaving recklessly in school in the hope that the consequences would be so nasty as to force me to leave, but nothing worse than the odd caning befell me. The Head himself stopped giving me special attention and no longer had any difficulty with my name. In fact, he addressed me only when it was unavoidable, averting his face as if my proximity was too disgusting to bear. If only they would torture me to become a Christian, or force me to eat pork. . . .

But the end, when it came, did involve principle. It was during break one Monday morning. Leoni and I were segregated as always in a corner of the school yard and began an argument over Italian fascists pouring castor oil down the throats of communists. Leoni paced around with his hands in his pockets, scowling. It served the communists right, he said ferociously. 'Look what they did in your country. They killed all the priests.'

A ball bounced across the yard. I fielded it and sent it back to the players with a drop kick before turning to deal with this unexpected statement.

'Whaddya mean, my country?'

'Russia. Your fatherland. You say "I'm English, I'm English," but even a Chinaman can be born in London.'

'Then he's an English Chinaman,' I said. Leoni pulled out a crumpled handkerchief and blew his nose in a highly contemptuous manner. His drawn-out shadow made a grotesque shape on the brick wall. 'Are you a fascist?' I asked, raising an eyebrow. Bash! right in the solar plexus.

'All Italians are proud to be fascists. *Dei et Patria*. Good on Mussolini! I hope he shoots all communists!'

I'd never met a fascist before and would certainly have expected visible signs of brutishness and depravity. Leoni didn't even have pimples.

'You like Mussolini,' I gasped. 'Even if he sucks the blood of the workers?' A distant fire glowed in his sooty eyes. Then he thrust two fingers in front of my face and began to walk away. 'Mussolini's a bastard!' I yelled after him.

He whipped round, tense and glaring, and pushed me clumsily against the wall. I pushed him back. We both took off our glasses carefully to show we meant business. Grindle, my chief enemy, strolled over with a group of his cronies.

'What's a marrer, Okey-Pokey?' he drawled solicitously. 'You and your pal 'aving trouble?'

'He – he insulted my country,' Leoni panted.

'Fucking Jewboy,' Grindle said. 'Why don't he go back to Palestine?'

I shuffled forward, fists up and chin tucked in, hoping to scare them off. It sometimes worked: but not this time.

'Look at 'im, Ted Kid Lewis,' jeered Grindle, and Leoni laughed gratefully. 'Muscles like sparrer's kneecaps and a cock like a peeled banana.' Encouraged by the applause this witticism aroused, he danced towards me, feinted, and flicked a light left at my jaw. I backed away with a belligerent scowl. 'Needle fight! Needle fight!' somebody yelled.

'Aah! not werf it,' he said.

'Gawn, Tom! You can 'andle 'im.'

Grindle still hesitated. Half lowering my fists, I tried to maintain an appearance of confident indifference. He had the knobbly face of a good fighter and shaved already. My irresolution must have got through. Grinning evilly, he said: 'Okay, then, yeah! I'll see you after school, Pissoffsky.'

They all began a frantic yelling. 'Now! Now!'

With unnerving calm, Grindle took a large watch out of his waistcoat pocket, consulted it in frowning concentration, then remarked: 'We got eight minutes. Awright.' I made the mistake of waiting. He put the watch away and hit me almost at the same moment. As my head jolted back, I caught a fleeting glimpse of Leoni, miserable and contrite. Grindle hit me again. I grabbed hold of his coat to restrain him and by some miracle he spun round, overbalanced and fell on his back. We were both astonished, but he was also alarmed.

'Cor! 'E knows Jujitsu,' someone exclaimed in awe and I was flooded by a premature feeling of victory.

Mr James came sprinting across the yard, the forelock of his blond, curly hair blowing in the wind, and pushed energetically into the centre of the crowd. He glanced from me to my reclining adversary in surprise.

'Get up, Grindle!' he commanded tersely. 'What's it all about?'

Like the True Sportsman he was, Tom Grindle kept mum but several other boys eagerly volunteered the information that the two of us were having a needle fight.

'A needle fight? Well, well, well!' Mr James made no attempt to conceal his satisfaction. For the first time ever, he gazed at me with approval. 'Good!' he said. 'That's the sporting way to get rid of bad blood. But it's got to be according to the rules. I'll speak to the Headmaster and we'll have it made official.' He gave us a chummy grin. 'You can bash each other's brains out in the gym at 4.30. If you got any. I'll be ref.'

All the rest of the day I was rocked by alternate waves of hope and panic, mainly the latter. I developed distressing physical symptoms. There didn't seem enough air to breathe; there was a hole in my stomach like a hundred-foot drop; I couldn't concentrate; my heart was pumping its heavy reluctant blood from somewhere outside my body; I felt faintly sick and kept wanting to pee all the time. At half past four Mr James smiled and nodded at me: 'Feeling in good shape, lad?' I grinned weakly and said yes in a shivering voice. It seemed to have got very cold for the time of the year.

The whole school tramped to the gym and formed up around the walls while Grindle and I stripped down to shorts and undervests. A hitch occurred when Mr James asked for someone to act as my second. Everyone became terribly quiet. Mr James repeated the request. There was a stir behind me as someone pushed his way forward.

'I'll do it,' said Leoni in a low voice. I don't know why he volunteered but he laced on the padded boxing gloves without once looking at my face as if to make it clear it didn't mean friendship.

All I wanted now was to end the suspense for better or worse, but we had to wait for the Headmaster. He trotted in at a brisk pace, a busy man attending to essential duty, and sat down in a chair placed deferentially at the ringside by Mr James.

'Right, lads,' said the latter, having called us into the centre of the ring. 'Two minute-rounds, needle-fight rules. That means,' he added alarmingly, 'fight to the finish or till someone gives in. Unless, in my opnion, one of you is too badly beaten up to carry on.' He slapped us on our backs encouragingly and the battle began.

As we advanced cautiously towards one another I noticed that Grindle seemed nervous. The hard muscles in his cheeks twitched and his eyes were screwed up uncertainly. Heartened, I rushed in, flailing my arms. He went back on the ropes and cowered behind his forearms. Except for the slap of leather gloves, there was a dismayed silence in the gym at the unpromising performance of the favourite. I knew a sweet surge of confidence. Grindle put his arms about my neck, his breath warm and close. Mr Sloper's mouth twisted in displeasure as I hammered my opponent's body.

'Break,' he said, looking peevishly over at Mr James. 'Break!' shouted the latter at the top of his voice.

We did so and Grindle swiped me smack in the nose. He was a strong boy. Blood and snot gushed out. As I staggered back, there were yells of excitement and all the bells of Christendom rang in my head. Grindle hit me again and again, a look of ecstasy on his blurred face.

In the midst of confusion, noise, helplessness, I felt disconnected and, somehow, resigned. There was so much shouting going on and some of it may have been meant as encouragement for me. But I couldn't believe it. Grindle was punching me, but I was fighting them all. Somewhere, in some deep recess of my being, I knew this was not for me: it was not my way.

Leoni mopped my bleeding nose with his own handkerchief. 'You better give in,' he muttered. 'He's murdering you.'

I went in throwing my arms about wildly, desperate to keep Grindle off. One lucky blow caught his eye. Or unlucky. Blotched and livid, he rushed past my pounding fists and drove me into a corner. In his reddened eyes I glimpsed something terrifying. Grindle really did want to kill me! Even if I could smash every bone in his face, the look of hatred would remain.

An excruciating pain sliced through me as he punched me in the stomach. I was clubbed on the face, the body, the head.

'That'll do,' Mr James said, forcing Grindle away. Through bloodshot darkness, I discovered a wryness in his expression which could have been pity, but the Headmaster was smiling.

There was no school for me the following day, nor ever again. I was fourteen years and three weeks old. Walking along Barbican, in the Clerkenwell district, one sunny morning, I saw a notice on a factory door. 'Strong boy wanted to learn the trade. Third Floor.' Summer was beginning, the height of the fur trade season.

Emanuel Litvinoff was born in London's East End, one of nine children of a Russian-Jewish mother, and grew up there in the 1930s, a bustling, painful and often hilarious experience as readers of his autobiographical sequence, *Journey Through a Small Planet*, will know. He left school at fourteen, worked in various trades, experienced unemployment and destitution, and, having acquired a dilapidated Remington for twelve shillings, was set for an apprenticeship as a writer when interrupted by the outbreak of war in which he spent almost six years in the British Army – Ulster, West Africa, the Middle East – leaving with the rank of Major and two books of wartime verse. His publications include: *The Untried Soldier, A Crown for Cain* and *Notes for a Survivor* (all verse), and *The Lost Europeans, The Man Next Door, A Death Out of Season, Blood on the Snow, The Face of Terror* and *Falls the Shadow* (all novels), *Journey Through a Small Planet* (autobiographical short stories) and several plays for TV. In addition Litvinoff has written extensively on the situation of Jews in the USSR and has edited the journals *Jews in Eastern Europe, Insight: Soviet Jews* and *Soviet Anti-Semitism: The Paris Trial*. He is also editor of *The Penguin Book of Jewish Short Stories*.

Last Rite by Neil Jordan

One white-hot Friday in June at some minutes after five o'clock a young builder's labourer crossed an iron railway overpass, just off the Harrow Road. The day was faded now and the sky was a curtain of haze, but the city still lay hard-edged and agonizingly bright in the day's undiminished heat. The labourer, as he crossed the overpass, took note of its regulation shade of green. He saw an old, old negro immigrant standing motionless in the shade of a red-bricked wall. Opposite the wall, in line with the overpass, he saw the Victorian façade of Kensal Rise Baths. Perhaps because of the heat, or because of a combination of the heat and his temperament, these impressions came to him with an unusual clarity; as if he had seen them in a film or in a dream, not in real, waking life. Within the hour he would take his own life. And dying, a cut-throat razor in his hand, his blood mingling with the shower water into the colour of weak wine he would take with him to whatever vacuum lay beyond, three memories: the memory of a green-painted bridge; an old, bowed, shadowed negro; of the sheer, tiled wall of a cubicle in what had originally been the wash-houses of the Kensal Rise Tontine and Workingmen's Association, in what was now Kensal Rise Public Baths.

The extraordinary sense of nervous anticipation the labourer experienced had long been familiar with him; and, inexplicable. He never questioned it fully. He knew he anticipated something, approaching the baths. He knew that it wasn't quite pleasure. It was something more and less than pleasurable, a feeling of ravishing, of private vindication, of exposure, of secret, solipsistic victory. Over what he never asked. But he knew, he knew. He knew as he approached the baths to wash off the dust of a week's labour, that this hour would be the week's high point. Although during the week he had never thought of it, never dwelt on its pleasures – as he did, for instance on his prolonged Saturday morning's rest – when the hour came, it was as if the secret thread behind his week's existence was emerging into daylight, was exposing itself to the scrutiny of daylight, his daylight. The way the fauna of the sea bed are exposed, when the tide goes out.

And so, when he crossed the marble step at the door, when he faced the lady behind the glass counter, handing her sevenpence, accepting a ticket from her, waving his hand to refuse towel and soap, gesticulating towards the towel in his duffle bag, each action was performed with the solemnity of an elaborate ritual, each action was a ring in the circular maze that led to the hidden purpose – the purpose he never elaborated, only felt, in his arm as he waved his hand; in his foot, as he crossed the threshold. And when he walked down the corridor, with its white walls, with its strange hybrid air, half unemployment exchange, half hospital ward, he was silent. As he took his place on the long oak bench, last in a line of negro, Scottish and Irish navvies, his expression preserved the same immobility as theirs, his duffle bag was kept between his feet and his rough slender hands between his knees and his eyes upon the grey cream wall in front of him. He listened to the rich, public voices of the negroes, knowing the warm colours of even their work-clothes without having to look. He listened to the odd mixture of reticence and resentment in the Irish voices. He felt the tiles beneath his feet, saw the flaking wall before him, the hard oak bench beneath him, the grey-haired cockney caretaker emerging every now and then from the shower to call 'Shower!', 'Bath!' and at each call the next man in the queue rising, towel and soap under one arm. So plain, so commonplace, and underneath the secret pulsing – but his face was immobile.

As each man left the queue he shifted one space forward and each time the short, crisp call issued from the cockney he turned his head to stare. And when his turn eventually came to be first in the queue and the cockney called 'Shower!' he padded quietly through the open door. He had a slow walk that seemed a little stiff, perhaps because of the unnatural straightness of his back. He had a thin face, unremarkable but for a kind of distance in the expression; removed, glazed blue eyes; the kind of inwardness there, of immersion, that is sometimes termed stupidity.

The grey-haired cockney took his ticket from him. He stuck it behind his ear, scratching his head with the same motion. He nodded towards an open cubicle. The man walked slowly through the rows of white doors, under the tiled roof to the cubicle signified. It was the seventh door down.

'*Espera me, Quievo!*'

'*Ora, deprisa, ha?*'

He heard splashing water, hissing shower-jets, the smack of palms off wet thighs. Behind each door he knew, was a naked man, held timeless and separate under an umbrella of darting water. The fact of the walls, of the similar but totally separate beings behind those walls, never ceased to amaze him; quietly to excite him. And the shouts of those who communicated echoed strangely through the long, perfectly regular hall. And he knew that everything would be heightened thus now, raised into the aura of the green light.

He walked through the cubicle door and slid the latch into place behind him. He took in his surroundings with a slow, familiar glance. He knew it all, but he wanted to be a stranger to it, to see it again for the first time, always the first time: the wall, evenly gridded with white tiles, rising to a height of seven feet; the small gap between it and the ceiling; the steam coming through the gap from the cubicle next door; the jutting wall, with the full-length mirror affixed to it; behind it, enclosed by the plastic curtain, the shower. He went straight to the mirror and stood motionless before it. And the first throes of his removal began to come upon him. He looked at himself the way one would examine a flat-handled trowel, gauging its usefulness; or, idly, the way one would examine the cracks on a city pavement. He watched the way his nostrils, caked with cement-dust, dilated with his breathing. He watched the rise of his chest, the buttons of his soiled white work-shirt straining with each rise, each breath. He clenched his teeth and his fingers. Then he undressed, slowly and deliberately, always remaining in full view of the full-length mirror.

After he was unclothed his frail body with its thin ribs, hard biceps and angular shoulders seemed to speak to him, through its frail, passive image in the mirror. He listened and watched.

(Later it would speak, lying on the floor with open wrists, still retaining its goose-pimples, to the old cockney attendant and the gathered bathers, every memory behind the transfixed eyes quietly intimated, almost revealed, by the body itself. If they had looked hard enough, had eyes keen enough, they would have known that the skin wouldn't have been so white but for a Dublin childhood, bread and margarine, cramped, carbonated air. The feet with the miniature half-moon scar on the right instep would have told, eloquently, of a summer spent on Laytown Strand, of barefoot walks on a hot beach, of sharded glass and poppies of blood on the summer sand. And the bulge of muscle round the right shoulder would have testified to two years' hod-carrying, just as the light, nervous lines across the forehead proclaimed the lessons of an acquisitive metropolis, the glazed eyes themselves demonstrating the failure, the lessons not learnt. All the ill-assorted group of bathers did was pull their towels more rigidly about them, noting the body's glaring pubes, imagining the hair (blonde, maybe) and the skin of the girls that first brought them to life; the first kiss and the indolent smudges of lipstick and all the subsequent kisses, never quite recovering that texture of the first. They saw the body and didn't hear the finer details – just heard that it had been born, had grown and suffered much pain and a little joy; that its dissatisfaction had been deep; and they thought of the green bridge and the red-bricked walls and understood –.)

He savoured his isolation for several full minutes. He allowed the cold to seep fully through him, after the heat of clothes, sunlight. He saw pale, rising goose-pimples on the mirrored flesh before him. When he was young he had been in the habit of leaving his house and walking down to a busy sea-front road, and clambering down from the road to the mud-flats below. The tide would never quite reach the wall and there would be stretches of mud and stone and the long sweep of the cement wall with a five-foot high groove running through it where he could sit, and he would look at the stone, the flat mud and the dried cakes of sea-lettuce and see the tide creep over them and wonder at their impassivity, their imperviousness to feeling; their deadness. It seemed to him an ultimate blessing and he would sit so long that when he came to rise, his legs, and sometimes his whole body, would be numb. He stood now, till his immobility, his cold became near-agonizing. Then he walked slowly to the shower, pulled aside the plastic curtain and walked inside. The tiles had that dead wetness that he had once noticed in the beach-pebbles. He placed each foot squarely on them and saw a thin cake of soap lying in a puddle of grey water. Both were evidence of the bather here before him and he wondered vaguely what he was like; whether the first impact of the wet tiles was as it was with him; whether he had a quick, rushed shower or a slow, careful one; whether he, in turn, wondered about the bather before him. And he stopped wondering, as idly as he had begun. He decided he would never know. And he turned on the water.

It came hot. He almost cried with the shock of it; a cry of pale, surprised delight. It was a pet love with him, the sudden heat and the wall of water, drumming on his crown, sealing him, magically, from the world outside; from the universe outside; the pleasurable biting needles of heat; the ripples of water down his hairless arms; the stalactites gathering at each fingertip; wet hair; the sounds of caught breath and thumping water. He loved its pain, the total self-absorption of it, and never wondered why he loved it; as with the rest of the weekly ritual – the trudge through the muted officialdom of the bath corridors into the total solitude of the shower cubicle, the total ultimate solitude of the boxed, sealed figure, three feet between it and its fellow; the contradictory joy of the first impact of heat, of the pleasurable pain.

(An overseer in an asbestos works who had entered his cubicle black and who had emerged with a white, blotchy, greyish skin-hue divined the reason for the cut wrists. He looked at the tiny coagulation of wrinkles around each eye and knew that here was a surfeit of boredom; not a moody, arbitrary, adolescent boredom, but that boredom which is the condition of life itself. He saw the way the mouth was tight, and wistful and somehow incommunicative, even in death, and the odour of his first contact with that boredom came back to him. He smelt again the incongruous fish-and-chip smells, the smells of the discarded sweet-wrappings, the metallic odour of the fun-palace, the sulphurous whiff of the dodgem wheels, the empty, musing, poignant smell of the seaside holiday town, for it was here that he had first met his boredom; here that he had wandered the green carpet of the golf-links, with the grey stretch of sky overhead, asking, what to do with the long days and hours, turning then towards the burrows and the long grasses and the strand, deciding, there's nothing to do, no point in doing, the sea glimmering to the right of him like the dull metal plate the dodgem wheels ran on. Here he had lain in a sand-bunker for hours, his head making a slight indentation in the sand, gazing at the mordant procession of clouds above. Here he had first asked, what's the point, there's only point if it's fun, it's pleasure, if there's more pleasure than pain; then thinking of the pleasure, weighing up the pleasure in his adolescent scales, the pleasure of the greased fish-and-chip bag warming the fingers, of the sweet taken from the wrapper, the discarded wrapper and the fading sweetness, of the white flash of a pubescent girl's legs, the thoughts of touch and caress, the pain of the impossibility of both and, his head digging deeper in the sand, he had seen the scales tip in favour of pain. Ever so slightly, maybe, but if it wins, then what is the point? And he had known the sheep-white clouds scudding through the blueness and ever after thought of them as significant of the preponderance of pain; and he looked, now, at the white scar on the young man's instep and thought of the white clouds, and thought of the bobbing of girls' skirts and of the fact of pain –.)

The first impact had passed; his body temperature had risen and the hot biting needles were now a running, massaging hand. And a silence had descended on him too, after the self-immersed orgy of driving water. He knew this shower was all things to him, a world to him. Only here could he see this world, hold it in balance, so he listened to what was now the quietness of rain in the cubicle, the hushed, quiet sound of dripping rain and the green rising mist through which things are seen in their true, unnatural clarity. He saw the wet, flapping shower curtain. There was a bleak rose-pattern on it, the roses faded by years of condensation into green: green roses. He saw the black spaces between the tiles, the plug-hole with its fading, whorling rivulet of water. He saw the exterior dirt washed off himself, the caked cement-dust, the flecks of mud. He saw creases of black round his elbow-joints, a high-water mark round his neck the more permanent, ingrained dirt. And he listened to the falling water, looked at the green roses, and wondered what it would be like to see these things, hear them; doing nothing but see and hear them; nothing but the pure sound, the sheer colour reaching him; to be as passive as the mud pebble was to that tide. He took the cake of soap then from the grilled tray affixed to the wall and began to rub himself hard. Soon he would be totally, bleakly clean.

There was a dash of paint on his cheek. The negro painter he worked beside had slapped him playfully with his brush. It was disappearing now, under pressure from the soap. And with it went the world, that world, the world he inhabited, the world that left grit under the nails, dust under the eyelids. He scrubbed at the dirt of that world, at the coat of that world, the self that lived in that world, in the silence of the falling water. Soon he would be totally, bleakly clean.

(The old cockney took another ticket from another bather he thought he recognized. Must have seen him last week. He crumpled the ticket in his hand, went inside his glass-fronted office and impaled it onto a six-inch nail jammed through a block of wood. He flipped a cigarette from its packet and lit it, wheezing heavily. Long hours spent in the office here, the windows running with condensation, had exaggerated a bronchial condition. He let his eyes scan the seventeen cubicles then. He wondered again how many of them, coming every week for seventeen weeks, have visited each of the seventeen showers. None, most likely. Have to go where they're told, don't they. No way they can get into a different box other than the one that's empty, even if they should want to. But what are the chances, a man washing himself ten years here, that he'd do the full round? And the chances he'd be stuck to the one? He wrinkled his eyes and coughed and rubbed the mist from the window to see more clearly.)

White, now. Not the sheer white of the tiles, but the human, flaccid, pink skin-white. He stood upwards, let his arms dangle by his sides, his wrists limp. His short black hair was plastered to his crown like a tight skull-cap. He gazed at the walls of his own cubicle and wondered at the fact that there were sixteen other cubicles around him, identical to this one which he couldn't see. A man in reach, washed by the same water, all in various stages of cleanliness. And, he wondered, did the form in the next cubicle think of him, his neighbour, as he did. Did he reciprocate his wondering? He thought it somehow appropriate that there should be men naked, washing themselves in adjacent cubicles. Appropriate to what, he couldn't have said. He looked round his cubicle and wondered: what's it worth, what does it all mean, this cubicle – wondered was any one of the other sixteen gazing at his cubicle and thinking, realizing, as he was, that he was nothing. He realized that he would never know.

Nothing. Or almost nothing. He looked down his body: thin belly, thin arms, a limp member. He knew he had arrived at the point where he would masturbate. He always came to this point in different ways, with different thoughts, by different stages. But when he had reached it, he always realized that the ways had been similar, the ways had been the same way, only the phrasing different. And he began then, taking himself with both hands, caressing himself with a familiar, bleak motion, knowing that afterwards the bleakness would only be intensified after the brief distraction of feeling – in this like every-thing – observing the while the motion of his belly muscles, glistening under their sheen of running water. And as he felt the mechanical surge of desire run through him he heard the splashing of an anonymous body in the cubicle adjacent. The thought came to him that somebody could be watching him. But no, he thought then, almost disappointed, who could, working at himself harder. He was standing when he felt an exultant muscular thrill run through him, arching his back, straining his calves upwards, each toe pressed passionately against the tiled floor.

(The young Trinidadian in the next cubicle squeezed out a sachet of lemon soft shampoo and rubbed it to a lather between two brown palms. Flecks of sawdust – he was an apprentice carpenter – mingled with the snow-white foam. He pressed two handfuls of it under each biceps, ladled it across his chest and belly and rubbed it till the foam seethed and melted to the colour of dull whey, and the water swept him clean again, splashed his body back to its miraculous brown and he slapped each nipple laughingly in turn and thought of a clean body under a crisp shirt, of a night of love under a low red-lit roof, of the thumping symmetry of a reggae band.)

There was one intense moment of silence. He was standing, spent, sagging. He heard:

'Hey, you rass, not finished yet?'

'How'd I be finished?'

'Well move that corpse, rassman. Move!'

He watched the seed that had splattered the tiles be swept by the shower water, diluting its grey, ultimately vanishing into the fury of current round the plug-hole. And he remembered the curving cement wall of his childhood and the spent tide and the rocks and dried green stretches of sea-lettuce, and because the exhaustion now was delicious and bleak, because he knew there would never be anything but that exhaustion after all the fury of effort, all the expense of passion and shame, he walked through the green-rose curtain and took the cut-throat razor from his pack and went back to the shower to cut his wrists. And dying, he thought of nothing more significant than the way, the way he had come here, of the green bridge and the bowed figure under the brick wall and the façade of the Victorian bath-house, thinking: there is nothing more significant.

(Of the dozen or so people who gathered to stare – as people will – none of them thought: 'Why did he do it?' All of them, pressed into a still, tight circle, staring at the whiplike body, knew intrinsically. And a middle-aged fat and possibly simple negro phrased the thought:

'Every day the Lord send me I think I do that. And every day the Lord send me I drink bottle of wine and forget 'bout doin' that.'

They took with them three memories: the memory of a thin, almost hairless body with reddened wrists; the memory of a thin, finely-wrought razor whose bright silver was mottled in places with rust; and the memory of a spurting shower-nozzle, an irregular drip of water. And when they emerged to the world of bright afternoon streets they saw the green-painted iron bridge and the red-brick wall and knew it to be in the nature of these, too, that the body should act thus –.)

Neil Jordan was born in Sligo in 1950. His first collection of short stories, *Night in Tunisia*, won the *Guardian* Fiction Prize in 1979. His subsequent two novels, *The Past* and *The Dream of a Beast*, established him amongst the most gifted writers of his generation. His three feature films to date have also established him as a highly talented film director. His first feature film, *Angel*, from its original screenplay, opened in 1980 to great critical acclaim. This was followed by *The Company of Wolves* in 1984, co-written with Angela Carter and starring Angela Lansbury and David Warner, and *Mona Lisa* in 1986, co-written with David Leland and starring Bob Hoskins and Cathy Tyson. He has just completed shooting of his fourth film, *High Spirits*.

People for Lunch by Georgina Hammick

'I must get up,' Mrs Nightingale said, but did not move. During the night she had worked her way down the bed so that her feet were now resting on the brass rail at its end. Two years ago today it had been Edward's feet striking this same brass rail with peculiar force that had woken her. 'I don't feel well,' he'd said, and she'd replied – sleepily? sharply? – she needed to know but could not remember – 'Then you'd better not go to work today.' When he'd gone on, haltingly, to murmur: 'No. I can't,' she'd sat up, wide awake and afraid. For Edward was a workaholic. Nothing prevented him going to the office. She'd leant over him and seen that his face and neck were beaded with sweat. She'd touched his forehead and found it as cold and green as marble. 'I've got a pain,' he said, 'in my chest.' Each word was a single, concentrated effort. 'I can't breathe.' Stumbling to the telephone which lived on Edward's side of the bed, she'd started to panic. How could she explain to the doctor, probably still in bed and asleep, how serious it was with Edward lying beside her listening? It was then that she'd begun to shake, and her teeth to rattle in her jaw like pebbles in a bag. She'd knocked the telephone directory on to the floor and misdialled the number half a dozen times. (It was not true that anxious, panicky people proved themselves level-headed under fire.) 'Be calm, Fanny. Go at it slowly,' Edward had said, lying still, his eyes unfocussed on the ceiling.

A shuddering sigh on Mrs Nightingale's left made her turn her head. Lying close on the adjoining pillow was the face of Bone. The dog's small body was concealed by the duvet, as was Mrs Nightingale's own. Mrs Nightingale stared at Bone's black nose, at the white whiskers that sprouted from her muzzle and chin, at her short sandy eyelashes. Bone's eyes were shut, but the left ear was open, its flap splayed on the pillow to reveal an intricacy of shiny and waxy pink coils. Mrs Nightingale leant across and blew gently in this ear. Bone opened one eye and shut it again. Mrs Nightingale put her arms round Bone and laid her head against the dog's neck. It smelt faintly of chicken soup. Bone jerked her head away and stretched her legs so that her claws lodged themselves in Mrs Nightingale's stomach. Mrs Nightingale kissed Bone on the muzzle just above the black, shiny lip. Bone opened her jaws wide in a foetid yawn and stretched again and went back to sleep. Mrs Nightingale got out of bed and left Bone, still covered to her neck by the duvet, sleeping peacefully.

Bone was not allowed in beds, only on them, and she reminded the dog of this. 'I don't like dogs,' she added untruthfully. The house was very quiet. Mrs Nightingale walked out bare-footed on to the uncarpeted landing and stood for a moment listening to the inharmonious ticking of the clocks downstairs. There was no sound from her children's bedrooms and their doors were uninvitingly shut. 'I hate being a widow,' she said aloud.

The bathroom door was blocked by a wrinkled dustbin sack full to overflowing with clothes intended for a jumble sale. She dragged it out of the way. From its torn side hung the yellowing arm of a Viyella cricket shirt. From its top protruded a brown Harris tweed skirt. Liza's name was still stitched to the tiny waistband. Had she ever really been that size? Mrs Nightingale had meant, before the move, to unpick the nametape from Liza's old uniform and take it back to the school for resale, but there had never been the time. This black sack was one of many about the house. Before moving she'd labelled them as to contents, but on examination recently they all contained the same things: outgrown clothes, single football boots, curtains originally made for Georgian sash windows that would not fit the small casements here, curtain hooks, picture hooks, bent wire coat hangers.

Lying motionless in the bath Mrs Nightingale saw Edward on the stretcher being carried into the ambulance. He had joked with the ambulance men. She would never forgive him for that. It had been his joking, and the doctor saying on arrival, just before he'd sent her out of the room: 'If you move, Edward, you're a dead man. If you lie still and do exactly what I say, you'll be all right,' that had given her hope. She could see Edward now, calling out from the stretcher to the twins, shivering in their night things on the front doorstep: 'Be good, monkeys. I'll be back soon.' And she could see herself, wrapped in his dressing-gown, bending down to kiss his cold cheek before the ambulance doors closed. She'd wanted to go with him, she'd needed to go with him, but had had to wait for her mother to come and look after the twins.

The bath water was by now tepid and Mrs Nightingale's finger ends were white and shrunk. As she lay there, unable to move, the church bells began a faint tolling through the shut window and at once the image of the ambulance with its frenetic blue light turning out of the drive was replaced by a picture of dead tulips and lilac in the vase beneath the lectern. She'd seen these on Friday when she'd gone to the church to check the Flower Rota List and found her name down for this Sunday. She forced herself out of the bath and pounded down the passage to Liza's room. She shook the mound of bedclothes.

'Liza – did you remember to do the church flowers yesterday?'

Liza was gliding through a dark lake on the back of a sea-serpent. She opened blank blue eyes for a second and then shut them again.

'Did you do the church flowers?'

The eyes opened again, flickered and then closed. Waking was a trial for Liza.

'Liza –'

'No. I didn't. Sorry.'

'You're the absolute end.' Mrs Nightingale was furious. 'You asked what you could do to help and I said –'

'Sorry, Mum.'

'You're not asked to do much. And you're eighteen, not six.'

'Don't flap' – Liza's voice sounded as though it had been dredged from the bottom of a deep lake – 'the congregation's geriatric. No one will notice if the flowers are dead.' She yawned. 'You're sopping wet,' she said incuriously to her mother.

'I need your help,' Mrs Nightingale cried. 'Get up at once, now, before you fall asleep again.' She stood for a moment awaiting results, but as there were none, left the room banging the door behind her.

Mrs Nightingale visited the twins' room next. They were fast asleep on their backs. Lily, on the camp-bed they took turns for, was snoring.

'Wake up, both of you,' Mrs Nightingale said. She trampled over their discarded clothes. 'Wake up now.' They sat up slowly, looking hurt and puzzled. 'It's late,' Mrs Nightingale said. 'Nine o'clock. They'll be here by half past twelve and there's a lot to do. You must get up. Now.'

'Who'll be here?' Poppy asked.

'Nine o'clock isn't late, it's early,' Lily said. 'It's Sunday.'

'Now,' Mrs Nightingale said and left the room.

When Mrs Nightingale opened Dave's door he was propped on one elbow, reading. His hair, which had been recently cut by a fellow student using blunt nail scissors, stuck out in stiff tufts. Here and there patches of scalp were visible. They'd had a row about the hair when he arrived. Usually Mrs Nightingale cut Dave's hair, and when she did he looked very nice. This present cut, which he'd admitted he wasn't that keen on himself, was an example of the perversity her son was given to and that Mrs Nightingale found exasperating and incomprehensible. He glanced up at her as she came in.

'Hallo, Mamma. How are you, darlin'?'

The question took Mrs Nightingale off-guard. Suddenly, she wanted to tell him. She wanted to say: 'Daddy died two years ago today.' She wanted to collapse on Dave's bed and howl, perhaps all day, perhaps for ever. Instead she stayed in the middle of the room and stared at the row of hats that hung from hooks above Dave's bed and which, together with the accents – foreign, regional – he adopted, formed part of her son's disguise kit.

'If you're awake, why aren't you up?' Mrs Nightingale heard herself say.

'Stay cool,' Dave said. 'I'm just tucking into Elizabeth Bishop.' He waved a paperback in the air that his mother recognized as her own and removed from its shelf without permission.

'How do you rate her? Compared to Lowell . . . ?'

'Get up, please,' Mrs Nightingale said.

'Okay, Marlene. Tuck in.'

Marlene, the second syllable of which was pronounced to rhyme with Jean, was not Mrs Nightingale's name, which was Frances. Marlene, which sometimes became Marlena, second syllable to rhyme with Gina, was the name Dave had bestowed on his mother some years ago when she'd started regularly cutting his hair. 'I'm due for a visit to Marlene's salon,' he'd say, ringing her from Leeds. 'Is the head stylist available?'

Mrs Nightingale moved backwards to Dave's door and fell over the bicycle wheel she'd noted on her way in and taken care to avoid.

'Shit. And your room's in shit, Dave.'

'Cool it.'

'Look, it is in shit and it smells. Do you have to sleep with the window shut? Why are you wearing that tee-shirt in bed?'

'I haven't any pyjamas, that's why,' Dave said reasonably.

'I know if I leave now you'll just go on reading –' Mrs Nightingale was getting desperate – 'so get out now, while I'm here.'

'I will as soon as you go. I've got nothing on below this tee-shirt, and the sight of my amazing, user-friendly equipment might unsettle you for the day. Tuck in, Marlene.' He yawned, showing a white tongue and all his fillings, and stretched his huge arms above his head.

Mrs Nightingale returned to her bedroom and dressed herself in scruffy, everyday clothes. Then she pulled Bone out of the bed and swept the bottom sheet with her hands. Being white, Bone's hairs did not show up well against the sheet but Mrs Nightingale knew they were there, and sure enough they flew around the room and settled on the floorboards like snowflakes in a paperweight snowstorm. Mrs Nightingale straightened the duvet and banged the pillows while Bone sat on her haunches, sorrowfully watching. As soon as the lace cover was on Bone leapt back on the bed and made herself comfortable among the cushions. Mrs Nightingale looked at her watch. This time two years ago she had just arrived at the hospital having driven at ninety most of the way. There'd been nowhere to park so she'd parked in one of the doctors' spaces. 'You can't park there,' an old man planting out geraniums by the hospital steps had told her, having watched her manoeuvre. Three floors up, on Harnham Ward, Sister had looked up from her notes and said: 'The specialist has examined your husband and would like to see you now.' Mrs Nightingale suddenly remembered the specialist's nose, aquiline and messily freckled. She'd stared at it as they sat opposite each other, divided by a desk. 'He's on the edge of a precipice,' the specialist had said. 'It was an almost total infarct – that means the supply of blood and oxygen to the heart has been severely reduced. A large part of the heart muscle is already dead. The next forty-eight hours will be crucial. If he survives, and I can give you no assurances, the dead muscle will be replaced in time by scar tissue, which is very tough and can do the same sort of job –'

I hate doctors, Mrs Nightingale thought as she went downstairs. Hate them. She took one look at the kitchen, then shut the door and went into the drawing-room, a room too poky to deserve the title that, from the habit of a lifetime, she had given it. It smelled of soot and damp and cigarettes, and of something indefinable that might have been the previous owners. Mrs Nightingale got down on her knees in front of the fireplace and swept the wood ash and cigarette stubs she found there into a dome. She stuck a firelighter on top of this, but the log baskets were empty except for two pieces of bark and several families of woodlice, so she got up again and started to punch the sofa cushions into shape. Dave came in while she was doing this. He was still wearing the tee-shirt but to his lower half he'd now added an Indian tablecloth which he'd wrapped twice round himself and tucked in at the waist.

'You left a filthy mess in the kitchen last night,' Mrs Nightingale said, remembering the slag heap of coffee grounds decorated by a rusty Brillo pad on the kitchen table. 'I thought you were going to get dressed.'

'Liza's in the bathroom.' Dave scratched his armpit, then sat down heavily on the sofa cushions and rested his head on his knees.

'Dave, I've just done that sofa. We've got people for lunch –'

'Yup. Sure thing. Sorry. What can I do?' He stayed where he was and Mrs Nightingale stared, mesmerized, at his large yellow feet. The toenails were black and torn. Black wire sprouted from his big toes. The same wire twined his calves, visible beneath the tablecloth. It stopped at the ankles, but continued, Mrs Nightingale knew, beyond his knees to his thighs, where it no longer twined, but curled. It was impossible that this huge male person had ever been inside her body. 'Well, the log baskets are empty, as you see,' Mrs Nightingale said, 'so when you're dressed –'

'Sure, sure.'

'I did ask you, you know,' Mrs Nightingale bravely continued,

164

'when you arrived, if you'd be responsible for getting the wood in, and you said –'

'Yeah. Yeah. Sure. Yup. Tuck in.' He sat for a moment longer and then got up, hitching the tablecloth which had slipped a little. He looked round the room. 'I like your little house, Marlene.'

'It isn't *my* house.' Mrs Nightingale was hurt by Dave's choice of possessive adjective. 'It's *our* house. It's home.'

'Yup.'

'No chance, I suppose,' she said as he padded to the door, 'of your wearing your contact lenses at lunch?' Dave stopped dead in his tracks and turned sharply. 'What's wrong with my specs?' He whipped them off and examined them myopically, close to his nose. They were bright scarlet with butterfly sides, the sort typists wore in the fifties. One arm was attached to the frame by a grubby Sellotape bandage.

'Nothing's wrong with them. It's just that you look nicer without them. You're quite nice looking, so it seems a shame –'

'Oh Christ,' Dave said and then hit his head on the beam above the door. 'Fuck. I hit my head everywhere I go in this fucking house. Cottage. Hen-coop. Hovel.'

By the time Mrs Nightingale had finished scrubbing the potatoes they were all down in the kitchen with her. The kitchen was too small for five people comfortably to be in at one time. She had once, when they were all tripping over each other, made this observation and had received a long lecture from Dave on the living conditions of the average farm-labourer and his family in the latter part of the nineteenth century. Her son was nothing if not inconsistent, Mrs Nightingale thought, remembering the hen-coop remark.

'Who's finished the Shreddies?' Poppy was on her knees on the brick floor, peering in a cupboard.

'Dave had them last night – don't you remember?' Liza said, sawing at a grapefruit with the bread knife. A pool of cloudy juice and pips spread over the table, soaking an unpaid telephone bill. Mrs Nightingale snatched it up.

'Here, have this' – Liza plonked the grapefruit halves into bowls and handed one of them to Poppy. 'This is better for you. You're too fat for cereal.'

'Speak for yourself, you great spotty oaf. At least I haven't got suppurating zits all over my face –'

'You will soon,' Dave interrupted cheerfully. 'You're into a pubescent exploding-hormone situation. Tuck in.'

'If you had, they might detract from your nose which, by the way,' – Liza glanced at it casually – 'is one big blackhead.'

There was a skirmish. Mrs Nightingale caught the milk bottle as it leapt from the table.

'Cool it, girls.' Dave had seen his mother's face. 'Marlene's trying to get organized. Aren't you, Marlene?' He was propped against the Rayburn, dressed now in one of his father's city shirts and scarlet trousers, the bottoms of which were tucked into old school games stockings, one brilliantly striped, the other grey, and shovelling Weetabix into his mouth from a bowl held within an inch of his face. Each time the spoon went in it banged horribly against his teeth. 'Is' the Rayburn *meant* to be off?' he asked, mock-innocently, between mouthfuls.

Mrs Nightingale was about to burst into tears.

'What? Out of my way please.' She pushed the red legs to one side, and knelt on the dog bed in front of the stove. Inside an erratic flame flickered. She turned the thermostat as high as it would go.

'Why's the heat gone down?'

'How the fuck should I know? The wind, probably –'

'Don't swear, Mummy,' Poppy said, grabbing a banana from the fruit bowl and stripping it.

'Put that banana back! It's for lunch.'

'We've got rhubarb crumble for lunch. I made it yesterday, remember.' Poppy took a bite out of the banana, folded the skin over the end and replaced it in the fruit bowl on top of a shrivelled orange.

'Look,' Mrs Nightingale said, 'we'll never be ready at this rate. Couldn't you all just –'

'Keep calm, Mamma. Sit down a moment and drink this.' Liza handed her mother a mug of coffee. 'There's nothing to do. Really. They won't be here till one at the earliest. All we've got to do is get the joint in –'

'Are we eating animals? Yuk. Unreal. Animals are people –'

'Shut up, Lily. Do the spuds and the veg and lay the table and light the fire and pick some flowers – five minutes at the most.'

'The whole house is in chaos,' Mrs Nightingale said, 'it's composed of nothing but tea-chests and plastic bags.'

'They're not coming to see the house. They know we've only just moved. They're coming to see *you*.'

'Actually, they're coming to inspect our reduced circumstances,' Dave said in a prissy voice. He picked up a piece of toast and stretched for the marmalade. Mrs Nightingale pushed it out of his reach. 'No, you've had enough.'

'Daddy couldn't bear them,' Lily said, staring into space.

'Couldn't bear who?' Poppy paused at the door.

'The Hendersons, stupid.'

'The Hendersons? Are *they* coming to lunch? Unreal.'

'Where do you think you're going to, Poppy? You haven't cleared up your breakfast things –'

'I'm going to the lav, if you must know. I'm coming back.'

'While you're up there, Fatso, take some of the gunge off your face!' Dave shouted at her.

'Have you got the logs in?' Mrs Nightingale asked Dave, knowing that he hadn't.

'I'm just about to. We shouldn't *need* a fire in May,' he said, resentfully as though his mother were to blame for the weather. 'Right, Marlena.' He rubbed his hands. 'Here we go-o,' he added in the manner of an air hostess about to deposit a snack on the knees of a passenger. He sat down on Poppy's chair and pulled a pair of canvas boots from under the table. A lace snapped as he put them on.

'Are you going to shave before they arrive?' Mrs Nightingale asked, eyeing him.

'Dunno. Oi moigh,' – Dave rubbed his chin so that it rasped – 'an' yere agine oi moigh na'. Don't you like me looking manly and virile?' Mrs Nightingale said No, she didn't much. No.

'Mrs Henderson will, though. She's got a yen for me. She'll really tuck in.'

'Oh ha ha,' Liza snorted from the sink.

'Mr Henderson has too. He's always putting his arm round my shoulder. Squeezing me. Kissing –'

'I don't suppose he's that desperate to get herpes. He hasn't seen you since you were about ten –'

'Do something for me, Lil, would you,' Mrs Nightingale said, as

Dave minced from the room flexing his biceps. Lily sighed. Did she know what today was? Mrs Nightingale thought perhaps she did. It was impossible to get near Lily at the moment. She resented everything her mother said and did, prefacing her argument with 'Daddy always said' or 'Daddy would have agreed with me that . . .' She'd been in a sulk since the move because the cottage was thatched i.e. spooky, witchy, bug-infested – and because her father had never been in it. 'Wake up, there' – Mrs Nightingale waved her hand slowly up and down in front of Lily's face. Lily managed not to blink.

'Go and get Bone off my bed and put her out. She hasn't had a pee yet.' Lily went on sitting there, expressionless. Then all of a sudden she leapt up, scraping back her chair, and ran out of the room.

'Bone, Bone, my darling one, I'm coming.' They could hear her clattering up the stairs, calling 'Bone, beloved angel, Bone –'

'She's mad,' Liza said, stacking plates in the rack. 'All my family's mad. And Dave is completely off the wall.' Mrs Nightingale kissed Liza's spotty face, pink and damp with steam. 'I love you, Liza,' she said.

As Mrs Nightingale rootled in the kitchen drawer looking for enough knives to lay the dining-room table with, Dave's face appeared at the window above the sink. He flattened his nose against the pane and drummed on it with his fingers. 'Open up! Open up!' he shouted. Liza leaned across the taps and biffed the window. It opened in a rush. Dave's face disappeared for a second, and then reappeared half in the window. 'Ladies,' he said with a South London inflexion and in confidential tones, holding up what looked like a piece of string and dangling it from between his fingers and thumb, 'do your hubbies' jock-straps pass the window test? If not –' he leered and let go of the jock-strap which fell across the sill and draped itself over the hot tap, and then held up a packet of something: 'Try new Weedol! Fast-acting, rainproof and guaranteed to erad-icate all biological stains for an entire season. Just one s*achette*' – he paused to consult the packet – 'treats 160 yards, or – if you ladies prefer a more up-to-date terminology – 135 square metres, of normally soiled jock-straps.' He backed away from the window, creased with laughter, and tripped over a flowerpot.

'Pathetic,' Liza said, tugging at the window catch, 'quite pathetic.'

'Logs!' Mrs Nightingale shouted at him, just before the window jerked to, scattering them with raindrops, 'Logs, logs, logs!'

Mrs Nightingale did her best with the dining-room which, not being a room they had so far needed to use, had become a dumping ground. There were ten full tea-chests stacked in one corner, her husband's golf clubs in a khaki bag, a clothes horse, innumerable lampshades and a depressed-looking cockatoo under a glass dome. Beneath the window precariously stacked books awaited the bookshelves Dave had promised to put up in the summer holidays. Everything in the room, including a dining-table much too large for it, was deep in dust. Mrs Nightingale looked at her watch. This time two years ago she'd sat beside Edward, who'd lain on his back without pillows, his chest and arms wired to a machine. Attached to the machine was a cardiograph that measured and recorded his heartbeat. The signal had gone all over the place, sometimes shooting to the top of the screen, and the bleeps, at each beat, had been similarly erratic – six, say, in succession followed by a silence which, each time it occurred, she'd felt would never be broken. 'The heroin was delicious,' Ed had murmured in a moment of consciousness, 'it took all the pain away, but they won't let me have any more in case I get hooked.' Why couldn't you have died at once, Mrs Nightingale thought, remembering her agony watching the nurse adjusting the drip, which had kept getting stuck, and checking the leads on Ed's chest which, because he rolled around a lot, were in constant danger of coming loose. This had happened once, when there'd been no nurse in the room. She'd been on the edge of her chair, her eyes alternately on Ed, and on the screen, when suddenly the bleeps had stopped and the signal had flattened into a straight, horizontal line. A red light had come on at the side of the machine and with it a whine like the unobtainable tone when you dial. He's dead, she'd thought. Sister had rushed in at once and checked Ed's pulse and then the leads and after a minute or two the crazy signal was back and the bleeps. 'Try not to worry, dear,' Sister had said. 'Worrying doesn't help.'

Mrs Nightingale forced herself out of her chair and went in search of a duster.

'The joint's in the oven,' Liza said. She had an apron on which bore the message I Hate Cooking, and was standing at the stove stirring a saucepan. 'I'm making onion sauce.' She looked up. 'Are you okay, Ma?' By way of an answer Mrs Nightingale enquired if anyone had seen the silver anywhere. Poppy knew. She and Lily were scraping carrots and glaring at each other across the kitchen table. She got up and helped her mother drag the despatch box from under the sink in the washroom. Back in the dining-room she stood and watched her mother dust the table.

'Mum – can I have a friend to stay – Julia, I mean, in the holidays?'

'Maybe. If we're straighter by then.' Mrs Nightingale didn't like Julia. On the child's last visit Mrs Nightingale had caught her in her clothes cupboard, examining the labels and checking to see how many pairs of Gucci shoes Mrs Nightingale owned, which was none. Mrs Nightingale didn't own a Gucci watch, either, and evidently wasn't worth speaking to: Julia hadn't addressed one word to her in five days. She'd managed a few indirect hits, though, as when at breakfast one morning, having accepted without comment the plate of scrambled eggs Mrs Nightingale had handed her, she'd leaned on one elbow to enquire of Poppy: 'Presumably your mother will be racing at Goodwood next week?' Mrs Nightingale was damned if she'd have Julia to stay again.

'I get bored without a friend,' Poppy moaned on. Mrs Nightingale wasn't having any of that. 'You can't be bored,' she said, 'and you've got Lily.' She unwrapped a yellowing candlestick from a piece of yellowing newspaper. 'Here, take this.'

'We don't get on,' Poppy said. 'We've got nothing in common.' That was rubbish, Mrs Nightingale told her.

'It isn't rubbish. She's so moody. She never speaks – just sits and stares.'

Since the truth of this could not be denied, Mrs Nightingale changed tack: 'As a matter of fact you don't deserve to have a friend to stay.' Poppy put down the spoon she'd been tentatively rubbing with a duster and stared at her mother with her mouth open.

'Your half-term report is the worst yet,' Mrs Nightingale continued, 'and we ought to discuss it. Not now. I don't mean now. Later. This evening, perhaps, when they've gone.'

'Miss Ansell doesn't like me. It's not my fault.'

'It isn't just Miss Ansell,' Mrs Nightingale said, more in sorrow than in anger. 'No one, no one – apart from Miss Whatsername – you know, games mistress – had a good word to say about you. You won't get a single "O" Level at this rate. Lily, on the other hand –'

'*Don't* compare me with her. She's quite different to me.'

'Different *from* me. Yes. She knows how to work, for one thing. And she reads. You never open a book.'

'I do.'

'The *Beano* annual. And you're *thirteen*.'

Poppy grinned sheepishly at that. 'Oh, Muzkin,' she said, and sidled up to her mother and put her arms round her waist.

'Muzkin nothing,' Mrs Nightingale said, disentangling herself. For it really was worrying. Poppy never did open a book. If ever she happened by some mischance to pick one up, she'd drop it again as soon as she'd realized her mistake. As a result of this her ignorance went wide and deep. Mrs Nightingale spent sleepless nights discussing the problem with Bone.

Liza's head appeared round the dining-room door.

'Bone's eaten the Brie, I'm afraid,' Liza said, 'so there's only mousetrap for lunch.'

'Where is she? I'll kill her!' Mrs Nightingale cried, preparing to do so.

'I've already beaten her,' Liza said. 'It's my business, she's my dog.'

Not when it comes to spending millions of pounds a year on Chum and Butch and Winalot and vet's bills, Mrs Nightingale thought. Not when it comes to clearing up mountains of dog sick and dog shit. Then she's my dog. She followed Liza back to the kitchen. 'Where's Dave?' she asked crossly. 'Where's the wood?'

'He's gone to get some milk and the papers,' Liza said, knowing what her mother's reaction would be.

'*What?*'

'I asked him to go because we're out of milk and you'll want the papers so that the Hendersons can read them after lunch.'

'Has he taken my car?' Mrs Nightingale was beside herself.

'Of course he's taken your car. How else would he go?'

Mrs Nightingale hated Dave taking her car. She hated him taking it because being stuck up a track with rusty bicycles the only means of escape made her feel a prisoner. She hated him taking it because he hadn't asked permission and because she didn't trust him not to drive like a racing driver – i.e. a maniac. It was her car. She hated Dave too because he ought to have remembered what the day was. There was something wrong with him that he hadn't. Something very wrong indeed.

'He has no business to take my car,' she said, 'he'll be gone for hours.'

Liza was taking glasses out of a cupboard. 'Don't be stupid,' she said briskly. 'He'll be back in a minute. He's only gone for the papers, for God's sake. He was *trying* to be helpful.' She held a glass up to the light. 'These glasses are filthy. I'd better wash them.'

'Get up, Lily,' Mrs Nightingale was now in a state of rage and panic. Lily was lying in the dog-bed on top of Bone, kissing Bone's ears. 'Get up! Have you made your bed and tidied your room?'

'You can't make a camp-bed.' Lily got up reluctantly, her navy jersey angora now with dog hairs.

'Answer that, would you, on your way,' Mrs Nightingale snapped as the telephone rang from the drawing-room. Lily returned almost at once.

'It's Granny. She wants to talk to *you*.'

'Fuck,' Mrs Nightingale said. 'Didn't you tell her we've got people for lunch?' Lily shrugged. 'Well, go back and tell her I'm frantic –'

'I'll say,' murmured Liza, putting glasses on a tray. 'These glasses are gross – did you get them from the garage?'

'– and that I'll ring her after tea. Go *on*. Hurry.'

'Granny sounded a bit hurt,' Lily said when she came back. 'She said to tell you she was thinking about you today.'

'What for?' Liza said.

What for, Mrs Nightingale repeated to herself, what for? 'What can Dave be doing?' she said. 'He's been gone for hours.' She opened the oven door. The joint seemed to be sizzling satisfactorily.

'Stop flapping,' Liza said.

'Did you put garlic on the joint? And rosemary? I couldn't see any.'

'Of course. Stop flapping.'

'Poppy, you're *soaked*! Couldn't you have worn a mac?' Poppy squelched into the kitchen and dumped a collection of sodden wild flowers on the table.

'*I* was going to do the flowers,' Liza said.

'God, the gratitude you get in this place.' Poppy fingered the limp cluster. 'What are these?'

'Ladies' smocks. *Must* you do that in here?' Liza said as Poppy found an assortment of jugs and lined them up on the table. 'I'm trying to get lunch. You can't put wallflowers in with that lot,' she added in disgust.

'Why can't I?' Poppy wanted to know.

'Because they're orange, stupid.'

'Piss off. I like them. I like the *smell*.'

Mrs Nightingale left her daughters to it and took the tray of glasses into the dining-room. Perhaps Dave *had* had an accident. Perhaps, at this very moment, firemen were fighting to cut his lifeless body from the wreckage. That was all she needed. It was typical of him to put her in this position of anxiety today of all days. 'If he's alive I'll kill him,' she thought aloud, knowing that when – please God – he did walk in she'd feel nothing but relief. As she went back into the kitchen he came in by the other door, accompanied by a smell of deep frying. The Sunday papers and two cartons of long-life milk were crushed against his chest. He uncrossed his arms and unloaded their contents into the watery mess of broken stems and leaves on the kitchen table.

'Hey – mind my flowers,' Poppy said. She sniffed. 'I can smell chips.'

'Whoops. Sorry.' Dave straightened up and caught sight of his mother. 'Hi there, Marlene.' He licked his fingers, slowly and deliberately. 'Finger fuckin' good,' he said when he'd finished. There was a silence, succeeded by a snort of laughter from Liza, succeeded by another silence.

'Dave, could I have a word with you, please –' Mrs Nightingale spoke through clenched teeth. She jerked her thumb towards the door. 'Outside.'

'Righto, Marlena.' He snatched up the *Observer* and followed his mother into the hall.

'Watch out, Dave,' Poppy sang out after him. 'You're in deep trouble, Boyo.'

'What are you so screwed-up about?' Dave asked when Mrs Nightingale, determined that they shouldn't be overheard, had shut the drawing-room door. Dave plonked himself into the nearest arm-chair.

'Get up out of that chair! Put that newspaper down!' Dave got up, very slowly. 'Take that smirk off your face!' Mrs Nightingale shouted. He towered above her, shifting from one foot to the other, while his eyes examined the ceiling with interest. 'I've had you,' Mrs Nightingale went on, her voice shaking. 'I wish you weren't here. You're twenty years old. You're the only so-called man in this house. I should be able to look to you for help and support. You had no business to take my car without asking –'

'Liza said we were out of milk –'

'It's not her car. It's *mine*. And I'd asked you to get the wood in. That's *all* I asked you to do. All all *all*!'

'Oh come *on* –'

'I won't come on.' Mrs Nightingale's voice rose . 'You were gone for hours while everyone else was working. Did you really eat chips, by the way?'

'I was hungry, I'm a big boy,' Dave said, perhaps hoping to appeal to that need (he supposed all women had) to mother and protect huge grown men as though they were babies.

'You didn't have breakfast till ten. And it'll be lunchtime any minute. You can't have been hungry.' Dave said nothing. He was bored with this interview and showed it by jiggling his knee. 'That finger business wasn't funny,' Mrs Nightingale said. 'It was disgusting. How could you, in front of Lily and Poppy?'

'Lily wasn't in the kitchen, actually,' Dave said. He started to pace about with his head down, a sure sign that he was losing his temper.

'Don't be pedantic with me, Dave.' Dave stopped pacing and swung round and pointed his finger at his mother in a threatening fashion.

'Fuck *you*,' he said. 'You're a complete hypocrite. No one in this house uses filthier language than you. It's "shit this" and "bugger that" all fucking day. We took the words in with your milk –' There was a pause, during which Mrs Nightingale considered reminding him that the twins, at least, had been bottle-fed, but Dave was quite capable of turning this fact to his advantage, so she said nothing. 'Well, I'm sick of your dramas and panics,' he continued, warming to his theme of self-justification. 'I can't stand the atmosphere in this place. I can't *work* here. I'm going back to Leeds. My tutor didn't want me to take time off to help you, and I've missed two important lectures already.' He made for the door.

'Typical,' Mrs Nightingale said, taking care not to say 'fucking well typical' as she would normally have done. 'You can't take any sort of criticism, ever. You just shout abuse and then walk out – it's too easy. What's more, you haven't been any help to me at all. You haven't lifted a finger –'

'Mum' – Liza's head appeared round the door as Dave reached it. He took two steps backwards – 'Shouldn't you be putting your face on? It's after twelve.'

'Go away,' Mrs Nightingale said, 'I'm talking to Dave.'

'Sounds like it. Poor Dave.' Liza's head withdrew. The door banged shut.

Mrs Nightingale and her son stood in silence, both waiting for something. Dave stared at the floor and at the front page of the *Observer* which lay at his feet. He pushed at it with the toe of one green canvas boot.

'Sorry I was rude,' he said at last without looking up.

Mrs Nightingale gave a sigh. Dave was good at apologies – much better than she was – and sometimes indulged in them for days after a particularly bloody row, castigating himself and telling anyone who'd listen what a shit he'd been. The trouble was, the apologies changed nothing, as Mrs Nightingale had learned. They never prevented his being rude and aggressive (and unfair, she thought, *unfair*) next time round. She didn't want his apologies. She wanted him to stop the behaviour that made them necessary. She watched him now get down on his knees and take off his specs and rub them on a dirty red-and-white spotted handkerchief and put them back on his nose. He picked up the *Observer* with his left hand and then struck at it with the fist of his right.

'I'm going to kill Mrs Thatcher,' he said, 'listen to this –' Oh dear, thought Mrs Nightingale.

Dave and newspapers did not mix. Cruise missiles, violence in inner cities, child abuse, drug abuse, vivisection, famine, rape, murder, abortion, multiple births, divorce rate, pollution, terrorism, persecution of Blacks and homosexuals, sex discrimination, unemployment, pornography, police brutality, rate capping – the stuff that newspapers were made of – were a daily cross he bore alone. 'You can't take the whole burden of the world on your shoulders,' she'd tell him when he rang from a Leeds call box desperate over the destruction of South American rain forests, or the plight of the latest hi-jack victims. 'The world has always been a terrible place,' she'd say, 'we just know more about it now because of the media. Horror used to be more *local*.' Then – since it seemed important to end on a positive note – she'd go on to remind him of ways in which the world had changed for the better, instancing the huge advances made in medicine this century (TB and polio virtually wiped out, infant mortality and death in childbirth negligible, etc) and reminding him that there were salmon in the Thames these days, and that people could fall into the river and swallow whole bucketfuls of its waters and not die. 'Try and get a sense of proportion,' she'd say, something she'd never managed herself. She knew that when she lectured Dave it was herself she was trying to comfort. The world was a far nastier place than it'd been when she was a child, even though there'd been a world war going on for some of that time. Far nastier.

Thinking about all this she was spared hearing Mrs Thatcher's latest pronouncement, although it was impossible to miss the passion in Dave's recital of the same. She came to when he stopped in mid-sentence, and put the paper down.

'It's the twenty-third today,' he said, 'Did you realize?'

'I know,' Mrs Nightingale said.

'Oh, Mum, I'm sorry. Why didn't you say?'

Dave, on his knees, began to rock backwards and forwards, his arms folded across his stomach. 'Poor old Dad, poor old Dad,' he said. Then he burst into tears. Mrs Nightingale got down on her knees beside her son. She put her arm round his shoulders which reeked of wet wool and chipped potatoes. She sensed that he did not want her arms round him but did not know how to extricate himself. After several minutes he blew his nose on the red-spotted handkerchief and licked at the tears which were running down his chin.

'I must get the wood in and light the fire.' He disengaged himself and got up. 'Then I'll shave. Sorry, Mum.' He gave her a pale smile. At the door he turned, and said in a sharper tone: 'But I still don't understand why you didn't *say*. And why didn't we go to church this morning – or did you, before we were up?'

'No,' Mrs Nightingale said.

'And why are the fucking Hendersons coming to lunch? You don't like them and Pa couldn't stand them. None of it makes sense.' He shook his head, spraying the room with water like a wet dog.

'Look, Dave,' Mrs Nightingale began. She explained that she hadn't asked the Hendersons, they'd asked themselves. She couldn't put them off for ever. Also she'd thought that having people to lunch might make the day easier in some way. And as for church – well, he didn't like Rite A any more than she did. It always put them into a rage, so there was no point, was there, in going.

'True,' Dave said.

It *was* true, she told him. But what she thought they might do, once they'd got rid of the Hendersons, was drive up to the churchyard and take Poppy's flowers perhaps, and put them on Daddy's grave.

Dave's eyes started to fill again. '. . . and then go to Evensong in the Cathedral, if there's time. It'll be a proper service with proper singing and anthems and sung responses.'

'Yup. Cool.'

'All right, sweetheart?' Dave nodded and fiddled with his watch-strap, a thin piece of canvas, once red and white striped. 'I suppose you realize,' Mrs Nightingale lied, 'that when I asked you to give me a hand this week, it was just an excuse for wanting you here today. I needed you.' But perhaps it was not a lie, she thought. Perhaps, subconsciously, she had needed him.

'I'm getting the wood now,' Dave said. He peered out of a dismal mullioned window, against which a yew branch flapped in the gale. 'I think the rain's stopping.'

The kitchen when Mrs Nightingale entered it was clean and tidy, everything washed up and put away. Liza was taking off her apron.

'All done,' she said.

She was a wonder, Mrs Nightingale told her, a real star.

'Mum you must get changed, they'll be here –'

Mrs Nightingale stopped in the doorway. 'Liza – do you know what today is?'

'It's the day Daddy died,' Liza said. 'Go on, Mum, I'll come and talk to you when I've done the ice.'

The back door banged as Mrs Nightingale climbed the stairs. She could hear Dave's grunts as he humped the log basket into the hall.

It was a relief to be on her own for five minutes. She needed to be alone with Edward who – she stood on the dark landing and peered at her watch – this time two years ago had been about to leave her. Suddenly, without warning and without saying goodbye. Not even a look. Not even a pressure of the hand. She'd hated him for this, until it had dawned on her that it was inevitable. He'd been hopeless at partings. The number of times she'd driven him to Heathrow and been rewarded not with hugs and the 'I'll miss you, darlings' and 'take care of your precious selves' other people seemed to get, but with a preoccupied peck and then his backview disappearing through the barrier. 'Turn round and wave, you bugger,' she used to will him, but he never did.

'You two ready?' she called, in hopeless competition with Madness, through the twin's bedroom door. Then she opened her own. The room looked as though burglars had visited it. The drawers of both clothes chests had been wrenched out; garments spilled from them onto the floor. A brassière, its strap looped round a wooden drawer knob, trailed greyly to the rug where two leather belts lay like coiled springs. Mrs Nightingale turned her gaze to the dressing-table. Here unnumbered treasures drooped from every drawer and orifice. The surface of the table was littered with screws of cotton wool and with unstoppered scent bottles, from which all London, Paris and New York disagreeably breathed. A cylinder of moisturizing lotion lay on its side oozing cucumber extract into the contents of her jewel case which sat, open and empty, on the stool. Three cotton wool buds, their ends clotted with ear wax, had been placed in the china tray which normally housed Mrs Nightingale's lipsticks. Only two lipsticks remained in the tray; the rest, which had been torn apart and abandoned with their tongues protruding, were umbled up with beads and cotton wool. Mrs Nightingale recognized her daughter Poppy's hand in all this. She opened her mouth wide in anger and despair, but no sound came. Instead, the telephone screamed from the table by her bed. When after the eighth ring no one had answered downstairs, Mrs Nightingale picked up the receiver.

'Mrs Nightingale? Mr Selby-Willis here.'

'Oh hallo, Jerry,' Mrs Nightingale said. (Fuck fuck fuck fuck fuck). How are you?'

'How are *you*?' Jerry Selby-Willis asked, in his best bedroom drawl.

'Well if you must know, I'm frantic. I've got people arriving for lunch any minute.'

'One normally does on a Sunday. Grania's just gone off to the station to meet our lot. I can't imagine *you* being frantic about anything –'

'It just goes to show how little –'

'When are you going to have luncheon with me?' Jerry Selby-Willis interrupted her. 'Or dinner?'

'Jerry, I've only *just* moved house –' Mrs Nightingale began. She had accepted none of his invitations. 'Then you're in need of a nice, relaxing dinner. Tuesday. Have you got your diary there?'

'No. Look, I'm afraid I must go. I haven't got my face on –'

'I'll ring you tomorrow, from the office.'

She must remember to leave the telephone off the hook tomorrow, Mrs Nightingale thought, as she wrenched garments from hangers, tried them on, examined the result in the looking glass, and tore them off again. Or else get the children to answer the telephone and say she was out.

'I've got nothing to wear!' she wailed, as Liza came into the room.

'That looks fine,' Liza said. 'Where's your hairbrush?'

While Liza brushed her mother's hair, Mrs Nightingale perched on the dressing-table stool and searched for her blue beads.

'I can't find my blue beads,' she said, turning out another drawer.

'Poppy's wearing them,' Liza said. 'She said you said she could. Time you dyed your hair, I think, or else made with the Grecian 2000,' she said kindly, putting the brush down.

'I think I heard a car,' Mrs Nightingale said, 'do you think you could round everyone up and go down and tell the Hendersons I'm coming. Give them a drink.'

Alone, Mrs Nightingale looked at her watch. It was ten past one. Edward was dead. He'd been dead a full quarter of an hour. At five to one, no doubt when she'd been fending off Jerry Selby-Willis, the signal on the cardiograph had flattened into a straight line for real this time, and the bleeps had ceased. She had not kept vigil; she had not been with him, holding his hand. She sat on the stool, twisting her wedding ring round and round her finger, for comfort. When at last she lifted her head she caught her reflection in the glass and was dismayed to see how pinched and wary and closed her face had become. 'Things have got to get better,' she said aloud. 'I must make them better.' There was a little moisturizer left in the bottle. She squeezed some into her palm and rubbed it into her forehead and cheeks, into the slack skin under her chin, into her crêpey neck. 'I am alive,' she said, 'I am not old. I am a young woman. I could live for another forty years yet.' She fumbled for the blusher, and worked it into her cheeks. 'I am a *person*,' she said threateningly into the glass. 'I am me, Frances.'

There was a thundering on the stairs, followed by Dave, out of breath at the door.

'Hi, folks, it's Lamborghini time,' he hissed. 'The Hendersons are in an arriving situation.' He had not shaved, after all, but on the other hand he was not wearing his red secretary spectacles either. You could not have everything, Mrs Nightingale supposed.

'Hurry up, Marlene,' he said. 'You can't leave us alone with them.' He vanished, and then immediately reappeared. 'You should know that Mrs H. is wearing a salmon two-piece, with turquoise accessories. Tuck in.'

Mrs Nightingale grabbed a lipstick from the table and stretched her mouth into the grimace that, with her, always preceded its application. At the first pressure the lipstick, which had been broken by Poppy earlier and stuck back by her into its case, toppled and fell, grazing Mrs Nightingale's chin as it did so with a long gash of Wicked Rose.

Georgina Hammick was born in Hampshire in 1939. She was educated at Limuru Girls' School, Kenya and Academie Julian, Paris. She is a sometime teacher and bookseller. Her poems have been published in various magazines and anthologies (*Pen*, *Arts Council*, *Poetry Book Society Supplement*, etc) and in *A Poetry Quintet* (Gollancz, 1976). She started writing short stories in 1984 and in 1985 was the winner of 4th Prize in the *Stand* International Short

Story Competition with 'People for Lunch'. Her collection of stories, under the same title, was published by Methuen in 1987. Georgina Hammick takes part in the Poetry Society's Poet-in-Schools scheme, tutors classes and workshops, is a member of the Southern Arts Literature Panel, and writes the Gardens column for *Books* magazine. She has three grown-up children and lives in the Deverill Valley, Wiltshire. At the moment she is writing more short stories.

The Dying by Iain Crichton Smith

When the breathing got worse he went into the adjacent room and got the copy of Dante. All that night and the night before he had been watching the dying though he didn't know it was a dying. The grey hairs around the head seemed to panic like the needle of a compass and the eyes, sometimes open and sometimes shut, seemed to be looking at him all the time. He had never seen a dying before. The breathlessness seemed a bit like asthma or bad bronchitis, ascending sometimes into a kind of whistling like a train leaving a station. The voice when it spoke was irritable and petulant. It wanted water, lots of water, milk, lots of milk, anything to quench the thirst and even then he didn't know it was a dying. The tongue seemed very cold as he fed it the milk. It was cold and almost stiff. Once near midnight he saw the cheeks suddenly flare up and become swollen so that the eyes could hardly look over them. When a mirror was required to be brought she looked at it, moving her head restlessly this way and that. He knew that the swelling was a portent of some kind, a message from the outer darkness, an omen.

Outside, it was snowing steadily, the complex flakes weaving an unintelligible pattern. If he were to put the light out then that other light, as alien as that from a dead planet, the light of the moon itself, would enter the room, a sick glare, an almost abstract light. It would light the pages of the Dante which he needed now more than ever, it would cast over the poetry its hollow glare.

He opened the pages but they did not mean anything at all since all the time he was looking at the face. The dying person was slipping away from him. She was absorbed in her dying and he did not understand what was happening. Dying was such an extraordinary thing, such a private affair. Sometimes he stretched out his hand and she clutched it and he felt as if he were in a boat and she were in the dark water around it. And all the time the breathing was faster and faster as if something wanted to be away. The brow was cold but the mouth still wanted water. The body was restlessly turning, now on one side now on the other. It was steadily weakening. Something was at it, and it was weakening.

In Thy Will is My Peace. . . The words from Dante swam into his mind. They seemed to swim out of the snow which was teeming beyond the window. He imagined the universe of Dante like a watch. The clock said five in the morning. He felt cold and the light was beginning to azure the window. The street outside was empty of people and traffic. There was no one alive in the world but himself. The lamps cast their glare over the street. They brooded over their own haloes all night.

When he looked again the whistling was changing to a rattling. He held the cold hands in his, locking them. The head fell back on the pillow, the mouth gaping wide like the mouth of a landed fish, the eyes staring irretrievably beyond him. The one-barred electric fire hummed in a corner of the room, a deep and raw red. His copy of Dante fell from his hand and lay on top of the red woollen rug at the side of the bed, stained with milk and soup. He seemed to be on a space ship hanging upside down and seeing coming towards him another space ship, shaped like a black medieval helmet in all that azure. On board the space ship there was at least one man encased in a black rubber suit, but he could not see the face. The man was busy either with a rope which he would fling to him or with a gun which he might fire at him. The figure seemed squat and alien like that of an Eskimo.

And all the while the window azured and the body was like a log, the mouth twisted where all the breath had left it. It lolled on one side of the pillow. Death was not dignified. A dead face showed the pain of its dying, what it had struggled through to become a log. He thought, weeping, this is the irretrievable centre where there is no foliage and no metaphor. At this time, poetry is powerless. The body looked up at him, blank as a stone, with the twisted mouth. It belonged to no one that he had ever known.

The copy of Dante seemed to have fallen into an abyss. It was lying on the red rug as if in a fire. Yet he himself was so cold, and numb. Suddenly he began to be shaken by tremors, though his face remained cold and without movement. The alien azure light was

184

growing steadily, mixed with the white glare of the snow. The landscape outside the window was not a human landscape. The body on the bed was not human.

The tears started to seep slowly from his eyes. In his right hand he found he was holding a small golden watch which he had picked up. He couldn't remember picking it up. He couldn't even hear its ticking. It was a delicate mechanism, small and golden. He held it up to his ear and at that moment the tears came, in the white and bluish glare. Through the tears he saw the watch and beyond it the copy of Dante lying on the red rug and beyond that again the log which seemed unchanging though it would change, since everything changed.

And he knew that he himself would change though he could not think of it at that moment. He knew that he would change and the log would change and it was this which more than anything made him cry, to think of what the log had been once, a suffering body, a girl growing up and marrying and bearing children. It was so strange that the log could have been that. It was so strange that the log had once worn dresses chequered like a draughtsboard, that it had called him into dinner, that it had been sleepless at nights thinking of the future.

So strange was it, so irretrievable that he was shaken as if by an earthquake of pathos and pity. He could not bring himself to look at the Dante, he could only stare at the log as if expecting that it would move or speak but it did not. It was concerned only with itself. The twisted mouth as if still gasping for air made no promises and no concessions.

Slowly as he sat there he was aware of a hammering coming from outside the window and aware also of blue lightning flickering across the room. He had forgotten about the workshop. He walked over to the window and saw men with helmets bending over pure white flame. The blue flashes were cold and queer as if they came from another world. At the same time he heard unintelligible shoutings from the people involved in the work and saw a visored head turning to look behind it. Beyond it steadied the sharp azure of the morning. And in front of it he saw the drifting flakes of snow. He looked down at the Dante with his bruised face and felt the hammer blows slamming the lines together, making a universe, holding a world together where people shouted out of a blue light. And the hammer

seemed to be beating the log into a vase, into marble, into flowers
made of blue rock, into the hardest of metaphors.

Iain Crichton Smith was born in 1928 on the island of Lewis. A
writer in both Gaelic and English, he has written novels, plays,
poems, short stories, and criticism in both languages. His latest
novel, *In the Middle of The Wood* was published by Gollancz, and his
latest book of poems, *A Life*, by Carcanet.

Tom Patrick by Sid Chaplin

One morning the cat led me out of the house into bright tingling sunshine. What's he about, I wondered. For once he didn't run, but high-stepped it down the yard, looking upwards and about him as he went. Even behind him I could see his whiskers twitch. Instead of streaking over the gate, the quicker to be in Grandma Richardson's and at his milk, he paused and reached up the wall with his two front paws. There he stretched, benignly looking at me. He almost smiled – and even a child knows how rare is the intimation of shared delight in a cat. Then, lowering himself, he went up and over the gate in a bound. Lifting the sneck I followed.

Grandma Richardson, who wasn't really my grandma at all but a grandma to everybody, put down his saucerful and Big Tom lapped. Straightening up, she announced: 'Well, here we are and it's spring again!'

'Spring?' I pondered, down on the proddy mat. In and out went the little red scoop of Big Tom's tongue.

'When all the flowers grow,' she said, as if that explained everything. But what use was that to one as green and unformed as me? I'd enough to do sorting out the puzzle of my own new-found identity.

A big man with rosy cheeks and a brown moustache rattled the sneck and walked in with the sunshine. 'Now, Nelly; now, canny bairn; by jo but Ah've got a thirst on me the morn!'

'Mind it would be summat different if tha' hadn't, Tom Pat!' she retorted. 'Tha' knows there's plenty o' watter i' the tap . . .' Nevertheless, all smiles, she brought out the grey hen and, with the George the Fifth Coronation mug she reserved for me, a pint pot for the man. 'Tack care of the bairn first!' The milky ginger beer gurgled and frothed to a top as she poured. I smiled at the spectacle.

'And what's thy name, canny bairn?'

'That's out of the ordinary,' he gravely informed me, unlike the majority of people, who looked startled, or burst out 'Any relation?' 'In fact, that's extra-ordinary!' I looked down at Big Tom. He had drunk every drop of his milk. When I looked up again the man had finished his ginger beer.

'You've got the same name as our cat, Mister,' I said. '*And* you drink fast as well.'

For the first time a grown man slapped his knee and laughed out loud, not at but with me. 'There's thy character in a nutshell,' triumphed Grandma Richardson.

'All the same, Ah'll have another.'

'The Lord help thi canny wife and bairns if iver thou tacks to drink, Tom Pat Gill,' she said, refilling his pot.

'The one that's on the way'll be the finish, Nellie.'

'There'll be more, Tom Pat; thou'll have a houseful.'

Standing up, he announced, 'One's enough for me: one wife, one bairn and one quart o' beer a day is enough for any man. Moderation in all things – that's my motto!'

'Off with ye!' she threatened, and with a grin he backed out into the yard. I followed him. Stopping short, he looked down at me, 'Noo, what's thoo after!'

For answer I took his hand.

'Tha's got thisel' a bairn before time!' mocked Grandma Richardson. I returned in triumph an hour later with stories of being swung on a gate, plump partridges clapping up from our very feet, and the perfect interior silkiness of a hedge-sparrow's nest. But what couldn't be told was the first glimpse of the smoky blue depths of the wood, the way his laughter rippled like the stream his name and nature had been endowed with, the interest in and affection for me his whole being exuded, as indeed it did for all the good things of life around him.

Our relationship brought about a friendship between Tom Pat and his wife and my parents. But he remained my particular friend. The trust between us was as inevitable as the blossom in the spring. It grew out of Grandma Richardson's obvious affection for him. Great shapeless mound of rectitude and comfort that she was, she was also the first woman I ever saw quicken to the life in a man. Time and time again I saw her become lovely in the presence of Tom Pat. Whenever I see the willow in the spring take on its splendid green-gold array I think of Grandma Richardson unfolding in the sunshine of Tom Patrick.

Tom Pat was quick and strong. A master of quoits, he ran fleetly and was a mighter hitter with a bat. But what endeared him most to me was the level he offered in friendship. Quick to sense a mood, he was never patronizing and knew the value of silence. When he made a pocket handkerchief rabbit hop from wrist to elbow then bound over his shoulder, it was as much to entertain himself as me. Weaving a rattle of rushes, a whip, or stripping away the delicate green skin to make a rose or lover's knot from the white pith, he was deep in his own delight and you were free to join in or not as you wished. Even when in the heat of the noon he made a little cap to preserve me from sunstroke he would hand it over so that I could put it on myself.

On the bad days it was sufficient for us to be together. A look was a conversation, and monosyllables spoke volumes. So to him belongs every spring wood in which I walk with its rife onion flowers, dusky red soldier's buttons and bluebells smelling of pleasantly doughy new bread. It may be hard for others to understand, but every good friendship since then and for evermore has the pungency of wild mint plucked by the water's edge.

That April Fool's day all the pits shut down, and in the beginning this helped to cement our friendship. The lockout lasted three months. Since my father worked at a pit which lay over the hill to the west and Tom Pat at another a mile eastwards out of view, I never saw the pulley wheels stop their interminable spinning and the winding engines fall silent, as if the giant slaves working inside the fortress-like winding towers had at last toppled over with burst lungs and cracked hearts.

But I did miss the caller on his courses and, with the slog of boots on the pavement outside when the foreshift came home the pit pungency, which is a compound of sweat of man and smell of pony on coaldust-impregnated work duds. I missed, too, my father's whistle as he wheeled out his bicycle in the morning, missed the tid-bits that came with Pay Friday and, if the truth be known, missed the calm of a woman-ruled household. Above all, the time came when I began to miss Tom Pat's cheerful hail from the yard gate, calling me out to a walk. 'Anybody seen the young'un?'

'Ah tell you what, we dinnat see ower much of Tom Pat these days,' said my father one morning, and my heart gave a leap.

'Her and her flamin' fire!' said my mother. 'She'll dee without nowt!'

'We'll toddle away up and see them this afternoon,' said my father. There was no holding me back when we set forth. 'Well, look who's turned up!' said Tom Pat, black as out of the pit when he opened the door.

Bessy Gill's house shone. You could see your face looking back at you out of the high shine of the tall press – unlike my grandmother's it didn't have mirrors on the doors, with white swans gravely swimming on them – and there was never a fly-spot on the big picture of Tom Pat's father with a beard so long that you could see only the bottom two buttons of his velveteen waistcoat. No matter where you sat the glow of the fire was reflected – how the blackleaded kitchen range resisted melting away is impossible of explanation! The only cool place in the kitchen was under the table, and looking out from there the fire roared away like an inferno. 'Thou should 'a' been colliery boilerman, Bessie!' charged my father.

I have never known anyone more prodigal of fuel. The great golden crust went almost up to the beginning of the chimney and the long flames curling away on each side relentlessly played upon the boiler and oven. How was I to know that I was looking at the enemy which had come between myself and Tom Pat? Day after day he was driven to gleaning on the peaks and low rambling ridges of Westerton pit-heap to feed this insatiable creature. There was no satisfying it.

But what a spread! Unlike my mother, who made once do, Bessie baked thrice weekly – twice for crusty bread and fresh teacakes and once for fancy. Her fairy cakes melted away in your mouth and her tarts were so crisp and light that it was only necessary to bite and let the pastry melt and merge with delicious jam or lemon curd.

'How do you manage – how?' demanded my mother in mingled delight and exasperation. Tom Pat was having his bath in the scullery.

'Ah sent him down to his mother's this morning,' returned Bessie significantly, then lowered her voice. 'Me being the way I am, they always tip up. Rub it in about me mornin' sickness, I tell him; and it always works. Then while he went for coals I walked through the woods to Bishop Auckland and enjoyed myself in Lingfords.'

'You must have spent a fortune, really!' cried my mother.

'Ah went in with ten bob an' came out with one and thrippence in me purse,' she replied. 'As long as Ah've a bit money to start with, me charms'll look after the rest.' With a flicker of her long eyelashes: 'It's my charm that makes me such a manager.'

And what a manager of managers she was! Every Sunday without fail during the long three months of the strike she would send up a helping of her rice pudding for my father. My father was always ready for it, and Tom Patrick would silently watch. But one day a touch of the old merriment came to the surface.

'Ah'm sure it does me heart good just to watch ye, Ike,' he said.

'Naebody can touch your lass's rice pudding,' said my father. 'Naebody!'

'Aye, trust Bessie for the finishing touch and the fal-de-rals,' rejoined Tom Pat gaily, but when I next looked his face was clouded. The enforced idleness which had put fat around the middle of all the other men had worn him down to a spare, tired leanness. The bone shone through his face.

'It's the heap-riddin' that gets you down, lad,' said my father. 'How about tryin' the cut?'

'She winnit hear on it,' said Tom Patrick. 'Says the pollis'll be down like a ton of bricks one of these days.' Against his will he allowed my father to persuade him to go.

'Let's go and see the men working,' said my mother. We looked over the bridge into the cool leafy canyon with its gleaming rails, now transformed into a mine with the lid off. The place swarmed with men. Naked to the waist and precariously balanced on the slopes they swung their picks at the narrow seam of coal, fixed like the lead of a pencil in the yellow strata. There was no need to shovel. Down it tumbled to pile up in the drainage channels, while the marrers of the pickmen above (no miner ever works alone if he can help it) joined forces to fill the sacks, or each with his burden toiled up the steep side of the cutting. Only the more fortunate who lived down the line were able to push their bicycles along and deliver almost at the coalhouse door. The place was a welter of picks and shovels and bicycles – and men who sang or jested as they worked. But there was no sign of my father or Tom Patrick. 'Where can they be?' asked my mother, screwing up her eyes.

Then the fields on each side erupted policemen who seemed nine feet tall in their helmets, swinging truncheons as they charged. Women screamed. Bairns started crying. Bicycles were abandoned and black coal spilled on the grass. Men dodged like coursed hares. Two forces entirely separate from those in the fields drove the men before them like sheep. One miner clambered up an almost perpendicular face of rock to where an Inspector, immaculate in white gloves and with his stick tucked back under his arm, impassively watched the melee below. When the miner reached the top he found first a pair of highly polished shoes, then, as his eyes travelled upwards, an officer resplendent and godlike. His mouth dropped open. The officer pointed with his stick, and the man went back down. This was the worst thing I saw. Then we hurried away home.

And there we waited. We whiled away the hours. 'They'll be gaoled for certain,' my mother wailed.

'Have a bite of pie,' suggested Bessie, 'while I put some coals on the fire.' In fact my father and Tom Patrick had been nowhere near the cutting. They had gone instead to the pit-heap, and after seeing the police march by, decided to wait it out.

'Ah told you to stick to the heap,' said Bessie.

And this was what he did. One day we went to see him. The great round barrows burned slowly with a smell like hell's judgement, and far up one smoking flank a small figure toiled with pick, shovel and small-meshed riddle. Tom Pat slid down to join us. We sat on the grass and talked. Down below lay the quiet pit with its spidery headgear and twin winding houses towering like empty castles. In full view was the gantry leading up to the cages. 'Ah never thought the day would come when I'd pray to get back down there,' said Tom Patrick.

The lockout ended and Tom Pat had his wish. Down the shaft he went, and one day never came back. Alive as ever, I came again over the brow of the hill with my parents. The pit lay before me and in my state of innocence death, having no meaning as yet, could hold no dominion. Like our own familiar Tom Cat, the pit stretched lazily out over the place whence my friend would never return. The two fireholes glowing like eyes in the night, it stretched itself out and seemed ready at any moment to purr. Never did it occur to me that there was any connection between the going away of my friend and the stretching out in the night of the great, black, beautiful creature. That had to wait upon my own experience of what might come of the careless flick of a paw, the implacable press of her immense belly.

The day after the funeral I accompanied mother on a visit to the bereaved wife, who greeted us at the door with be-floured arms and beaming face.

'Don't tell me you're bakin', lass!'

An unrepentant Bessie led us into a house which itself could have done service as an oven. 'Ah just took it into me head to bake a spice loaf for me mother,' she said. 'And then before Ah knew it Ah'd mixed enough pastry for a couple of pies and a baker's dozen girdle scones. The living have to be fed, you know. And it seemed such a waste – all that lovely fire.'

'Ah'm sure Ah don't know how you stand it – Ah'm sure you could fry an egg on that fender,' complained my mother.

'Here, take the bairn, and Ah'll bake you a nice bacon and onion pie for your tea.' Bessie thrust the baby into mother's arms. My mother, I noticed, made no complaint. And such a spread she made for us. It was the last of her great feasts, and she did it in style, proudly presiding over the teapot and queening it over us with face still flushed, and creamy arms yet pink from the heat.

After tea Bessie made preparations to leave with us, wishing to take the spice loaf to her mother. First mother washed in the cupboard under the stairs while Bessie changed and dressed the baby, then mother took the baby while Bessie completed her toilet.

'Do you like my soap, Elsie?' she enquired from the recess.

'Oh, but it's lovely. Ah do look forward to coming here for the soap!' I can hear them talking now. So long ago, and they were, after all, little more than girls.

Low and mysterious came Bessie's laugh; and even before she spoke I saw my mother turn sharply and look at the vague glow of womanhood out there in the shadows. 'Always look after your skin, Elsie. It's your face they look for first – a soft skin they like to touch . . .'

We left her with the child at the bottom of the street. 'Now did you ever hear the likes of that!' my mother demanded of me and then of a lark trilling high, in that order. 'Bessie's soap smells nice,' I firmly replied. We trudged along. To our left the pit lifted her standards high, and on our right the golden fields gently sloped to Binchester, a good two miles away.

'Ah wish it wasn't so far,' said my mother with a sigh.

And who should come spanking along but red-faced Butcher Wilkinson perched high up on the seat of his bright red van! The high wheels spun, the cabriolet-like box rocked on its springs, and the butcher, majestic below his bowler, shouted 'Whoa!'

'How about a lift?' he shouted, but already we were running to overtake him.

'Ye don't know what a welcome sight you are!' panted my mother as he helped her from the step to the seat.

'Oops-a-daisy does it!' he said. 'Now how about the nipper? Should we put him in the van to keep the beef and mutton company!' It was all God bless you, as far as I was concerned. I was already waiting at the other side, quite unafraid of the champ and twitch of the horse. A hand extended and in a trice, planted on the right of the butcher, I had been given command of the whip.

Then away we bowled while I, admiring the smooth rolling motion of the bay mare's hindquarters, wondered just what might happen if I dared touch them with the tip of the whip. The countryside was wide and open around us and blue smoke lifted perpendicularly from the chimneys of solitary farmhouses snuggled in the folds of little hills. A magpie flagged low over the railway field. Rooks cawed. In the September light all things were bright and clear. But I had no eyes for this. With the metal-bound wheels singing and the whip held high I rode along in triumph.

'– And him only buried yesterday,' my mother was saying. 'There she was, flour up to her elbows when we landed. "You can't bake for the dead, and that's a fact, Elsie," she told me; as sure as I'm sitting here.'

'It's a bonny funny carry-on – but then she always was a bit peecoolyar . . .'

'Peecoolyar isn't the word for it,' said my mother, unconsciously miming Butcher Wilkinson. 'You should have seen the carry-on when she got ready to go out – clear soap, two lots of water to wash with, the face cream, the scent!'

'She always did look like a woman that took care of herself,' ruminated the butcher. 'And she never did settle. Always ready to joke on.' My mother looked at him. 'Here, give us the whip, young 'un!' he demanded. That he didn't use it made me doubly resentful.

'It's sad,' he murmured at last.

'She'll pick, you watch!' said my mother.

'Oh, she'll pick – you need have no fears of that,' said the butcher robustly. And now he flicked the horse. Her ears went up. 'Hey, lass!' he said in an injured tone, and flicked her again. The mare's head went up and she stretched herself, licking us along to the brow at a fine pace. 'Whoa!' he cried, pulling. 'Now there's your lift home for ye!' he laughed. Picking me up he lowered me to the ground. At the other side he was one-handing my mother down. 'All the same, it's a sad case,' he said. Glancing down at me he said, 'Ye'd better come round and take hold of the lad.'

My eyes were fixed on bushes heavy with fruit. 'What's these black things, Mr Wilkinson?'

'What's them! What's them!' he demanded. 'Did you hear that, Elsie? Canny bairn, your education's been badly neglected. Tell him what the black things are, Elsie!'

'Why, they're blackberries,' she told me.

'Are they nice to eat?' Both adults looked down and laughed at me.

'You just try one,' said Butcher Wilkinson, watching as I picked and hesitantly took one to my mouth. 'Go on, pop it in,' he said. The berry was soft and yet firm between my fingers. 'Between your teeth,' encouraged the butcher, and oh, the smile that spread over his face as I tasted my first blackberry, the juice spurting out, taking its tart, faintly acid sweetness to a million instantly alert and rejoicing taste-buds. 'Was I right?' he demanded, but already my hand had darted to select another.

'Now you've started something,' said my mother. Laughing, Butcher Wilkinson whipped away.

We picked and picked until our teeth, our lips and fingers were stained and stung with the sweet pain of the insidious little thorns. There was no driving me home that evening. If I'd had my way we should have feasted on blackberries for evermore. So the pride and vain glory of the whip and the high seat, and the taste of all those fine ripe blackberries that hung heavy on the branch, quite jostled out of mind and memory the passing of Tom Patrick. Only tenuously was his living presence linked up in my mind with the words of Grandma Richardson: 'Such a beautiful skin. All those years in the pit and there wasn't a mark on him.'

And yet again the iron-bound wheels of the years carried me back to the churchyard where his gravestone leans, and Tom Patrick Gill aged twenty-three, fatally injured at Binchester Colliery. No more than a boy, he almost certainly went out as unblemished as on the day he was born. I am old now, but I can still hear his laugh. Surely this is a miracle. Tom Patrick is gone and the pit which overlaid him is obliterated, but still he walks beside me. 'Noo mind the bluebells; gan canny over the bonny flowers. Here, under the hawthorns where it's damp and cool, you're always sure to find them growing,' he says to the child I was then, and am no longer: that wild innocent creature who had still to taste his first blackberry. And to this day the sight of the cuckoo pints, each erect and sturdy, each guarding the life within it, has never yet failed to drive a pang like a nail through my heart.

Sid Chaplin was born in 1916 in the pit village of Shildon, County Durham, and after leaving school at fourteen worked as a miner. He won a scholarship to Fircroft College for Working Men and it was here that he started to write. His very first publication was a poem which appeared in *Penguin New Writing*, but it was as a writer of short stories that he first made his name. His first collection of stories, *The Leaping Lad* (1946), won him an Atlantic Award which enabled him to buy the time to write his first novel, *My Fate Cries Out* (1949). This was followed by six further novels: *The Thin Seam* (1950), *The Big Room* (1960), *The Watchers and the Watched* (1962), *The Day of the Sardine* (1961), *Sam in the Morning* (1965) and *The Mines of Alabaster* (1971). Throughout his career he contributed widely to magazines, periodicals and newspapers – both fiction and non-fiction – and also to several television series, including *When The Boat Comes In*. Sid Chaplin died in Grasmere, Cumbria, in 1986. A posthumous collection of stories, *In Blackberry Time*, was published in 1987.

The Toothache by Tony Harrison

Toothache on top of all this was too much. He had always taken great care of his teeth, even as a child. A child. His marriage was two months old and he wished that he was. Fifty years had passed in as many days. That made him seventy-three. Another two to go. His life was almost over. He had come to the right place. The door was divided, like a stable door, into two equal leaves. He knocked on the upper leaf, a frosted glass panel with the name and profession in heavy black capitals. The upper half opened. A clean, florid face appeared and disappointment pricked him.

—Yes?

—Would you . . . attend to this for me, please?

The slip of paper was carefully scrutinized. Himself. The paper. Himself.

—Are *you* the father?

—Yes.

—Come in.

The lower half of the door was unlatched to admit him into a room which seemed half church, half office. The ecclesiastical half was neat and shining, the official half untidy, strewn with papers. Nameless brass projections hung on the walls and looked as if they had been looted from a church. There were glossy photographs of the rest chapels in the city's crematoria. The funeral director busied himself among his littered papers, and, in a few minutes, with the air of having solved a problem, pronounced, as if he expected his client to haggle:

—That will be three pounds ten, young man.

—Yes.

He drew four new pound notes from his wallet, crossed the room, and placed them emphatically beneath the undertaker's eyes.

—It will be tomorrow. Will anyone attend?

—No.

—Has it got a name?

—No.

—Shall I inform you of the place of burial?

—No . . . thank you.

—Some people like to know, but best forgotten.

—If the child had lived only a few days or weeks it would have had a name. And a stone.

He felt he was apologizing for not bringing better trade.

—A different matter. But best forgotten.

He seemed to have solved a problem.

—It doesn't often happen these days.

He wondered how much a child of a few months would cost.

—Right. I'll see to it tomorrow for you.

—Thank you.

He turned to go. The business completed, the undertaker moved from the official to the ecclesiastical side of the room, and took his hand.

—Put it there. I know what it is. I'm a family man myself.

With his other hand the undertaker held out a small receipt for three pounds ten and a crumpled ten-shilling note. He took them and went through the divided door.

—Good afternoon.

—Good afternoon, young man.

It had been the same with the registrar of births and deaths, when he had collected the certificate for disposal at the hospital that morning. Names. Dates of birth. 1937. 1937. Professions. Schoolteacher. Schoolteacher. The registrar wrote the date of the stillbirth. 19 February, 1960.

—When were you married?

—December the Sixteenth.

—Nineteen Fifty Eight?

—No, last year.

The registrar smiled. Who had selected him to endure this? Time? Like an ever-rolling stream. There was comfort in that. His tooth ached. No comfort. There was time to kill before his dental appointment. There was always time to kill. You stood in the present and watched either the last moment die or the next being born. As they were ejaculated into being, his mind, like a spermicide, killed off the seeds of time. All *his* moments were dying. When you were seventy-three you could only look behind you. At that age you walked backwards into the future. There was time to kill before his dental appointment, before he died. He would walk.

To reach the dentist's, which he had not thought to change, he had to walk from Town to Beeston, up the long hill that overlooked the rest of Leeds. It was very near his old home. Since he had left so abruptly he had not returned. The lack of forgiveness would remain mutual. His resentment would consume his guilt. Supposing he was seen? Let them see him. Supposing he saw his mother at the greengrocer's on the corner? He would ignore her. He had written a terse postcard to tell them about the child and that was all. They would say it was a judgement. Besides if you were seventy-three, your parents would be dead. All the names that had been heaped on them! All the fragments of morality that had fallen about their heads! The fifth and the seventh commandments. They had burned his photograph and the Bible he had kept at his bedside. Such as he had no right to possess that, let alone read it. It had only been an ornament anyway. A tit bit. A miniature edition, inscribed *Joseph Carson*, 1841. He had picked it up in the market for a few pence, buried under the battered copies of Marie Corelli, Ouida and Hall Caine.

After only two months of absence the familiar streets showed signs of considerable change. Instead of the lines of gas lamps he was shocked to find overhead sodium lighting, and there was demolition in progress on a row of terrace houses, almost the same as his own street. He stopped to watch. There was time to kill. Ahead of him a man on crutches stood watching the houses being torn down. That had not changed. The afternoons were always peopled by mothers and children under five, or by the aged and the maimed. All the able-bodied, like the demolition men, were at work. He himself would be back at school tomorrow morning. After his slight indisposition. A chill? A bilious attack? The blood on the stair, the floor of the ambulance, the attendants' hands. At his feet on a pile of broken bricks, open at page 305, lay the grey remnants of *The Beauties of British Poetry*:

> 'The Assyrian came down like the wolf on the fold,
> And his cohorts were gleaming in purple and gold;'

He turned the stiffened pages with his foot. Another by Lord Byron. Mrs Hemans. Hogg. Two men with sledgehammers were poised on a high fragment of surviving wall. They might easily fall and kill themselves. This part of the city had worn badly. It was good to see it go. How doth the city sit solitary, that was full of people! Seventy-three. Fifty years *had* passed. You could expect changes in fifty years. Every change after fourteen years was for the worst. A plaque on the site testified that the work was being carried out by a member of *The National Federation of Demolition Contractors*. On it was a badge with a map of the British Isles. Great Britain and Ulster were in black. On the circumference of the badge, surmounting the Outer Hebrides, was a contractor's crane. A shovel intersected Sligo and traversed Ireland as far as County Cork, where it emerged into the ocean. A pick in the North Sea had its point curved towards some coastal town beneath the Firth of Forth. A crowbar, its point of balance opposite the Isle of Wight, floated in the English Channel, extending, at a rough guess, from Plymouth to Brighton. Beneath all this was the date, 1941 (he was four), and beneath that the motto, RESURGAM. The cripple had moved off. He overtook him quickly, imagining the cripple's envy at his straight, retreating legs. He turned round. The cripple's head, as if it always had, hung, like a cartoon Christ's, upon his breast.

He was nearer to his old home. You could see almost all of Leeds from the crest of Beeston Hill, the roofs, the chimneys and the steeples, the higher civic buildings, the clock of the black Town Hall, to which he had listened, in his attic bedroom, striking the small hours of those mornings immediately before he left. The slightest earth tremor could level them. He could see the familiar landmarks that he had passed on his way up. The Salem Institute, Hudson's Warehouse, formerly Wesley Hall, the gas cylinders, the truncated pinnacles of Christ Church. Some time ago, these had become insecure and the constant passage of heavy and rapidly increasing traffic had made them a danger to the community. The incumbent had sat for weeks at a trestle table, with placards ranged about him and fixed above the church porch on either side of what seemed to be a tinted photograph of Christ, beneath which was written in white capitals, COME UNTO ME. Who would go to that? The faded figure held out its arms in a gesture of welcome. AN APPEAL FOR RENOVATIONS TO THE FABRIC OF THE CHURCH. £10,000 URGENTLY NEEDED. PLEASE GIVE GENEROUSLY. SAVE YOUR CHURCH. Hardly a tithe was raised and, with no regard for proportion, the dangerous finials and crockets were removed, leaving four stunted growths of stone, projecting from a square tower. They should have left them to fall down. Nearer to him was the large dome of a building, formerly the Queen's Theatre, the Music Hall, the Queen's Cinema, now an unwanted fixture, described as an excellent site for future development, becoming more and more dilapidated, devoid of players, stars or audience. Of the advertisement board above the entrance, between what had been two giant tulips, there remained only the word, TODAY. Just visible below, however, the Palace Cinema, formerly the Tabernacle, was still assertive. Its prices had risen, so they said, from fourpence to one and six or two and three. It had risen in the world. The city was senile too. Let the everlasting stars go out. They would all pass away as one, a slow driftage of stardust, crumbled brick and plaster, powdered flesh and bone.

The dentist had his surgery in Cemetery Road on the very brow of the commanding hill. In the congested burial ground on his left the remains of his family from seventeen something were laid at rest, the butchers, the publicans, their wives, and some of their children. His father took flowers there almost every week and sometimes came home with the stains of clay on his trouser knees. The five sons, now dispersed in various parts of England, sent every year, with their Christmas cards, a subscription towards an elaborate wreath.

From the chair, as he was having his teeth tested and found wanting, he fixed his attention on the landmarks below him, to distract his mind from the pains of the dentist's probe. Four of his teeth required treatment. Three new fillings and one about twelve years old that needed repair. He had forgotten about that. The tooth that ached was not to be extracted. It would just be possible to fill it. Of course, they were paid more for a filling.

—Do you still clean your teeth regularly?
—Yes, of course. After every meal.
—And you don't eat sweets?
—No.
—Or a lot of biscuits?
—No. No.
—Mm. Your teeth are poorly resistant to decay.

They gave you nothing to numb the pain of drilling. No cocaine. No laughing gas. The drill began. He stared at the heavens and the higher landmarks. He pinched his hand beneath the protective sheet. Birds circled within his vision, circumscribed by the tilted position of the chair, seagulls fleeing the storms on the North Sea or the Irish Sea, sparrows, starlings circling the stunted pinnacles of Christ Church, the dome of the Queen's Theatre, the Music Hall, the Queen's Cinema, the derelict, wheeling backwards and forwards above the Gas Works cylinders, the Salem Institute, and, nearer, settling on the houses on the hill immediately beneath the window. Concentrate. Transfer the pain into the hand. The birds soar as the pain is sharp on the crumbling tooth. They settle and it is subdued. The drill. The drill. They rise, they wheel and turn, around the stunted pinnacles, poorly resistant to decay, the Queen's Theatre, poorly resistant to decay, the Queen's Cinema, poorly resistant to decay, the derelict, the excellent site for future development, for future buildings, future derelicts, that will survive my teeth, my flesh and bone, my son, who died before he saw the broken world, that may survive my second or my third, their first, or be demolished, excavated, filled, plucked out, root and all, teeth and children torn out of their roots, the nameless flesh interred in nameless ground, the dead to judgement torn, Christ torn from the tomb, the roots, the judgement, the welcoming, the faded Christ, poorly resistant to decay. Houses of people, of plays and pictures, and of prayer. Of prayer, like the birds, the birds in flight, that will not settle that this pain be stopped. Poorly resistant to decay. Slum clearance, demolition, and repairs, the plans of councillors and clerks, citizens and clergy, the aimless cockroach and the mouse, the pick, the crowbar, the shovel, the contractor's crane. The area of Great Britain dark, blacked out. Seventeen something. 1841. 1937. 1941. 1951. 1961. *Resurgam*. They rise. The pains. Love, poorly resistant to decay, like birds and pain together, rises, falls. Again, it rises, poorly resistant to decay, pain inseparable from flight. It must. Poorly resistant to decay, they fold their wings and perch on blackened houses and on generations, poorly resistant to decay. *Resurgam*. World without end. I will arise on painful or on broken wings.

Had he not been advised to eat nothing for three hours, he would have bought a penny apple at the greengrocer's on the corner, as he had done regularly when he was a boy. They were good for the teeth. There were holly wreaths, left over from Christmas, hanging in the shop.

—Hello, stranger. Not seen you for ages. Your mother told us you were married now. Says you've got yourself a nice girl. You're a dark horse. How are things?

His mouth was sore. He smiled painfully.

—Fine.

—Good. Just off to your mother's then?

—No. I'm just coming back. I want you to send two lots of flowers for me if you would. One home. You know the address. With love. And the other to . . . no, never mind. I'll take the others myself.

Bearing a bunch of many-coloured flowers, he caught an almost empty bus down Beeston Hill, along Victoria Road, and beneath the Dark Arches into City Square. There he walked past the dark horse itself, mounted by the Black Prince. There were sparrows perched on the horse's mane and on the Prince and, in bronze, a falcon brooded on his arm. It was growing dark. The naked nymphs, Morn and Eve, were bearing lighted lamps above their heads. Past the statues of Dr Priestley and Dean Hook. Over the square the wayside pulpit of Mill Hill Chapel bore its weekly message: POLITENESS IS LIKE AN AIR CUSHION. THERE'S NOTHING IN IT, BUT IT EASES THE JOINTS WONDERFULLY. They were going to rebuild the square. He caught another bus which took him past Quarry Hill Flats and Oastler House, past nameless lit and unlit windows, industrious or unfinished premises, darkened churches, cinemas, tall scaffolding and abandoned homes, and from the stop opposite the Cemetery Tavern, he walked through the lodge gates into the hospital waiting-room. They were seated indiscriminately on wooden benches, the

203

joyful, the anxious, and the near bereaved, waiting for the gatekeeper to admit them to see their dying for the last time, their sick, or their recently delivered. Was it true, as he scanned the faces, that those who were elated slightly subdued their joy, for the sake of those who were anxious or in mourning, and that those who were ridden with anxiety or bereavement allowed a little real or dissembled radiance to appear on their faces, for the sake of the elated, the fathers? If it was, then it was as it should be, and he belonged to both.

Tony Harrison was born in Leeds in 1937. He has published several books of poetry, including *The Loiners*, which won the Geoffrey Faber Memorial Prize in 1972, and *Continuous*. He has written much dramatic verse in the form of libretti for the Metropolitan Opera, New York, and for collaborations with several leading modern composers, including *Yan Tan Tethera* (with Harrison Birtwistle), which was shown on Channel 4 and had its theatre première on the South Bank in 1986. He has written verse texts for the National Theatre, including *The Misanthrope* (1973), *Phaedra Britannica* (1975), *Bow Down* (1977), *The Oresteia* (1981), which was performed at the ancient Greek theatre of Epidaurus and was awarded the European Poetry Translation Prize in 1983, and the much-acclaimed *The Mysteries* (1985). Both *The Oresteia* and *The Mysteries* were broadcast on Channel 4. He is the author of *Theatre Works 1973–1985* (1985, Penguin 1986) and two long poems *V.* and *The Fire-Gap*, both published in 1985. A new expanded edition of his *Selected Poems* was published by Penguin in 1987.

Stand Magazine

What is Stand Magazine?

Stand Magazine is an independent quarterly of new writing founded by the poet Jon Silkin in 1952. It is an international magazine publishing poetry, short stories, reviews, and occasional short plays. Stand Magazine Ltd is a non-profit making company registered with the Charity Commission, and it receives a substantial annual grant from Northern Arts, the regional arts association covering the North-East and Cumbria. *Stand Magazine* was given this name because it was begun as a stand against apathy towards new writing and in social relations.

What the magazine has achieved

Stand Magazine has a good record of promoting the work of talented writers long before they become well-known. Outstanding examples of this are Tony Harrison, David Mercer, Ken Smith, Jeffrey Wainwright, Tom Pickard, Lorna Tracy, Roger Garfitt and John Cassidy. The magazine has also published work by more established writers such as Samuel Beckett, Harold Pinter, Hugh McDiarmid, Richard Eberhart, Thom Gunn, Seamus Heaney, Norman Nicholson, Geoffrey Hill, Charles Tomlinson, Michael Hamburger, Iain Crichton Smith, Stephen Spender and Arnold Wesker – although the editorial policy has always been to publish only work considered worthwhile, regardless of the name on the manuscript.

The magazine has also brought to the attention of British readers important American and Australian writers such as William Stafford, Robert Bly, David Ignatow, Philip Levine, James Wright, Michael Wilding, Peter Carey and Robert Adamson. In addition, work by foreign writers in English translation has always been a feature, often when the writers were as yet unfamiliar to English-speaking readers. For example, we have published Johannes Bobrowski, Georg Trakel, Zbigniew Herbert, Leopold Staff, Eugenio Montale, Cesare Pavese, Giuseppe Ungaretti, Anna Akhmatova, Isaac Babel, Alexander Blok, Osip Mandelstam, Marina Tsvetayeva, Yuri Trifonov and Igor Pomerantsev.

Stand Magazine also produces special issues concentrating either on the work of a particular writer or on an area of literature little known or neglected by English-speaking readers, as in the issues devoted to Australian, Arabic, Israeli and Norwegian writing. The magazine has also consistently championed the work of the First World War poets, and brought out special issues celebrating their achievements long before their poetry gained its present popularity.

A recent development has been our biennial short story competition. The first was judged by Sid Chaplin and Penelope Mortimer; the second by Barry Unsworth and Fay Weldon; and the third by Angela Carter and Jack Trevor Story. Now in association with Harrogate International Festival, the competition has quickly established itself as the leading event of its kind in the English-speaking world. The fourth competition, judged by Beryl Bainbridge and Malcolm Ross-Macdonald, opens 1st October 1988. The first prize has been increased to £1,250/$1,875, and the total prize money is £2,250/$3,375. For a copy of the leaflet/entry-form (available August 1988) send a stamped addressed envelope (UK) or one international reply coupon (two for airmail).

What some critics have said

. . . a magazine with an internationalist outlook and a certain appetite for immediate social questions . . . It has a very distinct flavour, owing mainly to its breadth of hospitality. It concerns itself with literature in general and not only poetry, which immediately makes it less back-yardish and inbred, more of an open space, than the purely poetry magazine can be. Short stories, so hard to find these days, are a regular feature . . . Modest in format, ambitious in range, confident of itself without being cocksure. Stand *does a remarkably useful job.*

John Wain, Times Educational Supplement

. . . among essential magazines, there is Jon Silkin's Stand, *politically left, with reviews, poems and much translation from continental literature.*

Donald Hall, Parnassus (New York)

. . . generous to American writing, to European and Third World literatures in translation; always open to contributions from unknowns; as interested in the short story as in poetry . . . has long since earned its right to recognition for its scrupulous standards of discrimination . . .

Neil Corcoran, Times Literary Supplement

Please subscribe . . .

new subscribers will receive a free back issue

☐ one year (£6.15 + £1.10 p&p) £7.25 (UK), £8.00/$16.00 (Eire & abroad)
☐ two years
  (£12.05 + £2.15 p&p) £14.20 (UK), £15.70/$31.50 (Eire & abroad)
☐ student/unwaged
  (£5.15 + £1.10 p&p) £6.25 (UK), £7.00/$14.00 (Eire & abroad)
☐ single copy (£1.60 + 25p p&p) £1.85 (UK), £2.00/$4.00 (Eire & abroad)
I should like to subscribe to STAND MAGAZINE beginning with the
Spring/Summer/Autumn/Winter issue

Name_____

Address_____

_____

Cheque enclosed/debit my Visa account: £ _____ $ _____

Visa card expiry date: _____

☐☐☐☐☐☐☐☐☐☐☐☐☐☐☐☐☐

send completed form and payment/Visa card details to

STAND MAGAZINE, 179 Wingrove Road
Newcastle upon Tyne NE4 9DA, UK

KEN KESEY

Demon Box

Ken Kesey is something of a legend, the brilliant author of *One Flew Over the Cuckoo's Nest* and *Sometimes a Great Notion*, and the sixties' prankster who travelled on the magic bus and captured the spirit of a generation. Now, in this major new work of fiction, Kesey explores the rich territory of his own experience.

Since he was released from jail in 1967 Kesey has written continuously, following the contradictions and lost dreams of American life in the seventies and eighties. In *Demon Box* the persona of Devlin Deboree links stories, poems and essays closely comparable to Kesey's own life and perception.

Here are accounts of a search for human dimension among Egypt's geometric monuments, of a hard lesson learned after the murder of John Lennon, and, in *The Demon Box: An Essay*, a description of the positive energy of madness.

Kesey is a unique stylist and storyteller. His many fans will welcome this latest book, and will find much to celebrate within it.

'Very fine writing indeed' NEW STATESMAN

'Kesey writes with enormous vigour and humour, but, above all, with an endearingly unrepentant optimism' SUNDAY TIMES

MICHELE ROBERTS

The Book of Mrs Noah

'A woman visiting Venice with her pre-occupied husband fantasizes that she is Mrs Noah. The Ark is a vast library, a repository not only of creatures but of the entire knowledge and experience of the human race. She is its curator (or 'Arkivist'), and her fellow voyagers are a group of five Sibyls and a single man, the Gaffer, a bearded old party who once wrote a best-selling book and has now retired to a tax haven in the sky. Each Sibyl tells a story and each story is about the way men have oppressed women down the centuries.

'I have not felt so uneasy and so guilty about my gender since I read Margaret Atwood's *The Handmaid's Tale*. To say that *The Book of Mrs Noah* is a superb novel sounds impertinent or patronizing. But it remains the case' Kenneth McLeish, DAILY TELEGRAPH

'Sharply but sympathetically observed . . . both down to earth and visionary. Roberts' writing is rich, troubling and audacious . . . the female imagination at its best' CITY LIFE

'A feast of inventive imagery . . . it's not unusual for a woman writer to pitch for brave humour, but to strike the note as truly as Roberts does is a marvel' COMPANY

'A strange and interesting book, pouring the subject matter of Virginia Woolf into a form designed by Boccaccio' INDEPENDENT

'Like the best of new women's writing, takes a generous view of the widely different ways in which women find their salvation, and avoids feminist clichés . . . a poetic, visionary book, and humorous as well' COSMOPOLITAN

'A slow, rich read of pleasurable complexity' GUARDIAN

SIEGFRIED LENZ

The Heritage

First published in English in 1981 this haunting and passionate novel from the prize-winning author of *The German Lesson* and *The Lightship* is now published in paperback for the first time.

'An old man, badly burnt, lies in a hospital bed and lets his mind range back over his experiences. We know from the start that the burns were in a sense self-inflicted, because Zygmunt himself deliberately began the fire which caused his injuries. What he burned down was the local museum (*Heimatmuseum* is the German title of *The Heritage*) whose collections he had assembled so carefully over the years. What he destroyed was a phoney, exploited sense of the past. . . . A spellbinding narrative, full of memorable scenes, some of them touching, some comic, some – such as the wartime evacuation in face of the Russians – with the crowded imagery of a lurid panoramic painting.' Anthony Thwaite, THE OBSERVER

'I greatly enjoyed this intelligent, skilfully organized novel.' Norman Shrapnel, THE GUARDIAN

'*The Heritage* deserves comparison with *Dr Faustus* and *The Tin Drum* as a comprehensive analysis of Germany's cultural disintegration.' S. N. Plaice, TIMES LITERARY SUPPLEMENT

MAUREEN DUFFY

Change

'[Maureen Duffy] shows at once broad and deep understanding of what the war of 1939–45 meant for ordinary English men and women, both in and out of uniform: a delight to read.'
M. R. D. Foot

To different people in Britain in 1939 the coming of war meant different things. To Hilary at a London grammar school it meant her father joining the Home Guard and later, her school moving to the country and reaching adulthood in a dangerous and exciting world. To Alan it meant learning to fly and risk his life nightly, as well as trying to respond with his poetry to the challenges of new experience. To Daphne it meant separation from her army officer husband and making a new life for herself as an ambulance driver in the Blitz. . . .

'It's as if our parents' and grandparents' treasured photograph albums had been tossed in the air and their snapshots, frozen moments in time, had landed heaped and entwined. Maureen Duffy has picked through these fragments of life and fitted them into the mosaic of *Change*.' TIME OUT

'In *Change* Maureen Duffy demonstrates her ability to be simultaneously involved and yet distanced. It is this merging of the implicated and prophetic voice that makes her writing continually and unpredictably challenging.' FICTION MAGAZINE

'The telling is vivid, very readable.' FINANCIAL TIMES

'An experienced, prolific novelist; nothing she writes can fail.'
DAILY TELEGRAPH

BENEDICT KIELY

A Letter to Peachtree

Benedict Kiely is one of those rare writers who can portray the unexpected, the comic and the tragic sides of life, often in the same person and in the same moment of hilarity and doubt. In this, his fourth collection of stories, he teases his readers as happily and as wickedly as ever.

'There are fine things all over this collection, lives to brood about and glorious gallops down every interesting looking diversion . . . There are so many Irish people who write short stories, and so few who are real storytellers. Ben Kiely is one, and he should be preserved in aspic or crowned high king or just bought in huge numbers.' SUNDAY INDEPENDENT

'This is a splendid collection, confirming Kiely as a master of the oral tradition.' IRISH PRESS

'They are as much occasions of sin as any Ben Kiely story ever was' IRISH INDEPENDENT

'The stories are full of the sort of verve you would expect from Ben Kiely, overflowing with wit, erudition, a sense of the absurd, a tenderness for beauty, whether of people or places' EVENING PRESS

'Sheer magic' Dominic Behan, DUBLIN EVENING HERALD

'Stylish, gabby, using language like a fallen angel, he mixes his feelings with a true storyteller's verve that looks like superb skill but is in fact something better. Call it instinct.' Norman Shrapnell, GUARDIAN

BARBARA COMYNS

Mr. Fox

Mr Fox is a spiv – a dealer in second-hand cars and black-market food, a man skilled in bending the law. When Caroline Seymore and her young daughter Jenny are deserted at the beginning of World War II, he offers them a roof over their heads, advice on evading creditors and a shared – if dubious – future. . . .

'I recommend it for its hilariously accurate descriptions of war . . . Barbara Comyns had me by the throat in that chokey state between laughter and tears given us by all too few writers' Mary Wesley, LONDON DAILY NEWS

'An extremely funny book' LITERARY REVIEW

'It has great charm' THE TIMES

'I enjoyed her story . . . for its innocence, its straightforwardness, its charming lack of guile' Nina Bawden, DAILY TELEGRAPH

'Delicate poignancy wrapped up in beautifully elegant prose' WOMEN'S REVIEW

'A minor classic . . . hunt down *Mr. Fox* forthwith for its peerless evocation of an era' DAILY MAIL

MICHEL TOURNIER

The Erl-King

The Erl-King is a novel of immense reputation and an international bestseller. On one level it is an engrossing adventure story. But many levels and layers of meaning are unfolded as it delineates the personality and career of Abel Tiffauges, on his journey from submissive schoolboy to 'Ogre of Kaltenborn' and a mystic destiny set in the apocalypse of the Third Reich.

'Prodigious imaginative power . . . unforgettably rich and vivid' Maurice Wiggin, SUNDAY TIMES

'A beautifully and vividly written book, a joy to read on nearly every page' Auberon Waugh, SPECTATOR

'Must be one of the best novels published anywhere since the War' NEW STATESMAN

'One of the few major European works of the past decade' George Steiner